BLUE HALO SERIES BOOK SIX

TYLER

D1452906

NYSSA KATHRYN

TYLER
Copyright © 2023 Nyssa Kathryn Sitarenos

An NW Partners Book
eBook Cover by L.J. Anderson at Mayhem Cover Creations
Paperback Cover Deranged Doctor Design
Developmentally and Copy Edited by Kelli Collins
Line Edited by Jessica Snyder
Proofread by Amanda Cuff and Jen Katemi

Sometimes, the biggest secrets can bring both salvation and destruction.

Emerson Charles grew up luckier than most, going from a difficult life to finding safety and a true home with her stepmother and stepbrother. Years later, when Levi's in trouble, Emerson will do anything for the brother of her heart, her greatest protector. Even seek the expertise of people who could be more hinderance than help—the men of Blue Halo Security. But she'll have to play her cards close to her chest. Telling the whole truth could see the team unwilling to assist, and Levi in more trouble than ever.

Tyler Morgan's career in the special forces had barely begun when he was kidnapped by the people behind Project Arma. With that chapter of his life finally put to rest, he runs a security business with men he considers brothers, all of them using their enhanced physical abilities to assist others. But their newest client seems to be harboring secrets behind her pretty amber eyes. He can't trust Emerson, but that doesn't stop him from wanting her. Nor can he let her out of his sight when the danger surrounding her brother increases.

As the risks get higher, and their attraction stronger, Tyler and Emerson are soon embroiled in a deadly race to locate a man only one of them believes is worthy of redemption.

ACKNOWLEDGMENTS

Thank you, Kelli. I am always grateful to have you fixing my stories and making them make sense, but this one in particular.

Thank you, Jessica. Your line edits always take my writing to the next level.

Thank you to my wonderful proofreaders, Amanda and Jen. You tidy everything up and help me send my book babies into the world with confidence.

Thank you to my ARC team. Your beautiful reviews and words of kindness never cease to amaze me.

Thank you to my readers. It is because of you that I write the next book.

And thank you to the two most important people in my life, Will and Sophia. Your support and love keep me going.

PROLOGUE

 leven Years Old

HER EYES POPPED OPEN. Her chest moved up and down so quickly, she couldn't get a single deep breath in.

It was the dead of the night, but her puppy-shaped nightlight cast a dim glow over the room.

Alone. She was alone. No one was trying to hurt her. She was safe.

She swallowed, trying to wet her dry throat which felt like it was stuck together. Her gaze shifted to the side table, a trickle of unease settling in her belly when she saw the empty glass of water.

For a moment, she was still. So still, all she could do was breathe and try to figure out whether she could fall back to sleep without water. She'd tried before. It had never worked.

With a deep breath of courage, she climbed out of bed. The springs of the mattress squeaked, causing her to cringe. She paused, not wanting to wake her father. She waited for the whisper of footsteps. The creak of a door opening.

When all she heard was the lull of the wind outside and the gentle rattle of her window, she wrapped her fingers around her flashlight and stood, allowing the cold of the wooden floorboards to seep into her feet and trickle up her legs. Then she crossed the room, each step more silent than the last.

As she passed her closet, she gave it a wide berth. She'd come to hate that thing. The clothes inside had long stopped fitting her since she used her chest of drawers for everything she needed now. The closet was a dark, scary place inside. Her father had taught her that.

She swallowed, turned on the flashlight, and left her bedroom.

Waking in the night wasn't unusual. Sometimes she preferred it to the nightmares that riddled her sleep. Sometimes she begged herself to wake up.

But it wasn't just the nightmares. She used to awake in fear her father would enter, drunk and angry, yelling at her for whatever her last mistake had been. Sometimes it was leaving a glass somewhere it didn't belong. Others, it was that she'd forgotten to complete a chore.

He was the man who was supposed to love her. He didn't. She'd learned that very early on in her life.

She crept down the stairs and into the kitchen, careful to avoid any floorboard that would give her movement away. Her gaze constantly darted around the crevices of the house, searching for the man she was forever trying to remain invisible from.

When she made it to the kitchen, her fingers twitched to turn on the light. She didn't. She'd made that mistake once. Two heartbeats later, her father's voice had boomed from the hall.

The memory made her shudder.

With trembling fingers, she opened the cupboard door and gently lifted out a glass. The soft hum of the fridge was backing noise to her thundering heart. Then she moved over to the tap, turned it on slowly, and let the dribble of water fill her glass. If she turned it on with too much force, the groan of the pipes would churn throughout the house.

The glass was a quarter full when she shut off the water. Then she turned and took a sip, letting the cool liquid wet her dry throat. She only took a couple sips because she didn't dare stay out of bed too long.

When her thirty seconds were up, she turned and emptied the rest of the liquid down the sink. The sweep of relief that she hadn't woken him was just spidering through her limbs when a floorboard creaked down the hall.

She whipped around so fast that her elbow caught on a vase, sending it flying into the sink. The glass shattered, cutting through the quiet like a million little explosions.

Her world stopped, and a familiar fear broke into her chest, making her heart do an ugly thrash against her ribs. Her knees felt so weak, she was sure she'd fall. Tumble to the floor and struggle to rise again.

She almost scrunched her eyes closed, not wanting to see her father's intimidating form appear. But she wasn't sure what would be worse—the dark surprise of a fist or seeing it coming.

The panic was just digging its claws into her skin when a form appeared in the hall. But it wasn't her father. It was Pixie, her new stepmother.

Little snippets of her new reality began to creep back into her consciousness. Her father wasn't around anymore. Hadn't been around for over a month.

She opened and closed her mouth three times before her words sliced through the air. "I had a nightmare and I forgot."

God, how had she forgotten that he was gone? About her new life. Her new safety.

A sad expression turned the older woman's lips down. She crossed the room and pulled Emerson into her arms. Security.

Protection. It cocooned her. Slowed her heart, and let the forgotten warmth coat her skin.

"Oh, darling. We'll be out of this house soon."

She rested her head on the woman's chest, listening to her heart as a new set of footsteps sounded behind her.

Her gaze cut across the room to Levi. He was her stepbrother, but he also wasn't. If this last month had taught her anything, it was that blood didn't make people family. It was loyalty. Trust. And love. Pixie and Levi were all those things. *They* were family.

The bruises on Levi's face had faded, but he still cringed when his broken ribs were nudged. Broken ribs her father had caused when Levi had saved her. Her brother had only been released from the hospital a few days ago. He'd protected her against a monster. Because that's what family did, they protected each other, regardless of the cost. She was *alive* because of Levi. Even at eleven years old, she knew it was a debt she'd spend her life trying to repay.

CHAPTER 1

 oday

EMERSON CHARLES TOOK three deep breaths as she traced the letters on the Blue Halo Security sign with her eyes.

This was it. Her last-ditch effort to catch Levi and get him the help he so desperately needed. Nothing else had worked. Not catching him herself. Not hiring a normal private investigative firm. Ha, she could still remember the investigators' call last night. The call she'd known was coming because the investigators had been quiet for a month. *Sorry, we keep locating him then losing him, but we're still going to charge you squillions of dollars for our services.*

Okay, they didn't say those exact words, but close enough.

She clenched her jaw, her gaze lowering to her seat belt as she unbuckled.

What good was it to locate him and lose him? That didn't help Levi. That didn't help anyone.

The problem was, he was too fast for the average person to catch.

With a sigh, she climbed out of the car. The guys who ran Blue Halo also weren't normal. Not only were all eight men former Special Forces, they'd suffered through Project Arma. The non-government-sanctioned project that had drugged unsuspecting soldiers. Made them faster. Stronger. Able to do things men shouldn't be able to do.

They were what she needed. *They* would catch her stepbrother.

With steady determination, she walked to the door and pushed inside to find a set of stairs. Her hands felt clammy as she jogged up. Then, with a single breath of courage, she walked inside Blue Halo.

A woman with long brown hair that fell around her shoulders sat behind a desk. Her intelligent green gaze flashed up and she smiled. The woman wasn't just pretty. She was beautiful.

"Good morning," she said cheerily. "Welcome to Blue Halo Security. My name's Cassie. How can I help you today?"

Nerves fluttered in her belly. Nerves because she knew this was her last shot. If the men of Blue Halo couldn't capture her brother, *no one* could.

You've got this, Em.

With the last whispered words of encouragement, she stepped up to the desk. "Hi, Cassie. I'm Emerson Charles. I have a nine a.m. meeting."

"Yes! Our first appointment this morning. Bear with me for a moment. It's my first day." Cassie looked at the computer, her smile slipping and a tiny crease marring her smooth brow. "You were scheduled with Logan, but there was a last-minute change and now your appointment is with—"

"Me."

A deep, familiar voice sounded from the hallway. A voice she'd heard for the first time just last night at the bar. It made awareness skitter down her body and tiny goose bumps rise over her skin.

She turned her head and looked up at the tall man. Not just tall. Huge. Well over six feet, maybe even closer to six and a half. But he wasn't just huge in height. His shoulders were wide, and he wore a white T-shirt that stretched across a thick chest and hard biceps.

And then there was his face. She swallowed at the brightest blue eyes she'd ever seen. They were contrasted by his dark brown hair.

She hadn't been planning on going out last night. She'd been sitting in her Airbnb, feeling sad and sorry for herself. It had been a split-second decision. All the men from Blue Halo had been there. But it was this man who'd approached her.

He stepped forward and held out his hand. "Tyler Morgan. It's nice to see you again, Miss Charles."

She reached out her hand and placed it in his much larger one. Heat spiraled up her arm, tingling across her shoulders. It was the same heat she'd felt last night when he touched her. It made her cheeks flush and her stomach knot.

"Emerson, please. And it's nice to see you again, Mr. Morgan."

"Tyler."

His name carved its way inside her, making her pulse beat to a new rhythm. "Tyler."

His eyes flashed to the woman behind the desk. "Thanks, Cass." Then his attention returned to her. "Follow me."

She smiled at Cassie, not missing how the woman watched them closely, a look of something indefinable in her expression... interest maybe?

They headed down a hall with doors on both sides. Tyler stopped halfway down and held out his hand, ushering her into an office. "Come in."

As she passed him, a wave of sandalwood scented the air. He even had to smell good? God.

7

She dropped into the chair opposite his desk, a soft thud sounding through the room as the door closed behind her. Then Tyler folded his large body into the chair behind the desk. He smiled, flashing a hint of a dimple on his cheek.

"So, before we begin, I'd love to find out more about you."

She swallowed. She was sure the man had run a background check already. Wasn't that something all security companies did? So he'd know a bit about what had happened with her father when she was younger. About her stepmother adopting her, and the fact that she had a stepbrother. But very little of Levi's last five years was available. In fact, she was pretty sure people had gone to great lengths to make sure his activity was off the record.

"I live in Vermont and work as an artist. Mostly commissioned paintings. And I'm divorced, no kids."

She still kept in contact with her ex-husband. Just like everything else about their marriage, the split had been perfectly amicable. No fiery arguments. Nothing thrown across the room or broken when she'd asked for a divorce.

Tyler nodded. "You've come quite a distance to see us."

She had. But then, she would have traveled to the other side of the world if necessary, to help her stepbrother. "I hear your team is the best, and I need the best." She cleared her throat. "I'm sorry about Project Arma."

The second the words were out, she regretted them. His smile slipped, dimple disappearing, and those bright blue eyes darkened a fraction. "Thank you. Fortunately, that's just about behind us."

Her brows twitched. Just about? Meaning it wasn't quite behind them? Did he know there were people who'd received the DNA-altering drugs still out there?

She tried for a small smile. "Hopefully everyone who worked for the project was either arrested or rehabilitated."

This time, Tyler frowned. "Rehabilitated?"

He watched her so closely, she wanted to squirm. Or maybe

she did. "Well, yeah. I followed the news reports. It sounds like the man who ran things didn't give anyone involved much of a choice. The subjects, the scientists... I'd guess even some of the guards were coerced."

The smile returned to his face, but this one had a dangerous edge to it. "Those guards and scientists had a choice, Emerson. And after making that choice, they needed to face the consequences. I have yet to meet a person involved in the actual running of Project Arma who didn't need to die."

It took everything inside her not to flinch at his words. At the way he said *die*, like it was a vow. Like he'd promised himself long ago no one working for the project would live.

She worked hard to control her breathing and pulse, two things she knew he could monitor with his advanced hearing.

He cleared his throat, the smile on his face relaxing. "Let's talk about why you're here. What can I do for you today?"

The words she'd planned to say died in her throat. If she told Tyler the whole truth, would Levi become one of those people who needed to die? But if she didn't say anything, who was going to find him? Who was going to bring him in and save him?

Panic and desolation swirled inside her like a tornado. She needed Tyler's help. *Levi* needed his help.

Her mouth opened and closed twice before she got words out. "I need your help catching and subduing my stepbrother."

Her heart pounded. This was a risk. A big one. She knew she couldn't lie to any of these men...but maybe she could fudge the truth for now.

Tyler leaned forward. "Is he missing?"

God, that was a loaded question. "Have you done a background check on me?"

"We've done some research."

"What did you find?" She was genuinely interested in knowing.

"Your father raised you on his own in Vermont before

marrying your stepmother when you were nine." His eyes hardened, and she knew what was coming next. "There was an incident. Your father hurt your stepbrother, and the neighbor shot him to save Levi."

She breathed through the pain that memory brought. So much had been left out of that police report. Yet she remembered every second of that fateful day. The day Levi had saved her. The day Levi had almost died for her.

"Then your stepmother raised you," Tyler finished softly.

She nodded. "That's correct. Levi's my brother, even though we're not blood related. He joined the military after graduating from high school, then went into the Special Forces." This is where she had to be careful with what she said. "On his final mission…he made a mistake."

Her heart ached for Levi. She was sure Tyler's research had extended to her family and he knew this, but she explained anyway.

"Instead of shooting the enemy, he shot two team members and killed them. It was an accident, and because of that, he wasn't charged." Friendly fire incidents were rarely punished. Apparently, it was unfortunate but common. "But he still left the military because he just couldn't stay."

Most thought he'd gotten off lightly. But she knew the truth. That was the beginning of the end for Levi. He'd shot his brothers. And those deaths plagued him. Tormented him. Destroyed him.

Tyler tilted his head. "That would have been really difficult for him."

She nodded and forced the next words out. Words that would shock him. "Two years after that incident, while he was still suffering from PTSD, a man named James Hylar took him."

It wasn't a lie. Hylar *had* taken him. He'd taken advantage of a man in pain. Promised him something he could never deliver—to give Levi purpose again.

Tyler's reaction was immediate. He straightened, steel entering his eyes. "Your brother was a prisoner at Project Arma?"

Sweat beaded her forehead. She knew these men could detect a lie, so she was careful to avoid saying anything that would give away the truth. "He was in there for two years, and during that time, he was given the DNA-altering drugs." She fiddled with a thread on her jeans. "I don't know the details of what happened the day the compound was raided, but Levi disappeared soon after. And I need you to help me help *him*."

Everything she said was true. Yet, nothing gave away the full truth.

"Why isn't he already home with you?"

That was a good question. Her brother should've known he could stay with her. That she would do anything and everything to help him.

"He *did* stay with me for about a month after the project was shut down. But I've only seen him a couple of times since then, and each time I'm more convinced he's suffering from mental illness. He talks about people still being after him. About people watching him." It was heartbreaking. "I think he's suffering from psychosis. Delusions. He needs psychological help."

And she needed to get him help before it got worse. Before he did something, hurt someone, he shouldn't.

"He sounds dangerous." Concern swept over Tyler's face. It made her skin tingle.

"He is. His mental state has been deteriorating since he was discharged from the military, and after Project Arma, it seemed even more rapid. He could be a danger to himself and others. That's why I'm here. To force my brother to stop running and seek treatment, which can only be done with help from men of equal speed and strength."

There. She'd said it. And God, she felt lighter having the words out. She was one step closer to saving him.

"Are you safe?"

Something hot swept through her limbs and settled in her belly. "Yes." Levi had never hurt her. He'd always been her protector. And she still believed that was true. In fact, maybe even more so now that Pixie had passed away. "But that doesn't change the fact he needs therapy of some kind."

"Do you have any idea where he might be?" Tyler asked.

"His mother, my stepmother, died a few months ago. I've felt him close to me ever since. I even catch glimpses of him at times. I think he was watching over Pixie a lot, and now he's switched his protection to me. I'm the only family he has left."

"So you think he might be here, in Cradle Mountain?"

"Yes." She was counting on it.

CHAPTER 2

$\mathcal{T}$yler watched the array of emotions flicker across Emerson's face. She was hiding something. What, exactly, he wasn't sure. But there were secrets behind those pretty amber eyes. Every time he asked a question, she didn't fully answer. He could almost see her carefully crafting her response in her head before giving him anything.

In case she gave away too much? In case she said something she shouldn't?

The guys on his team would be alarmed by that because it was suspicious as hell. And yeah, he also wanted straight answers, especially because she'd admitted her stepbrother was tangled up with Project Arma. But he was also intrigued. And something told him if he pushed too hard, too fast, she'd leave. And he didn't want her to leave. So he had to be smarter. Softer.

He leaned forward again, not missing the small hitch in her breath. A smile played at his lips. She felt it too. The pull. The heat that danced in his gut when he got close to her. It had been there last night, and it hadn't died with the light of day.

"I'd like to set up a meeting with my team and discuss strategy. Because our target is a Project Arma man, we'll have to approach this a little differently than how we normally would."

She gave a quick nod and continued to pick at a thread from her jeans. A nervous gesture?

What are you hiding, Amber Eyes?

"I'd also like to get assistance from the Feds."

That had her eyes bulging and her fingers pausing. "The FBI?"

"We have a contact in the Intelligence department with whom we work regularly. We actually have a meeting with him after I'm finished here. I might ask him to extend the call so we can all talk strategy."

Her eyes darted between his, fingers now wrapped around the seat of the chair, knuckles almost white.

The idea of involving more people made her nervous. Why?

"Are you sure that's necessary?" she finally asked, voice quiet.

"It would certainly help."

The woman gave a slow nod. Her hesitancy made him want to reach out and comfort her. With a touch of the hand. A graze on the arm.

He shook it off. "Do you mind hanging around for half an hour?"

"Of course not. I really appreciate anything you can do. Thank you."

Relief. It threaded through her voice and shone in her eyes. She was nervous, but also relieved they were helping.

"You're welcome." He stood. "I'll get Cassie to make you some coffee while you wait."

She stood too. At almost six-four, he towered over the woman. She wet her lips again. *Fuck.* He needed her to stop doing that. She had full, rosy-colored lips that made his dick twitch just looking at them.

As he led her to the reception area, her citrus scent hung in the air, toying with him. Cassie smiled at them when they stepped into the room.

"Could you make Emerson a coffee, Cass? I'll be back to get her in about twenty minutes."

She nodded. "Of course."

He flashed the woman a final smile, his eyes catching on Emerson's one last time before moving down the hall.

Here at Blue Halo, the team members weren't just private and corporate protection agents. They also did off-the-books jobs for the government through their FBI contact, Steve. Usually, jobs that couldn't be completed by ordinary people. Today, Steve had requested a meeting because he was stuck with a case and needed more brains on it.

When he reached the conference room, he stepped inside to see Aidan, Callum, Liam, and Flynn already sitting around the long table.

He clamped a hand on Aidan's shoulder before sitting beside him. "Cassie's doing well out there. You must be happy to have her close."

Aidan blew out a breath, leaning back in his seat. "After everything that went down over the last month, I want her as close as possible at all times."

Tyler didn't blame him. Cassie had almost been killed by a crazy cult and its leader. Aidan and the team had only just made it in time to save her.

"How'd the appointment go?" Flynn asked from across the table.

Tyler opened his mouth to tell them about Levi, but the video call came through before he got a word out. A second later, Steve was on the large screen hanging on the wall.

The older FBI agent shuffled in his seat. "Hey, guys." As usual, he looked tired. He always seemed to have too much shit on his plate.

"What do you have for us, Steve?" Flynn asked.

He ran a hand through his hair. "This is a strange one. We've got next to nothing. No suspects. No motive."

"Tell us," Liam said.

"Three incidents. In each one, two people kidnapped. They're kidnapped separately—first one and then the other, just hours apart—but are connected in their personal lives. Usually related, but one incident involved best friends. They both turn up dead together."

"Dead how?" Tyler asked.

"Both are found in a burning house, but autopsies reveal victim one always has a stab wound, with no smoke in the lungs."

Aidan frowned. "So victim one is killed prior to the fire."

"Yes. While victim two dies in the fire beside their loved one. The front door to the burning house is always open, it's always a two-story structure, and the two bodies are found upstairs."

What the hell? "If the door's open, why doesn't victim two leave?" Tyler asked.

"Our thoughts exactly. Our best guess is victim two runs in to try to save victim one and gets trapped when the fire spreads."

Jesus.

"Are the homeowners connected?" Liam asked.

"No. We've ruled all of them out. The owners are always away from the home, often for an extended period of time, when someone breaks in and sets the fire."

Steve ran a hand through his hair. "We're really struggling with this one. There seems to be no gender preference. No sexual assault. Although, I should mention, victim one is always either a convicted criminal or accused of a felony. The last incident involved a man who'd been charged with the murder of three people but got off because there wasn't enough evidence to hold him."

Tyler frowned. "Maybe some sort of Robin Hood?"

"That would make sense if the second person was suspected of wrongdoing, but none of them have been. In fact, one of the people who died by fire was a doctor."

"Where are these deaths taking place?" Aidan asked.

"Maine, Philadelphia, and Kansas."

"And no connection between the pairs of victims?" Callum asked.

"None."

Shit. That didn't leave them with much.

"I'm gonna send the case files," Steve said, shuffling some papers in front of him. "We'd appreciate it if you could look them over. See if there's anything we've missed. We'd also like your team to question some of the victims' loved ones. Listen to see if they're lying or hiding something."

"You got it," Flynn said.

"His pattern has been to kill every two weeks."

Liam frowned. "When's the next two weeks up?"

"In three days."

Shit.

"All right. I'll send those files over within the hour."

Before Steve could click out, Tyler cleared his throat. "I actually have a case I'd like *your* help on, Steve."

The agent stopped, then nodded. If he was surprised, he didn't show it. The team hadn't asked much of him since they'd been working together.

"I've just had a new client ask our team to catch and subdue her stepbrother." He felt his team's eyes on him. "The man was part of Project Arma, and he's a security risk."

There was a beat of silence.

"Why does he need to be caught and subdued?" Liam finally asked.

"His mental health is declining. Emerson believes he suffers from delusions and, therefore, won't accept the help he needs. He's also former Special Forces."

Flynn cursed softly under his breath. Yeah, they all knew how dangerous that made him.

"I'm happy to help in any way I can," Steve said.

He nodded. "I'll go get the client."

As he moved down the hall, he could hear Cassie talking about the town, telling Emerson that she'd just moved here.

He entered the foyer to see Emerson looking just as nervous as when he'd left her. He tried for an easy smile. "Ready?"

"Yes."

Even if he *couldn't* detect a lie, the woman had answered too quickly for that to be true.

When she reached him, he lightly touched a hand to the small of her back, and he was almost sure he felt her lean into him just a bit. But it wasn't until they stepped into the conference room that he felt her go almost rigid. The guys could be a pretty intimidating sight. Even though everyone was sitting, there was no mistaking their sizes.

"Emerson, this is Liam, Aidan, Callum, and Flynn. And on the screen is Steve," Tyler said, introducing everyone.

She smiled at each man before Tyler ushered her into a seat at the table.

His gaze moved to Steve as he spoke.

"Hi, Emerson. Tyler's filled us in a bit. Your stepbrother has declining mental health and has advanced speed and strength. Is that correct?"

"Yes. He needs psychiatric help."

She'd said the same to Tyler. Like she wanted to emphasize that part. Did she think they wouldn't help him otherwise?

"We'll organize a person to be on you at all times," Tyler said quietly, his fingers twitching to touch her. "That way, if he's around, we can see and catch him."

"We can also keep tranquilizers on us," Liam suggested. "So we have a means to stop him without harming him."

She seemed relieved by that. "That sounds good."

"I can tap into our resources here to track any movement via street surveillance," Steve offered.

Callum nodded. "I can do the same."

"That all sounds great." There was a but coming from Emerson, he felt it before she said it. "Although, I don't have a lot of money. You guys are my last resort, which means my resources are already pretty drained. Detail during daytime hours should be enough. I normally feel him when I'm out in public anyway, which is usually during the day."

Tyler tensed. He didn't like that. Danger didn't stop at night.

Like she sensed his disapproval, she hurried to continue. "He looks a bit different from his old military photos. He has a scar beside his right eye. His hair's a bit longer. Shaggy and down to his ears."

Tyler dipped his chin. "That's helpful."

"Is there anything else you can tell us that might help?" Flynn asked.

"Just that he's confused and will probably mistake you for the enemy. So please be careful. I don't want anyone getting hurt."

Tyler almost reached out and touched her, again wanting to offer comfort. Instead, he softened his voice. "We can take care of ourselves."

She looked at him like she wasn't sure.

They spoke details and schedules for another ten minutes, then Tyler stood and led her from the room. When they passed his office, he ducked inside and grabbed his card before handing it to her. "This has my personal number on it. Call or text if you need anything."

When she slipped the card from his hand, their fingers grazed, and he heard her pulse spike. So damn responsive to his touch, just like he was to hers.

When they reached the reception area, he opened the door for her, but she stopped and turned. "Thank you again. For listening to me and agreeing to help."

He touched her arm, and that same shot of awareness ran through his body again like a damn spark of electricity. "It's what we do. I look forward to helping you get your stepbrother back, Emerson."

A flicker of emotion rolled over her face. Uncertainty. Maybe even fear?

It disappeared as quickly as it had come. She gave him a small smile before thanking Cassie, then leaving. He watched her head down the stairs. Just before she disappeared, she glanced back up at him. Their gazes caught. There was a small pause as her chest rose and fell, then she kept moving.

His smile grew. He looked forward to working with the woman. Learning more about her. But then, he'd known he would. It was exactly why, after meeting her in the bar last night, he'd rearranged her appointment to be with him.

When he looked up, it was to see Cassie watching him closely, a huge-ass grin on her face.

"She's cute," Cassie said with a raised brow.

She wasn't just cute. She was fucking gorgeous. He wouldn't be admitting that out loud just yet, though. He closed the door. "First morning going okay?"

She chuckled. Yeah, he was avoiding her statement, and she knew it.

"Yep. You guys were pretty organized, although I'm tidying up a few things in your system."

He heard the footsteps from the hall before he saw his friend. A second later, Aidan was behind Cassie, kissing her neck.

Tyler smiled. His friend had just gotten Cassie back after years of separation. He was glad they were happy.

"Are you doing okay?" Aidan asked her.

Another of her huge smiles, this one all for Aidan. "Perfect."

When Aidan spun her chair and kissed her, Tyler groaned. He was thrilled for the man, but he didn't need front-row viewing. "That's my cue to leave."

He made it halfway down the hall before Aidan caught up with him.

"Hey." Aidan paused briefly before asking, "Did you sense she was hiding something?"

He knew his team wouldn't have missed it.

"Yes. And I'm interested to find out what it is when she's ready to share." No way was he pushing her into running. This was too important.

Something crossed Aidan's face, and Tyler knew he wasn't going to like what he said next, even before any words left his mouth. "Maybe someone else should take the lead on this. I know you wanted the job after meeting her in the bar last night, but—"

"I can remain professional." Yes, he was attracted to her. But he also needed to know what she was hiding. There was no way he was handing over this job.

CHAPTER 3

*E*merson touched her paintbrush to the canvas. As Levi's brown eyes looked back at her, memories skittered through her mind of the last time she'd spoken to him. Well, the last time she'd spoken to him while he'd been in his right mind. Just before the project was shut down.

"Em, what are you doing here?"

Emerson wrapped her arms tight around her waist, studying Levi's wide eyes and tense muscles. "I'm here because I'm worried about you."

She stood in front of his door, blocking his way inside. She'd waited for him for hours. Had been willing to wait all night if she needed to.

He wore a black shirt that bore a little emblem on the left chest. The emblem was a shield with an odd weapon running through it. One end of the weapon was a knife blade, the other, the muzzle of a gun. Levi had told her he worked for a military commander, but that was it. Rowan had told her the rest.

Her gaze traveled back up to his face.

His jaw clenched. "You need to go before someone sees you here."

He tried to step around her, but she gripped his arm, stopping him. "I'm your sister. Why would it matter if someone saw me at your home? Are you in danger?"

"No. But what I'm working on isn't public knowledge. It's also dangerous. Go home, Em." He pulled his arm from her grasp.

"Rowan told me about your visit last week."

Levi stilled. Her stepbrother had contacted her husband. Not her. It still hurt. She understood Rowan and Levi had grown close during her marriage. Even now, they often talked on the phone. Texted regularly. But sharing important personal information with him—and not her?

She took a small step closer. "He told me you haven't been feeling good. That you think people are watching you."

"You need to go home," he repeated in a tone so dark it caused the fine hairs on her arms to stand on end. But she didn't stop. She couldn't.

"Come home with me. Quit your job and let me take care of you."

He stared straight at her, and for a moment, she almost thought he was considering her request. Then he blinked. The lethal hardness returned. "What we're working on could change the face of warfare. It could tip the odds in our favor and ensure men no longer have to go fight losing battles. That soldiers don't get so tired they kill their own team members."

She flinched at the way he said kill. Like he was a coldblooded murderer, when she knew a part of him had died with his friends.

Her voice lowered. "You told Rowan that innocent men are suffering." Another slash of pain that he'd shared the information with Rowan and not her. "Are you hurting people, Levi?"

Rowan said Levi hadn't gone into a lot of detail. Just that it was called Project Arma and experimental drugs were involved.

Levi stepped closer, and she almost shrank back. He'd been so different since leaving the military, but the way he was looking at her right now...it almost made her think he might hurt her. But that wasn't possible. Levi had always been her greatest ally.

"There are no lengths I wouldn't go to, to make sure others don't go through the hell that was Iraq. If that means a few good men are sacrificed so that many others live, then that's just what has to happen."

Even now, two years later, his chilling words moved through her mind like quicksand. She hadn't known exactly what Project

Arma was until later, when it had been all over the news. Before that, she'd thought Levi's work was government sanctioned.

Had Levi known? Almost certainly. At least at the end. There had been something wild in his expression that night. Something so unlike him.

She believed with everything she was that he'd been taken advantage of. He'd been vulnerable and hurting, suffering from PTSD, and then he was fed lies about history never having to repeat itself.

She touched her brush to the canvas once more. She'd painted his image countless times over the last year. For this portrait, she'd been working on his eyes for hours, trying to get the shade just right. They were deep brown with specks of green. They were eyes she used to look at and see safety in. Sanctuary.

There are no lengths I wouldn't go to, to make sure others don't go through the hell that was Iraq.

God, she hated those words and the pain that came with them. Levi may not have been imprisoned for shooting his team members in Iraq, but he'd still paid dearly for his crimes. He'd spent two years torturing himself and mentally deteriorating from the guilt, and that was something Arma had preyed on. Capitalized on.

He needed therapy. And she needed to make sure he got it.

She smudged the paint in his left eye.

Some would never understand her need to help him. But he'd saved her from an abusive father, a man who still gave her nightmares even when he was deep in the ground.

A shudder rocked her spine, and her gaze flicked to the overhead lights. Still to this day, she couldn't sit in the dark or in small spaces. Not after being locked in her closet for hours on end, beaten and bruised.

Taking a deep breath, she dipped her brush into the green and added more specks to his right eye. Then she sat back and studied the curve of his nose. Imperfect, just like the rest of him.

Dented from a few breaks in the military. And his face... She'd drawn his expression like she remembered it—confused. Like he saw the world and everything in it as an enemy. As a threat he needed to conquer.

"What happened to you, Levi?" she whispered, wishing she could ask the man himself.

Her gaze caught on the little emblem on his shirt.

She blew out a breath and added some shading beneath his eyes before finally lowering the brush. When she glanced at her phone beside her, the ten p.m. readout surprised her. She'd been at this for hours, even skipping dinner.

He wasn't quite done, but she'd keep working. He was forever her work in progress.

The phone vibrated, and she smiled when she saw a message from Mrs. Henry, the owner of the Airbnb. The middle-aged woman had stopped over earlier because the heater wouldn't turn on. Apparently, Emerson hadn't been pressing the right button on the digital thermostat. She almost laughed at her own ridiculousness. Mrs. Henry had been lovely about it, though. She'd even brought Emerson a basket of muffins.

Everything okay? Warm?

Emerson typed in a quick response.

Super toasty. Thank you again for coming, Mrs. Henry.

The house was kind of isolated and on the outskirts of town, but the woods and mountains made for a beautiful backdrop while she worked. It was a small cabin, the front door opening into the kitchen, which then shared an open space with the living room. There was no dining table, just a tall kitchen island with a couple of stools. Two bedrooms were right off the living room, one for painting and one for sleeping. So basically, it was perfect. She'd rented it for three months, because who the heck knew how long it would take the guys to catch Levi.

You're welcome, dear. Have a good night.

She was just about to set her phone down when it rang. Jeez, she was popular tonight.

Her ex-husband's name popped up on the screen, and she answered on the second ring.

"Hi, Rowan." Even though she'd divorced the man over two years ago, they remained good friends. They'd been more friends than anything else during their marriage anyway.

"Hey, Emerson. I would ask if I woke you, but knowing you, I'm guessing you're up getting lost in a painting?"

She smiled, rising to her feet and stretching her back. "Not lost. I know exactly where I am."

Painting, though? Always. It was how she processed life. Her ultimate passion since the first paintbrush had been slipped into her hand.

"But you're painting, right? Probably have been for hours. Maybe even missed a meal or two?" Amusement tinged his voice.

The man knew her too well. She stepped into the living room. "Did you call just to tell me how predictable I am? Because that's not news to me."

"No. I called to check in on how your meeting went today."

Rowan knew everything. He'd gone through it all with her, both before and after their marriage ended. Witnessed Levi's pain after shooting his teammates, saw him spiraling down in the ensuing years, then watched the man they knew almost disappear entirely while working for the commander.

"It went…" She paused, trying to think of the right word. "Okay."

"Uh-oh. What happened?"

She pinched the bridge of her nose. "The guy basically told me everyone who was part of the project deserved to die, so I…I couldn't tell him the whole truth. I let him believe Levi was a prisoner of Project Arma."

She still felt awful about it. She hadn't directly lied, but she'd let him believe the inference, so it was kind of the same thing, wasn't it?

There was a beat of silence, then Rowan sighed wearily. "It's risky to involve the team from Blue Halo if they want to kill everyone involved."

Oh, she was well aware.

A part of her was always waiting for Rowan to outright tell her she shouldn't be trying to help her stepbrother at all. The two men had been friends, yes, but Rowan had a strong sense of right and wrong. When the media exploded with details about Project Arma's atrocities, long after the project itself had been raided and shut down, he'd cut all ties with her brother.

"It was literally a last resort. And Levi told us he never worked with prisoners, so I'm counting on these guys never having seen him."

In the month Levi had stayed with them after Project Arma was raided, his mental health had taken a nosedive—before he just disappeared.

"But if any of them had caught even a glimpse of him during their captivity, and they remember—"

"I know!" she interrupted. "But what choice did I have? No one else can catch him. He's too fast."

Another sigh. "Do you need me to come out there and help?"

This was mostly why she'd married him. Because he was so incredibly kind and supportive. "No. I'm okay. But thank you. Are you doing all right?" The guy was knee deep in obtaining his PhD, something he'd been working toward for a while.

Her phone vibrated in her hand with a text message.

"You know me," Rowan said. "Studying and researching hard, as usual."

Oh, she did know him. The man lived and breathed neuropsychology. By the end of her marriage, she'd come to realize he loved his work more than he would ever love her. But she couldn't really judge; it had been the same for her and her art.

Exactly why they weren't married anymore. Why they probably shouldn't have married in the first place.

"All right. I'm going to leave you to it, then," he said quietly. "But call if you need *anything*."

"I will. And thanks for checking in, Rowan."

"Of course."

She hung up, expecting to see another text from Mrs. Henry. Her pulse jumped when she saw the name in the message.

Not Mrs. Henry.

Hey. It's Tyler. Just wanted to check in, make sure you're doing okay out there?

Heat danced over her flesh. She'd given his company the address of her Airbnb in paperwork she'd filled out online before her meeting. But even if she hadn't, she was sure Tyler would have been able to source the information.

She typed, then retyped a reply, nibbling her bottom lip the entire time.

Hey. I'm safe and sound. Just painting.

There was something so sexy and seductive about the man. He was younger than her. Probably a good seven to eight years younger. Not to mention gorgeous. So she was pretty sure he didn't feel the same attraction. Hell, he probably had twenty-something-year-old models vying for his attention.

Her phone vibrated again.

Good. We're going to start trailing you tomorrow. I thought I might pick you up and show you the town. Is that okay?

Him and her. Together. All day. Her mouth went dry. She'd thought he would tail her from a distance.

Her attention drew back to the painting before typing out a response.

Sounds great. Although, could we make it afternoon? I've still got some more painting to do tonight.

She'd always been a night owl. That was when she did her best work.

Done. I've got a couple of meetings in the morning, so that works well. If you need anything before then, call.

Man, she should really stay away from him. Something told her he'd be too easy to fall for. And considering she'd been less than honest at their meeting, that was not a good idea.

I will. Thank you for checking in.

His response was instant.

Sleep well, Emerson.

Her heart gave a little trill. Oh God, she was screwed.

She was still smiling down at her phone when a rustling noise sounded from outside the house. With a frown, she looked out the window but saw nothing in the dark.

Was that an animal? Probably. There'd be plenty around here.

She was just turning back to the painting when it sounded again. Except this time, her skin tingled.

Something that *always* happened when Levi was close. Apprehension trickled up her spine.

Switching on her cell's flashlight feature, she moved to the front door and stepped out onto the porch. Her throat tried to close, and sweat beaded her forehead. Christ, she hated the dark.

She pushed the fear down, focused on her breaths, and scanned the area. She had light. She was okay.

"Hello?"

Nothing. Not the rustle of leaves or a whisper of movement.

She took two steps off the porch, forcing her feet to move farther into the darkness. "Levi? Is that you?" She spun the flashlight around the nearby woods. "If it is, you don't need to hide from me. I want to help you."

One more step.

"Please, Levi."

Suddenly the rustle of leaves sounded again, this time behind her.

She spun so quickly, her foot caught on a random branch on the ground, and she dropped with a thud. She barely paid attention to her aching backside, instead scrambling for her phone and shining it toward the house. But there was nothing.

Dammit! He was here. She knew it. She'd felt him.

Carefully, she pushed to her feet and headed back inside. She'd just shut and locked the door when she saw it. A notepad on the otherwise empty kitchen counter. And writing scrawled across the top page...

Stay away from them.

CHAPTER 4

*T*yler pulled up outside Emerson's house and scanned the wooded area. The place was too isolated. He didn't like that. Isolation meant no neighbors to run to or call for help if needed. It meant trees and bushes for predators to hide behind and questionable phone signals.

He turned his attention back to the small cabin. He knew from the team's check on her that she'd rented the house for three months. Three months was a long time. It meant she'd come here expecting this job to take a while.

The woman she'd rented it from was actually his neighbor, Mrs. Henry. He'd laughed when he saw that. That's what you got in small towns.

His team had done a more in-depth background check on Levi Campbell's life. They'd found that two years after leaving the military, he'd disappeared, which matched what Emerson said about him being taken by Hylar. There was no trace of him after. No car registration. No credit cards or bank accounts. There wasn't even a rental or mortgage in his name.

So, since the project had been shut down, where had he been living? How had he been paying for things? They were questions he needed answers to. Questions he wondered if Emerson knew more about than she'd let on.

He climbed out of the car and crossed to her door, then rang the bell. A few seconds of silence passed. When no noise came from inside the house, he knocked.

That was when his advanced hearing picked up the rustle of what sounded like sheets, followed by a quiet, "Shit!"

An almost silent laugh escaped his chest. Was she just waking up? It was the middle of the day.

There was the distinct thud of feet hitting floorboards, heading in his direction, before the door opened.

Desire slammed into his gut—hard. The woman was in silky sleep shorts that showed off almost the entire length of her toned, creamy legs. Her top was wrinkled and so low cut that he wanted to groan at how much cleavage was on display. And then there was her hair. It cascaded over her shoulders like a fountain, wild and rumpled.

Fuck, she was gorgeous.

Concentrate on her face, Tyler. Not that it would help him calm the hell down. Her eyes were half-hooded, making his jeans feel too damn tight.

"I'm so sorry," she said in a rush. "I was up late painting. Make yourself at home. I'll jump in the shower and be ready in a couple of minutes."

His groan was loud inside his head. He was going to have to listen to the woman *shower*?

Before he could respond, she turned, and it took everything inside him to tear his gaze off her ass, which almost poked out from the legs of her shorts as she ran into what he assumed was a bedroom.

Blowing out a long, steadying breath, he moved inside and closed the door behind him. The shower turned on in the other room, and images of her stripping off those shorts and top and stepping under the stream ran through his head, torturing him.

Dammit. He needed to stop.

He took in the living room around him. It was a typical wooden cabin, but there were splotches of color here and there. Color he was almost certain Emerson had put there. A red owl candle holder. A clay mug on the counter. Had she made that?

A framed photo on a side table caught his attention. Slowly, he walked over and lifted it. A younger Emerson stared back at him. On one side of her stood an older woman with a wide smile, and on the other, a tall teenage boy. Levi. He looked similar to the old military photo his team had pulled up. Except here, he was smiling. They all were.

Questions flickered through his mind about her father. The police report said Levi had just gotten home after school, broken a glass, and the man starting swinging. Emerson had been home. She ran to get a neighbor, who'd shot her father to save her stepbrother. Her father had died at the hospital from his wound, and Levi had *almost* died. His injuries had been significant.

Anger thrummed through Tyler's veins, and he shoved his hands into his jean pockets to keep from fisting them. He couldn't stand men who used their strength against women and children. Was Emerson still affected by that day? Had her father ever hurt *her*?

Tyler was pretty sure he knew the answer. A man didn't just go from model father to almost beating a kid to death.

Five minutes later, Emerson stepped out of the bedroom. Her hair was wet but pulled up into a ponytail. She wore jeans that hugged her hips and a purple knit sweater that highlighted her features.

Beautiful. The woman was damn beautiful.

She smiled. "Ready?"

He cleared his throat, trying to get some damn air into his lungs. Even that smile could easily destroy him. "I am." He nodded toward the frame. "Is that you, your stepmom, and Levi?"

Her eyes softened. "Yeah."

"You look happy."

She walked over to it and seemed to trace the people in the picture with her eyes. "It was the night before Levi left for the military. I was so sad to see him go, but I was also so happy for him. The military was all he ever spoke about. He wanted to fight for his country. You know the saying, do more, be more."

Her eyes turned sad, and immediately, Tyler wanted to erase that sorrow. He wanted to bring the smile back, see the lift in the corners of her mouth and the joy in her eyes.

He couldn't stop himself. He reached out and ran his thumb over her cheek.

Her tiny gasp wisped through the room. When she looked at him, her eyes could slay him.

"I'm sorry," he said.

"Why?"

"Because you lost him." The second Hylar had taken Levi, she'd lost him, and he'd been lost ever since.

"I did." She said it like she was surprised. Like it was the first time anyone had recognized how great that loss had been.

When she stepped away from his touch, it took a lot of self-control to not reach for her again. To not touch her silky-smooth skin.

He trailed behind her as they made their way to his car, then touched a hand to her back before she slid into the passenger seat. Her pulse picked up.

Yeah, I feel it too, Amber Eyes.

He slid behind the wheel and pulled out of the long drive.

"So where are you taking me?" she asked.

"I thought we could park at a coffee shop called The Grind. The woman who owns the place is dating Jason, a man from my team. We can walk around for a bit, see if we catch a glimpse of Levi. If not, we'll grab a coffee."

"Do they have good coffee?"

He grinned. "According to Courtney, it's the best."

She raised a brow. "And according to you?"

"It's still the best."

She laughed, and that lyrical sound hit him right in the gut.

"You have nice hands," she said out of the blue as they headed into town.

Her statement had his lips twitching. "Nice hands?"

"Strong. Masculine." She leaned over and ran her index fingers over a thick vein on the back of his right hand. The heat of her touch snaked up his arm. "I might have to paint them."

He swallowed, and his voice came out gruff. "You'll have to show me how it turns out."

He realized he liked the idea of her painting him, even if it was just his hands.

When he glanced over, their gazes caught. Her eyes widened almost imperceptibly. Then she snatched her hand away like the contact burned.

Well, honey, it burned me worse. He was certain of it.

It took the rest of the drive for Tyler to calm the hell down. When he reached town, he parked near the coffee shop, and as promised, they walked around for about an hour. They also spent a bit of time in the park, sitting under the sun. Every so often, the breeze would brush hair onto her face, and he had to physically stop himself from pushing it away.

He was on high alert the entire time. Watching. Taking note of his surroundings. If he wasn't so well trained, that would have been a hard feat considering how transfixed he was by the woman in his company. She made him laugh. And when *she* laughed, it was like every part of her brightened with her smile.

The only time she stopped smiling was when they headed back toward The Grind. The shift in her energy was instant.

"I was really hoping we'd catch a glimpse of him."

"We will." He'd make sure of it.

Her eyes ran over his body. "Are you wearing a…"

"Tranquilizer gun?" he finished when she seemingly couldn't.

She nibbled her bottom lip. "Yeah."

"I am." It was concealed in a holster. The dart contained a much higher dose than he'd use on a regular man, but then, if he used a lower dose, it wouldn't stop Levi.

He nudged her shoulder. "I've decided to let you paint my hands."

As he'd hoped, the corners of her lips quirked.

Ah, there it is.

"Let me? Buddy, when I want to paint something, I paint it. No permission needed. I might even add in the rest of you."

"That's not fair. You'll have a painting of me, but I don't have anything of you."

They stopped outside The Grind, and she looked up at him. "Well...then maybe I'll paint *you* one too."

Yeah, he definitely liked that idea. But he didn't want just a simple painting.

Images flashed through his mind of them together. Of Emerson in his arms, his mouth on her neck.

Shit. He seriously needed to stop.

Her focus on him was oddly intense. "Although, I'd need to study your face." She stepped closer and, to his surprise, reached up and traced a faded scar on his forehead near his hairline.

He sucked in a quiet breath, forcing the air into his lungs.

"There's a story behind a person's face. The scars and wrinkles and ridges." Her finger shifted to his nose. "The beautiful dents." Then she stroked a line beside his right eye. "The way the eyes are a window to a person's inner self."

"What do my eyes say?" he asked, voice gruff. The look she gave him, the way she seemed to see all the little parts of himself that he kept hidden... It was weighted...heavy...but he didn't mind the heavy.

"That you've seen and experienced a lot in your life, but those things don't scare you away from experiencing more. That you're open to pain if it gets you where you need to go."

Shock hit him so hard it was an effort not to flinch. How did she do that? See right into his damn soul?

Almost of its own volition, his hand went to her hip and tugged her closer. It felt right. Touching this woman. Having her close. All of it felt like he was exactly where he was supposed to be, with exactly who he was supposed to be with.

Her lips parted slightly. And every inch of him wanted to kiss her. Taste the beautiful woman who'd bounded into his life from seemingly nowhere.

He lowered his head, his lips just hovering over hers, when a voice sounded.

"Well, hello, Tyler!"

CHAPTER 5

*T*yler had been about to kiss her. Emerson could almost feel his lips on hers. And she'd wanted him to. There was nothing she'd wanted more, in fact.

But the moment was gone. Still, a smile tugged at her mouth at the way Tyler's chin dropped to his chest and a small growl vibrated from his throat.

She turned her head to see a pretty woman with pale blue eyes and long golden hair. Beside her was a tall man with short brown hair and almost silver eyes, whom she remembered from the meeting. Flynn. Even if he hadn't been at the meeting, though, she would have known he was a Blue Halo man. He had the same height and breadth. That dangerous I-could-end-a-man-without-breaking-a-sweat vibe. God, they were cut from the same cloth.

The woman smiled at her. "Hi. I'm Carina."

She returned the smile. "Emerson."

"Good to see you again, Emerson," Flynn said. His voice was just as deep and smooth as Tyler's. Definitely the same cloth.

Carina's smile grew as her gaze flicked between Emerson and Tyler.

Tyler sighed as he opened the door. "Come on. Let's get coffee."

She stepped inside the bright shop. It was busy, and the smell of coffee hit her right in the face. It smelled incredible. She hadn't had a good coffee in too long. There was no coffee maker in Mrs. Henry's Airbnb, so she'd been making do with instant. And no, she was not a fan of the stuff.

When Tyler pressed a light hand to the small of her back, awareness skittered up her spine. His large hand felt like it covered her entire back. She'd been telling herself all day that she needed to be immune to the man. He didn't know the truth about Levi. She couldn't start a flirtation with someone she was lying to.

The logical side of her brain knew that, but the rest of her was proving harder to convince.

A woman smiled at them from the other side of a long counter, looking at her and Tyler in the same way Carina had. With interest.

Tyler smiled. "Hey, Courtney. This is Emerson."

Courtney's gaze shifted to her. "Emerson. What a cool name. I like it."

"Thanks. I've grown quite fond of it over the last thirty-four years."

Courtney chuckled. "Can I tempt you with a coffee? I don't like to float my own boat, but it's the best in town."

"I heard. I've been looking forward to this since Tyler told me." Not only looking forward to it. Just about salivating at the thought.

Courtney's smile grew as she glanced at Tyler. "You told her how good my coffee is?"

"Of course."

"I knew I liked you."

"You own this shop?" Emerson asked when the woman looked back at her.

"I do. She's a labor of love."

It was impressive. Courtney didn't look too old, maybe late twenties, yet it appeared she ran a very successful business, if the packed shop was any indication. "Well, I'm looking forward to trying the best coffee in town. Could I get a double-shot iced latte?"

Her brows rose. "Fancy. I like it." She looked at Tyler. "Usual?"

"Thanks, Court." He turned his head to look at Emerson, and her skin almost broke out into full-body goose bumps at his attention. "I'm just gonna talk to Flynn for a sec."

She nodded and watched him walk to the end of the counter. She absolutely did not focus on his perfect ass or the way the material of his shirt pulled against his muscled back.

Or at least, she told herself she didn't. But when she finally dragged her gaze back to the women, it was to see them looking at her with knowing smiles.

Oh jeez. They'd caught her staring. She took a seat at the counter beside Carina. "I didn't—"

Courtney held up her hands. "You do *not* need to explain. All those boys are eye candy."

Carina sighed, propping her chin in her hand. "They're beautiful. God's gifts to women."

Emerson chuckled. "I would agree, but I understand they have really good hearing."

On cue, she glanced at Tyler from below her lashes. He winked at her, and her tummy did a little flutter. *Oh Lord.*

"Your usual, too?" Courtney asked Carina.

"Actually, that double-shot iced latte sounds really good. I might try that too."

"They're amazing," Emerson promised. "But be careful, they can become addictive, especially with a dollop of whipped cream on top." She didn't like to admit it, but she may have started indulging in one a day back in Vermont. A habit that was probably better broken.

"A dollop?" Courtney laughed as she turned to the coffee machine. "I'll add more than a dollop. Otherwise, what's the point?"

Emerson grinned. She was going to like these women.

"So you're dating Flynn?" she asked Carina.

"I am. And this gorgeous coffee shop owner is dating Jason." Carina nudged her shoulder suggestively. "You were pretty close to Tyler out there."

"He's just helping me track down my brother." And if she was smart, it would stay that way. Problem was, anytime Tyler was around, she forgot what smart was.

Courtney laughed. "It always starts as a job or a protection detail. Certainly started like that for me and Jason."

"Oh, me too," Carina said. "Except, I was Flynn's mother's in-home nurse."

Emerson could see how the men could fall for these women. She'd just met them minutes ago and she already liked them. Lowering her voice, she said, "Nothing will happen between Tyler and me." She scrambled to come up with a reason that didn't end with, *I'm letting him believe a lie.* "There's a bit of an age gap."

Yeah, that worked.

Both women frowned, but it was Courtney who spoke. "You said you're thirty-four. What's he? Twenty-six? Twenty-seven? That's nothing."

Carina nodded. "Jay-Z and Beyonce are twelve years apart, and they're goals for most people."

She laughed. Was Jay-Z the older one? Didn't really matter, she was no Jay-Z *or* Beyonce.

She swept another covert glance his way. This time, he wasn't looking back. In fact, he seemed so deep in conversation he wasn't paying them any attention. Good.

She shook her head. "We've known each other a day." Making

her attraction even crazier. She'd almost kissed a man, in public, who she'd only known for *a day*!

Courtney scoffed. "It took me and Jason no time at all."

"One meeting for me," Carina said. "He pretended to hate me, but I knew the truth."

Emerson's heart thumped. Then she gave herself a mental shake.

No. She had to stop these thoughts. It was a good thing the almost-kiss was interrupted. The relationship would be built on lies.

Courtney set two glasses of ice on the counter and poured shots of coffee over the top, then milk.

"You said he was helping you track down your brother. Everything okay?" Carina asked.

The mention of the case—of Levi—made her stomach turn. "Not really. My stepbrother needs help but doesn't want it. Unfortunately, if no one helps him, he could pose a danger to himself or others."

Not ideal. The note left on her kitchen counter flickered back into her mind.

Stay away from them.

She hadn't told Tyler about it yet, but that was mostly because he'd distracted her with his beautiful blue eyes the moment she'd opened her door. She would. She needed to. If she wanted him to find her brother, she needed to share everything she could with him.

Carina touched her hand, pulling her out of her thoughts. "Well, if there's anyone you want on your side to find a loved one, it's one of them."

"Exactly right," Courtney agreed. Then she moved down the counter, grabbing a small can from the fridge before returning. She sprayed some whipped cream onto the drinks. No. Not some. *A lot.*

Emerson's eyes widened. "Okay, that has to the biggest iced coffee I've ever seen."

"And no doubt the best," Courtney said, setting straws into the glasses. "I'm not modest, by the way."

Emerson took a sip. Holy crap, it *was* the best. "God, why would you be modest when your coffee's so good? This is amazing."

Carina groaned. "A hit of caffeine and sugar is exactly what I needed today."

Emerson agreed. So much yes. She turned to Carina to respond—but something behind the other woman, through the coffee shop window, caught her eye. Her breath stopped.

Levi.

For a moment, the people, the movement, and the sounds around her died, and he was all she saw. He stood across the road amongst several people at a bus stop. It was the first time he'd remained still, allowing her to stare at him, for months. He looked scruffy, and he was touching his right shoulder with his left hand. Scratching it. He also seemed angry.

Then his mouth moved.

She frowned. Had he just said *leave*?

The word had no sooner left his mouth when he disappeared down the sidewalk.

No...

She didn't think. She rose to her feet and ran. There was the faint sound of her name being called behind her, but it was background noise. She couldn't concentrate on anything but Levi.

She rushed outside without looking where she was going and ran smack bang into a man's chest. Her foot landed on top of his and her ankle rolled. The stranger grabbed her to stop her from falling, then another set of hands steadied her from behind.

The older man frowned. "Ma'am, are you okay?"

"Yes. Sorry." The words tumbled from her lips as she started to step away, her eyes on the spot she'd seen Levi, but the second she put weight on her foot, she stumbled, pain spiraling up her leg.

The strong hands on her hips tightened. "Emerson, your ankle."

She turned to look at Tyler. "Did you see him? Levi was here!"

Tyler straightened, instantly alert. "Where?"

"By the bus stop." Her gaze flicked back across the road before scanning the street. Gone. He was gone.

Her heart dropped. They'd lost him.

Flynn appeared beside them.

"Search the streets," Tyler said to his friend. "Levi was here."

Flynn's eyes turned hard, and he took off. Tyler looked back at her. "Why didn't you get me?"

That was a damn good question. Why hadn't she gotten him? She should have. But she'd been so startled to find him standing so still, allowing her to see him. When he'd disappeared, she'd panicked. "I'm sorry. He was looking at me, and I just couldn't look away. Then he took off and I...I just moved without thinking about what I was doing."

Dumb. She was so dumb. She knew she wasn't fast enough to catch him, exactly why she'd hired Tyler and his team. But in the moment, she'd just reacted.

She ran a hand over her face. "I'm so sorry."

The pain in her ankle started to throb. *And* she'd injured herself. Great.

Tyler's voice softened. "Come on, you need ice." He slid an arm around her waist, and she leaned into him for support, still wanting to kick her own ass for her mistake.

CHAPTER 6

yler turned into Emerson's long driveway. Courtney had given them a pack for her ankle, and Flynn had returned empty-handed. Wherever Levi had gone, it was far enough that they wouldn't catch him today.

Frustration thrummed through his veins that her stepbrother had been right there, across the road, and Tyler hadn't seen him. He wanted to find the guy. Emerson believed she was safe with Levi, but her stepbrother wasn't the same man he'd been when they were younger.

Once he parked in front of the cabin, he was out and around her side before she could even open the door. Without hesitation, he scooped her into his arms.

She sighed. "Tyler, you really don't need to carry me everywhere."

"You can barely walk, and you shouldn't be putting weight on your ankle." Plus, having her against his body felt too damn good, so he didn't need much more reason than that.

"I've rolled my ankle so many times in my life, I'm used to it." When he frowned at her, she lifted a shoulder. "I was into sports.

Some days I'd literally roll my ankle, strap it, take some pain meds, and be back on court the next day."

"Which sports?"

"Mostly volleyball, but I dabbled in basketball too."

He wanted to see her in those volleyball shorts. "Well, lucky for you, you have me now and don't need to do that."

When they reached the front of the house, he lowered her to her feet so she could unlock the door. The second the door was open, he lifted her again. She gave a half protest but then sighed and leaned her head against his chest.

His heart gave a big kick. *Jesus,* she felt too good.

Gently, he placed her on the couch, and she untied the icepack Courtney had given her, then handed it to him. Their fingers grazed, and he ignored the shot of awareness that tried to distract him yet again. He went to the freezer and popped the partially melted pack in before grabbing a tray of ice cubes.

"There's a plastic bag in the first drawer," Emerson called.

He opened the drawer—then stopped. There *were* bags inside, but sitting on top of the box was a small, scribbled note.

Stay away from them.

The writing was messy, like it had been done in a rush, but the letters were bold. The pen nib had been pressed so hard it almost went through the page. Anger. Yeah, there was definitely some of that on the page.

"Who wrote this?" he asked, turning and pinning her with his eyes.

Her gaze zeroed in on the note in his hand, and her eyes widened. It took a moment for her to respond, and when she did, the single word was quiet. "Levi."

His muscles tightened. "When?"

"Last night, shortly after you texted. I heard a noise outside, so I went to check. I couldn't see anyone, and when I came back, the note was on my kitchen counter."

His gut twisted. The guy had been moving around outside her

home. *Entered* her house. While she'd been out here alone. He didn't like that one fucking bit.

He slotted the note back into the drawer and was quiet as he prepared the bag of ice. When he sat beside her, he lifted her foot onto his lap. It was wrapped tightly. Gently, he pressed the ice on top of the bandage.

His voice remained low when he spoke. "Why didn't you tell me about the note?" He started a gentle massage on her ankle, something he'd learned from the medical team during his military days when he'd sprained his own ankle a couple of times.

Her gaze focused on his hands. "I planned to."

Truth. Next question. "Why didn't you tell me right away?"

"You distract me. And when it comes to Levi, I have to think things through a bit."

"Why?"

She wet her lips. "Because he's important to me, and I want him to be safe."

So, a part of her thought her brother wasn't safe with him? Then why had she come to Blue Halo for help?

So many emotions flickered over her face as she watched his hands on her foot. The main one...desperation. She was desperate to locate her stepbrother.

"Has he hurt anyone since he's been out, Emerson?"

Her eyes flashed back to his. "I don't know."

Not *no*. Not *of course not*. She wasn't sure. Meaning, it was possible. Maybe even more likely than not.

He shifted his hands to her calf and continued to knead. "I think we should organize an around-the-clock detail for you."

She responded as he'd known she would—by shaking her head. "I can't afford that."

"I wasn't asking for more money."

"I can't take charity from you. I have you on speed dial. I promise to call at the first sight of him."

His jaw tightened. It wasn't enough. It would take him too

long to get here. He wanted to argue. Hell, he wanted to push the issue until she agreed. But he wasn't anything to her. Not a friend. Not a partner.

Frustrated, he pulled his phone from his pocket. "It's going to be evening soon. Let's order some food."

EMERSON WASHED her hands at the bathroom sink. Tyler was still here. He'd ordered Thai food, and they'd chatted all night. Just like during the walk around town, it was so easy to talk to him. He'd told her about his time in the military. How he'd been raised by a single mother.

He'd asked about her art. Listened while she talked about her passion and watched her like he really cared about her words. Rowan hadn't been capable of that. He'd listened to her, of course, but never really seemed like he was taking anything in. His attention had usually been somewhere else. A book. A computer screen.

With a sigh, she dried her hands and limped out of the bathroom. Tyler was drying dishes. Dishes he'd washed. Because of course he cleaned. He couldn't be the perfect man without cleaning.

She'd crossed half the room when he was suddenly beside her. He slipped his powerful arms around her once again and lifted her off her feet.

She told herself to object, but her lips only separated for a second before snapping closed again. The truth was, she was already getting used to his touch. Addicted to it, even.

He placed her on the couch and handed her a glass of red wine. She'd opened the bottle during dinner. Tyler had barely drunk any. He told her that he rarely drank, especially while on the job. Because he considered *this* "on the job"?

Her gaze went to the kitchen. "Tyler, I can help you tidy up."

"I'm almost done."

Again, she could have argued some more, but he'd already returned to the kitchen and continued drying the dishes, his thick muscles pulling at the material of his shirt. Man, oh man, he was pretty.

When he finally returned to the couch, he lifted her ankle onto his lap and restarted that torturous massage. Lord, his hands felt good. She wanted to lean back, close her eyes, and just get lost in the feeling.

"Do you still keep in contact with your ex-husband?" he asked.

She sipped her wine. "I do, actually. We're friends. Probably should have stayed friends instead of marrying." She swirled the wine around in her glass. "We're opposites. He's all science, and I'm all art. He's studying for his PhD in neuropsychology. He lives and breathes the stuff. And he can afford to be a lifelong learner because he has a lot of generational wealth. Money inherited from his parents and grandparents."

"So it was an amicable divorce, then?" Tyler's deep voice brushed over her skin like soft velvet.

The small smile was automatic. "It was probably the most amicable divorce in the history of divorces."

He watched her closely, like he took in everything she said... maybe even the words she *didn't* speak. "Who initiated the divorce?"

"Me. It was a Wednesday night. We were sitting at the table, eating dinner. Neither of us had spoken a word in twenty-three minutes. I remember because my last question to him had been, 'What's the time?'"

His powerful hands moved over her calf, drawing her focus. They pressed and massaged and soothed her skin.

"He was reading some psychology dissertation. And out of nowhere, the idea of divorce slipped into my head. It was like this whisper inside me. But instead of feeling sad or scared, do you know what my first thought was?"

"What?" Soft. The man's voice was soft. The only soft thing about him.

"Who would mow my lawn."

His brows twitched, like he wondered if she was telling the truth.

She swallowed. "I didn't feel sad about losing him or being divorced. My lawn was literally my biggest concern at that moment. Oh, and I was worried about who would change his tires. I'd always been the tire changer in the relationship." She chuckled at the memory. "And that was when I knew it was time to leave."

Looking up, she met his dark, intense gaze, before adding, "You should care about more than lawn and tire maintenance when you consider leaving a man you supposedly love."

Tyler pressed his thumb into her skin and ran it down the side of her leg. "Are you happy now?"

Happy? She hadn't asked herself that since the divorce.

No. The word was loud and firm in her head. But that had more to do with Levi than Rowan.

"I'm happier than I would have been if I'd stayed with him. Marrying Rowan was a mistake. A safe choice. Something I did because he asked, and I was getting older."

"And what did he say when you told him you wanted a divorce?"

Even that memory made her smile, but it was more sad than anything else. "He looked at me, and I could almost see him dissecting the idea in his head. Dissecting *me*. He does that to everything. It's the scientist in him. A full thirty seconds passed, then he nodded and said he agreed. And that was it. There were no tears. No arguments. We sold the house and off I went."

Easy. So much easier than it should have been.

"I even moved into an apartment. No lawn to mow."

He chuckled.

"What about you?" she asked. "Any great loves?" Her stomach did a little roll at the thought of this man loving another woman.

"No great loves yet."

Yet... The word rolled over her skin, causing the hairs on her arms to stand on end. Did he expect to fall in love? Did he want to? She wanted to ask, but fear kept the question at bay.

"I meant what I said in your office the other day," she said softly. "I really am sorry about Project Arma." She felt awful for every person whose life had been touched by that stupid project.

"Thank you. It wasn't all bad. For most of our time in captivity, we were kept on a large property in a big house. We were only put in cages at the end."

Jesus. Had Levi known about the cages?

Her stepbrother's words played in her head yet again.

If that means a few good men are sacrificed so that many others live, then that's just what has to happen.

Tyler was one of those "few good men."

She swallowed. "But you don't think you could ever forgive any of the men who worked for Hylar?"

A steeliness entered his eyes. "Any person who knew what Hylar was doing, and still made the conscious decision to work for him, is beyond redemption."

Her heart dropped, and all the warmth that had been sweeping through her limbs disappeared. There was so much anger in his voice. It was like a bucket of cold water. After the day they'd had, a part of her had started hoping, praying, that she could build trust with this man. Maybe try to explain how Levi's experiences led to the decisions he'd made. That they'd affected his judgment.

But there was no softness in his tone. Did that mean it wouldn't be possible?

She straightened, not wanting to think about the answer. "I should be getting to bed now."

A crease formed between his brows. "Are you sure you'll be okay alone? I can sleep on your couch."

His kindness was too much. She shook her head, probably too quickly. "I'll be okay. But thank you."

She stood and began to hobble to the front door, but his arm swept around her waist, taking most of her weight as she walked. And God, all she wanted to do was lean into him. Let this beautiful man support her.

He opened the door and paused, worry glazing his features as he stared into the dark night.

Without thinking, she cupped his cheek. "Really, Ty. You don't need to worry about me."

The hand on her waist tugged her closer. "I do worry about you."

She sucked in air, his woodsy scent infusing the air around her. "I'll be okay." Her words were almost a whisper, yet he heard.

Step back, Em. Get some distance.

But instead of listening to her own advice, she leaned closer.

His head lowered, and every fraction of distance his lips crept toward hers, her heart pumped harder. Her skin felt that much more sensitive, and her lungs tightened. She screamed at herself to pull away. But she just...*couldn't*. Attraction for this near stranger overwhelmed her, as crazy as that seemed.

She remained perfectly still as he pressed his mouth to hers.

Oh God. The man's lips...they were perfect and made her heart roar to a new rhythm.

His other hand swept up her back and held her so close, she could feel his entire front press against hers. And when her lips parted, and he swept his tongue inside her mouth, she moaned.

Safety. Desire. Heat. It all melded together in the most intoxicating way. It pulled her in and demanded she give all of herself to this man.

As his tongue continued to swipe against hers, she eased her fingers into the soft strands of his hair, holding him close. His hands traversed her back, one slipping up to her neck, holding her head.

She liked being held by him and could already feel it would be very easy to become addicted.

She didn't know how long they stood like that, getting lost in each other, but all too soon he lifted his head. Her breathing was labored, and she was almost certain her eyes were hooded.

He swept his fingers through her hair. "I'll see you tomorrow."

Words tickled at her throat, but a nod was all she could manage.

"Lock the door after me, Amber Eyes," he whispered.

Amber Eyes... She wanted to sigh at that intimate nickname.

He lowered his head and pressed his lips to hers once again. One more gentle kiss. One more somersault of her belly. Then he whispered against her mouth, "Sleep well, honey."

She watched him until his car disappeared down the driveway. And even then, she remained where she was.

She shouldn't have kissed him. Mistake. One big fat mistake.

Then why had it felt so right?

CHAPTER 7

Tyler's gaze ran over the notes of the latest killings in Steve's case.

Daniel Spencer and his mother, Jenny Spencer.

Daniel had been stabbed and left to bleed out on the second floor of an isolated house on the outskirts of some small town. He was the number one suspect in the rape and murder of an ex-girlfriend. Unfortunately, the DNA sample from the crime scene hadn't been stored properly and had deteriorated, so there wasn't enough evidence to convict. He'd been all over the news.

His mother died in the same house, but unlike Daniel, the fire had killed her, which was arguably a worse fate than a stabbing.

Why? Why stab *him*, a potentially heinous criminal, and let her suffer in the fire? She attended church. Lived a quiet life. Had no convictions or complaints against her. Was she killed solely because of her relationship to Daniel?

Had the house been on fire when she'd arrived? It had to be. The door was open, like all the others, and she'd died beside her son, making Tyler suspect she'd gone in to save him but was unable to get him out.

He ran a hand over his face in frustration. He was still trying to get his head around it when his phone rang from the table. Liam.

Liam and Flynn were in Kansas, where the latest murders had taken place.

He answered on the second ring. "How'd it go with the kid?"

Jenny's other son, Daniel's brother, was twenty, so not really a kid, but he was young.

"He had a lot to say," Liam said, wind blowing in the background. "He hated his brother. Said he was an asshole and should've been in prison. He was also angry at his mother for constantly defending him. Said she always stood by him, even when she shouldn't have."

"So, he wasn't close to either of them?"

"Nope. Moved away from home two years ago and barely visited. Unfortunately, that means he didn't know a whole lot about who might have killed them. Said a lot of people hated his brother, though. Gave us a couple of names. We're going to check them out now, but I'm not feeling optimistic."

Tyler figured as much. "Keep us posted."

"You got it."

When the call ended, Tyler leaned back in his seat and closed his eyes. Steve usually only asked them to step in on cases that required muscle or speed, but with this one, he was lost for motive, and Tyler could see why.

A voice floated down the hall. A soft voice that hit him right in the gut.

Emerson.

A few days had passed since she'd rolled her ankle. In that time, there'd been no more kisses but plenty of touches. Grazes on the arm. Hands on the small of her back.

For some reason, she was hesitant around him now. But in the tiny moments when he touched her, that hesitancy melted.

This morning, she'd insisted on going on a short walk, even though her ankle was still a little swollen. He'd only allowed it for about twenty minutes. They spent some time in the park. Some time at The Grind. They'd returned to Blue Halo an hour ago. She was working on her laptop while he worked in his office. It was hard to concentrate when he knew she was just steps away.

He could hear her talking to Grace, Logan's partner, two doors down. His muscles twitched to get up. Go talk to her.

His gaze flicked to the clock on his wall. Five. Time to take her home.

He was about to get up and go to her when another call came through. He sighed. Blue Halo had been busy lately. A lot of people needed their help because there were a lot of scumbags in the world.

～

"HEY!"

Emerson's attention shifted from her laptop screen to the voice behind her. A short woman with long brown hair fanning around her shoulders stood in the doorway.

The woman smiled. "Sorry, I was just walking past and saw you in here. You're Emerson?"

Emerson smiled from where she sat at a small table. "Yes, I am."

"I'm Grace. I'm dating Logan."

God, all these men had such gorgeous partners. Not a surprise, really.

Grace's gaze shifted to her foot, which was resting on another chair. "Courtney mentioned you rolled your ankle outside her shop. How's it healing?"

She lifted a shoulder. "It's fine, just a bit fat. I probably wouldn't even have it elevated right now, but the two times I've put it down, Tyler just happened to come in a minute later and demand I put it back up."

Grace chuckled. "Crazy, isn't it? It's not enough that they can hear things they shouldn't. Sometimes it feels like they can see through walls. I swear, the second I feel upset over anything, Logan's beside me asking if I'm okay."

"Oh, that's sweet." Like, ridiculously sweet.

Grace grinned. "Yeah, he's a good guy. They all are. Well, I'll leave you to it. It was nice to meet you."

Emerson smiled as the woman left and turned her attention back to her laptop.

She'd spent her day responding to requests and queries about commissioned pieces, some small, some large. She'd also caught up on a few admin tasks. The type of tasks she hated. She was currently in the middle of a commissioned painting, which she would prefer to be working on, but every so often she had to force herself to stop and complete more mundane stuff.

Blowing out a breath, she got back to work. These emails weren't going to answer themselves.

She didn't know how much time had passed when a hand touched her shoulder.

She jumped and turned, air whipping into her lungs on a gasp. When she saw Tyler, she almost deflated. "Oh my gosh. Either you walk like a cat, or I was too deep in my own world to hear you."

"Maybe a bit of both." He crouched beside her. Her stomach fluttered at the proximity of his lips. At the way his hand shifted from her shoulder to her knee. "I'm sorry I'm late. I lost track of time."

She swallowed, trying to wet her suddenly dry throat. "I didn't even notice it was late."

His gaze darted between her eyes, and when it slid down to her mouth, the fine hairs on her arms stood on end.

Her lips separated, and memories of their kiss the other night fluttered through her mind. A kiss she'd promised herself wouldn't happen again, and she'd done a damn good job of making sure of that...so far.

"I should get you home," he said quietly. "It will be dark soon."

Her heart jumped as her gaze shot to the window. Walking on a well-lit street was okay, but her heart rate always picked up and fear trickled into the dark places inside her when it was too dark. Usually, she was good at hiding that fear, but with Tyler, it would be harder.

She plastered a smile onto her face. "I'm ready when you are." Hopefully, if there was a shake in her voice, Tyler would think she was just nervous about his proximity.

He watched her for another beat. Man, his eyes were intense. Beautiful, but intense. She had to get up before she did something stupid...like touch him. Cup his cheek. *Kiss* him.

Argh. She pushed to her feet. Tyler rose slowly, towering over her as he usually did.

"How's the admin work going?"

She scoffed at his question. "I hate it. Give me a paintbrush any day, but a laptop? No, thanks. An unfortunate consequence of being self-employed."

"But all worth it when you get to do what you love."

The way he said *love*—the smooth, raspy tone of his voice— made her swallow hard. She took a quick step away from him. Or a limp away. "You're right. Art is my world, and I would do anything to make sure I can keep doing it."

His gaze darkened. Suddenly, he looked at her like *she* was a piece of art.

Get out, Emerson. Before it's too late.

She turned and headed toward the door, and immediately Tyler's thick arm slid around her waist, taking her weight.

It wasn't completely dark outside when they left, but by the time they got to her place, it was. It was the kind of dark where there wasn't even a moon or star in the sky to brighten the ground in front of you. Fortunately, Tyler didn't question her when she turned on her phone's flashlight before she climbed out of the car. Or when she stuck close to him and put all her focus on the beam of light.

She breathed a sigh of relief when she finally flipped the switch to illuminate the kitchen and living area. She turned off the flashlight and set her phone on the island before giving her attention to Tyler. He stood by the half-closed door, again doing that "watching her too closely" thing. He was good at that.

"I'm sorry it was another wasted day," she said quietly.

There'd been no sightings of Levi. Not on their walk or at the park. And not at The Grind, although she'd watched outside the window the entire freaking time.

"We have time." The deep rumble of his voice washed over her skin.

Did they? Every day that passed made her worry that Levi was falling deeper into the dark space in which he'd found himself. She constantly wondered if he'd hurt anyone. Done anything he would regret later.

She didn't share any of those fears with Tyler. "Maybe tomorrow."

He stepped closer...and it was like a repeat of the other night. The slowing of her breath. The thumping of her heart.

He'd just touched her hip when the lights suddenly flashed off in the living room.

Her reaction was instant.

Throat closed.

Heart raced.

A roar blasted between her ears.

"Emerson?"

Phone. Flashlight.

She ran her fingers over the kitchen island in desperation.

She needed her phone! She swept things off the surface, her movements clumsy.

"Hey...Emerson..."

A hand touched her waist, and her entire body jolted.

"I can't...breathe!" she gasped.

No phone.

The panic was closing in, but she frantically shoved it away. She couldn't let herself drown in her fear. She'd seen a therapist for this. She knew what to do.

Deep breaths were key.

In...and out...

Next, she forced her muscles to relax. First her shoulders. Then her jaw. She was just unclenching her fingers when light hit her closed eyelids.

She opened her eyes. Tyler stood beside her, at first a blur, then she blinked. He held his cell, the flashlight on. His expression was soft, worried.

"Are you okay?"

No. She wasn't. And she hated that he'd seen her like that.

Embarrassment heated her cheeks. "I'm okay." A whispered lie. Another to add to the tally she was telling this man.

"Can I touch you?"

She swallowed. There was still a shake in her limbs and fear swimming in her belly, but she wanted his touch. She wanted everything he could give her. Warmth. Safety.

"Yes," she whispered.

He took a small step closer, setting his phone on the counter so the flashlight shone at the ceiling. Then he touched her hip with one hand and cupped her cheek with the other. "There you are."

The heat of his hands... God, she wanted to let it thaw every inch of the ice inside her. To pull the ragged edges of her brokenness back together.

So instead of stepping away like she knew she should, instead of creating space between them, she stepped closer. His ribs were solid, warm against her fingers, and she touched her forehead to his chest. His arms wrapped around her.

And there it was. Protection. Calm. Peace.

The lights flicked back on, but she didn't lift her head, and Tyler didn't lower his arms. He knew she needed him. Knew she needed them to remain exactly as they were just for a bit longer.

Eventually, she'd lift her head. Check the fuse panel. Give Mrs. Henry a call. But for now, clutching Tyler was all she had the strength to do.

CHAPTER 8

*T*yler kept his steps silent as he moved through the wooded area around Emerson's Airbnb. A night had passed since the power outage. Fire still scorched his veins at the memory of her fear. She hadn't been able to see anything, but with his enhanced vision, he'd seen *everything*. The color leach from her face. The raw terror in her eyes.

He hadn't just seen the fear though, he'd felt it. The way her limbs trembled so fiercely, her teeth had rattled. Her jolt at his touch like he was a demon in the dark. An enemy she couldn't run from.

She'd gone somewhere else. Somewhere dark he hadn't been able to reach her. And he wanted to know where.

When she'd finally returned to him, he'd wanted to ask about her fear of the dark and kill whoever instilled it. Tear them to fucking shreds. But the second she pulled out of his arms, she'd flown into action. Calling Mrs. Henry. Checking the fuse box. All the while, never quite meeting his eyes.

According to Mrs. Henry, the power went out often. The Airbnb host had apologized, even offered to refund for some of her stay. A little part of him wondered, though, if there was more to it than that. He hadn't heard anyone outside that night, but the incident made him uneasy enough that he wanted to stick close by, even if she insisted he didn't need to.

His gaze flicked to the time on his phone. Almost one in the morning. He started to return the cell to his pocket when it vibrated with a message from Callum.

Everything okay out there?

He sent a quick text back to his friend.

All is quiet.

Callum was coming to take over in about half an hour. A part of Tyler wanted to stay. He trusted his friends to guard the house. Hell, he trusted every man on his team with his life. But being close to her felt right, and it eliminated the pit in his gut.

He didn't need much sleep, but he knew he'd be more alert if he went home and got at least a couple hours.

He'd just slipped his phone into his pocket when he heard it. The crunch of leaves beneath shoes.

His gaze shot up in the direction of the noise. A beat of silence passed.

Then he saw the distant shadow of a person.

Tyler took off. He didn't try to mask the noise of his feet pounding the ground or the branches whipping across his body, he just ran.

The guy matched his speed, and when he turned his head, Tyler caught sight of his face. It was a brief glimpse, but that was all he needed.

Levi. And the guy was running full tilt away from Tyler. Away from the cabin.

Cool air whipped across his face, and branches snapped beneath his feet. He ignored all of it, putting his entire focus on the man in front of him.

Levi was fast and athletic, jumping over large rocks and fallen trees like they were nothing. But Tyler was fast too. And he was driven. Driven to keep Emerson safe. To catch her stepbrother for her.

Levi glanced over his shoulder again, and Tyler caught another glimpse of his face. Definitely him. He even had the scar beside his right eye, which Emerson had described in the meeting. He looked older than his military photos and less...tamed.

Tyler pushed his body to move faster. He was gaining, but he was doing so too goddamn slowly.

They'd just reached the outskirts of the woods when Tyler was close enough to lunge. He grabbed Levi around the middle and sent them both to the ground. Levi was only under him for a second before spinning them around.

The knife appeared from nowhere, swiping at Tyler's throat.

Tyler whipped his head aside just before the sharp blade could slice skin. He grabbed Levi's wrist, rolling again so the man was under him once more.

"Stop!" Tyler shouted. "I want to help you."

Levi growled and spluttered, his eyes savage and unfocused. "You're one of *them*. I'll never stop!"

"I'm not your enemy!"

The hit to the ribs caught Tyler hard enough for him to lose his hold on the man's wrist. Instead of swinging the knife again, Levi threw Tyler to the side, jumped to his feet, and ran.

Tyler rose too, but by the time he gained his feet, the guy was gone.

Fuck!

There was a dull ache in his ribs, but he ignored it, instead letting the anger and frustration over losing the man take hold. He'd been right there, goddammit!

He grabbed his phone from his back pocket, ignoring the pain from the slight twist of his torso. Callum answered immediately.

"Hey."

"Levi was here. I just chased him through the woods around Emerson's place."

Movement sounded on the phone. "I'll come now. You okay?"

"Yeah, I caught him, but he got me in the ribs and I lost my grip." Another blast of anger and frustration melded in his gut.

"Won't be long."

"Thanks." He'd just hung up when a call came through. His brows twitched when he saw who it was.

Emerson.

~

No problem with the lights tonight?

The text from Mrs. Henry made her smile. It was late, yet the woman was still texting. Mrs. Henry was a self-proclaimed night owl, and when Emerson had told her she was the same, she'd taken to texting at all hours. Emerson didn't mind. Working into the night could get lonely. It was nice to have someone to message.

She typed in a quick response.

I've had power all night.

Thank God. She'd also kept her phone on her at all times. Just in case. She *did not* want a repeat of her panic attack from the other night. She couldn't even think about that without feeling the overwhelming need to bury her head into the sand.

Her phone vibrated again.

Oh, good. I can rest easy. Have a good night, dear.

Emerson pushed the phone into her pocket and lifted the paintbrush. She should go to bed. She should have gone to bed long ago. But she couldn't stop. She'd worked on a commissioned piece for a while when she got home, but now she was starting a new one of Levi, this time as she'd seen him at the bus stop.

Her strokes became stronger, faster, flying over the canvas. Emotions swirled inside her. Frustration. Love. Fear.

God, so much fear.

More dark strokes. She usually painted in color. Bright and

vibrant. But today, everything was black and gray and charcoal. The darkness matched the look she'd seen in Levi's eyes. He seemed nothing like the boy who'd cared about her and protected her from her father.

Her chest rose and fell in quick succession as she painted dark clouds around him. Endless minutes passed. Endless strokes of the brush. All the while, music blasted through the room, blocking out the world.

"Don't touch her!"

She frowned, pain filling her chest at the memory of that day. The day Levi had stepped in front of her father. Protected her. *Almost died* for her.

"Get out of my way, boy. This has nothing to do with you."

Her father's voice was as evil in her head as it had been in that moment. She slashed her brush against the canvas.

"If you touch her, I'll break you!"

He'd only been twelve, yet Levi's voice had been so fierce. Like he had no fear even though he was standing in front of a monster twice his size.

Images flashed in her mind of what had happened next. Of the angry fists of her father. Of Levi continuing to rise to his feet and shield her body with his own.

More slashes of her brush.

He'd protected her. Yet she hadn't been able to protect him. From the heartache of what had happened in the military, then Project Arma.

She kept painting. Kept moving her brush, even as tears pricked her eyes. As a familiar devastation rose in her chest, choking the air out of her.

More than anything, she hadn't been able to protect Levi from himself. From his own mind.

By the time she was finished, tears blurred the canvas in front of her, threatening to fall, but she scrubbed them away.

She would not fall apart. She was stronger than that.

For the first time that night, she sat back and studied the painting carefully. Beneath Levi's intense focus, beneath his anger, she saw...fear.

"Oh, Levi."

Fear and pain mixed together, making him look like a bomb about to explode.

God, she wished she could make it better. Like Levi and his mother had made her life better through their love.

She frowned when her gaze caught on the hand on his shoulder. He'd been touching his shoulder the entire time during those brief seconds. Scratching and digging his fingers into his skin. Like he was in pain of some kind.

With a long exhale, she stood. God, every muscle creaked and ached. How long had she been painting? She checked her phone.

A bit past one in the morning. And another night of missed dinner. Argh, she needed to get better at looking after herself. She stretched her stiff muscles, then moved over to the light switch and flicked it off.

She was just pulling the door closed when she saw eyes watching her through the window.

A terrified gasp wrenched from her throat, and she took three big steps back, hip hitting the couch. Before she could stop herself, she called Tyler. Even though it was the middle of the night, he answered on the first ring and sounded wide awake.

"Emerson, are you okay?"

"I just saw him. In the window." Usually, her stepbrother didn't scare her, but this time, he did. Because he'd been watching her from the darkness. How long had he been standing there?

Wind whistled over the line. "I'm coming now. Make sure the doors are locked and grab a weapon if you have one."

A relieved exhale rushed from her chest. The relief was mixed with guilt, of course, because it was the middle of the night. But still... "Thank you."

"Two minutes."

Wait, what?

The line went dead.

Two minutes? How was the guy going to get to her house in two minutes?

Unless he was already close...

CHAPTER 9

Tyler wanted to kick his own ass. Levi had circled back. Why the hell hadn't Tyler gone straight back to her cabin?

He reached the house in minutes, but before knocking, he took a moment to listen. Only one heartbeat from inside the house. Good.

He knocked on the door. When Emerson opened it, she stood in front of him in leggings and an oversized shirt. There were splatters of paint on her clothes and hands, and a streak of black on her cheekbone, like she'd rubbed her face or brushed hair behind her ear, leaving a trail of paint as she went.

"Are you okay?"

Her chest rose and fell. "Yes."

"Good. I'm going to do a quick perimeter check. Stay inside, and if you see him again, make noise. I'm going to stay close enough to hear you."

She gave a quick nod.

He stepped back, then circled the house. At a window on the side of the cabin, there were footprints in the grass.

He trailed them back into the woods. Yeah, the guy had definitely circled back and returned. He'd given himself a wide enough berth that Tyler couldn't hear him.

Stupid. So damn stupid. He'd been so fixated on the fact he'd lost Levi that he hadn't been thinking straight.

He jogged back to the door and knocked again. Emerson let him in, and the second he stepped inside, he was hit by the scent of lilacs. He worked hard to control the twitch in his fingers to touch her.

"I found his prints in the yard, but he's gone now."

"I figured," she said softly. Another nibble of her lip. "You were out there, weren't you? It's how you got to me so quickly."

He considered his words, not sure how she'd react. "My team and I have been watching your house since the power went out." No surprise on her face. He took a small step toward her. "I'm sorry I didn't tell you. I did it because I want you safe. And I'm not leaving."

Her brows twitched. "I told you, I can't afford—"

"I don't care about money, Em." He took hold of her hips. Touching this woman felt right. He literally couldn't *not* touch her. "You hired me to find and bring in your stepbrother. If he's remaining close to you, I need to be close to you as well."

And more than that, he needed to know she was okay.

Her gaze went to his shirt. There was another twitch of her brows. Carefully, she lifted a small leaf from the material, then brushed dirt from his shoulder. "Why do you look like you've been rolling around on the ground?"

"Because I caught him."

Her breath hitched, her eyes flashing back up to his.

"But then I lost him," he quickly added.

Concern transformed her expression. "But you're both okay?"

"Yes. He clearly circled back while I was still out there. I'm sorry."

She shook her head. "Don't say sorry." She stepped away, her hands dropping from his chest, his leaving her waist. And damn, he wanted to pull her back.

"I only have one bed."

Her statement caused one side of his mouth to kick up. "I can sleep on the couch, honey."

She laughed, and that sound hit him dangerously low in his gut, heating him from the inside. "It's a two-person couch, and you're a million feet tall. There's no way you'll fit."

"I'll make it work." Hell, he'd slept worse places.

She scoffed. "Unless you can fold yourself into a pretzel, that's not happening. I'll sleep on the couch." She started to walk away, but he snagged her wrist and pulled her back. Her eyes widened, her hand yet again pressing to him.

"You're not sleeping on the couch." He grazed his thumb across her wrist. "The gentleman in me would never allow that."

There was a beat of silence. The kind of silence you wanted to pause and get lost in.

"I guess we could both sleep in the bed," she said quietly. "It's big."

Something flared to life inside of him at the thought of sharing a bed with this woman. He sure as hell wouldn't say no. "Whatever you're comfortable with, Amber Eyes."

Another swipe of his thumb. Her intense stare punched right into his chest before tugging her arm away. "Okay. I'll just go change."

He watched as she headed into the bedroom, a smile playing on his lips. The smile disappeared when he glanced out the window. She was too vulnerable out here. What the hell was Levi doing? Just watching her? If he thought she wasn't safe with Tyler, would he attack any of the Blue Halo team? Or would he try to take her? He was hoping for the former.

A couple minutes later, the bedroom door opened, letting him know she was ready. His insides warmed at the sight of that familiar camisole. At the miles of golden leg exposed by those shorts. Her throat bobbed when she met his gaze. Did she see in his eyes everything he was feeling? Heat...need...desire?

She quickly turned and retreated back into the room.

Yeah, she saw it.

He switched off the lights in the living area before moving into the bedroom. A text came through from Callum. He was out there. Good. For tonight at least, there were two of them here. He felt better about that.

When he tugged his shirt over his head, her gasp sliced through the quiet. His gaze shifted across the room to see her looking at his torso. He looked down, spotting the large purple bruise already visible from where Levi had hit him.

Damn. He shouldn't have let the guy get a punch in. He was better than that. He shifted his attention back to her. "It looks worse than it is." And more than that, he was a quick healer. It would be faded by tomorrow.

Slowly, she crossed the room. When she stopped and grazed the discolored skin with the tips of her fingers, his muscles tensed so hard he was sure they'd snap. Her touch left a trail of fire burning across his stomach.

Her gaze lifted, but there wasn't desire in her eyes, there was something else. Concern. Worry. "I don't want him to hurt you."

He slipped his hand on top of hers. "He won't."

"You can't be sure of that. He's dangerous, and he thinks you're a threat." There was a small pause. "Maybe I shouldn't have brought you into this."

He stepped closer, his hand curving around hers, holding her. His other touched her cheek. "I'm glad you did. You don't need to worry about me. He may be dangerous, but so am I. And I won't stop until we get him the help he needs."

Her lips separated like she was going to say something. Then she stopped. Blinked. Whatever it was, became lost as her mouth snapped shut and she stepped away.

He wanted to pull her back, ask her what was going on in that pretty head of hers. But it was late. They both needed sleep. So he let her go...for now.

As she slid between the sheets, he switched off the light and climbed in beside her. He noticed she had a small nightlight on her side that shone a warm light across the ceiling. She didn't move to switch it off.

His hand twitched to pull her near. Hold her. The thought had no sooner entered his mind when she shuffled closer and lay a hand on his chest.

"Thank you," she whispered.

He wrapped an arm around her waist and pulled her into him. There. That felt better. "You don't need to thank me for protecting you."

∽

EMERSON WOKE to a steady thump in her ear. Not only that, but she was warm. So warm, she wanted to snuggle down and stay right where she was longer. Let the seconds trickle into minutes.

It took a few beats to recognize the thumps as Tyler's heart and the warmth as his smooth skin. That should scare her. It should make her pull away. It didn't. Because the more she got to know this beautiful man, the more she believed, hoped, and prayed he would understand. If she was open and vulnerable with him and she told him everything Levi had been through, he might still be willing to help. But first, she needed the courage to be open and vulnerable. And she needed to hope like hell he didn't hate her for not being honest from the beginning.

The hand on her back grazed the skin beneath her top, cutting her thoughts off in their track.

She bit back a groan. God, that felt good.

He did it again. Same thing.

Instead of pulling away or leaning into him, she remained perfectly still. Perfectly caught between what she should do and what she wanted to do. She let his strong heart thrum beneath her ear and the burn of his hand cast a trail of goose bumps along her back.

Slowly, the strokes lengthened, hovering at the waistband of her shorts before rising up to her shoulder blades.

Endless minutes of those long, slow strokes passed. Of her skin tingling and her breaths shortening. It wasn't until she was on the brink of losing her mind that she looked up to meet his gaze. Tyler was watching her closely. There was no smile on his face.

Her throat closed. The way he looked at her...it was like he saw her need and he approved. Like he wanted her to want him.

Her heart kicked against her ribs, and when her gaze lowered to his lips, the fingers on her back spanned and nudged her that bit closer to him.

"You shouldn't look at me like that."

She swallowed and met his eyes. "Like what?"

"Like you want my kiss as much as I want to give it to you."

Her heart stopped. *I do.* The words were a breathless murmur inside her from a place she needed to lock away from him and the world.

Unable to stop herself, she stroked a hand across his chest. "Why do I want to forget about everything and get lost in you whenever we touch?"

She probably shouldn't have asked that question. It was as dangerous as this man's proximity. But the words tumbled out before she could stop them.

With his other hand, he trailed a finger from her shoulder to her elbow. Every hair stood on end.

"I don't know," he said, his voice raspy. "But if you're lost, I want to be lost with you."

His words were like an arrow to her chest. Digging into her, claiming her as his.

He felt it too. But she'd already known that. She'd already felt the connection.

The finger trailed back up her arm, passing her shoulder before cupping her cheek. "You're so beautiful, Em."

Why did he have to be so perfect and say all the right things?

His fingers threaded into her hair, and his thumb grazed the back of her ear. She couldn't stop herself. She stretched up and kissed him.

His hold on her neck tightened, the fingers of his other hand spreading, taking up almost her entire back. His soft lips swiped across hers, and God, in that moment she couldn't give him up. Not the kiss, not the hold he had on her. None of it.

Heat danced in her belly, and lava burned through her. She leaned into him, hand skirting up his skin, grazing every inch of his rock-hard chest.

When her lips separated, his tongue slipped inside her mouth and stroked hers.

She hummed. Christ, this man and the things he did to her. The things he made her feel. It was unlike anything she'd experienced before him. Like a storm of fire and yearning and rightness. Yes, so much right.

The second the word hit her consciousness, though, the questions came. How could it be right when the foundation of the relationship was built on a lie? A lie he might hate her for?

"I can almost hear you thinking," he whispered against her lips.

It was too late. Cold had replaced the heat in her chest, and she pushed herself up slightly, breaking the contact. It shouldn't take as much strength as it did. It shouldn't take her remembering why she was here.

This time, her heart thumped for a different reason. His hands remained behind her head and back. She was so weak that she didn't even want him to drop them. He didn't seem annoyed that she'd stopped kissing him. More intrigued.

"What's going on in that beautiful head of yours, Amber Eyes?"

He knew. Not what she was hiding, but that she was hiding *something*.

Yet he didn't push. Because that was the kind of guy he was— good. He was all good. Whereas she...

She had to stop. The kisses. The touches. Everything. At least for now.

"We should get up," she said quietly. "I have to finish a commissioned piece this week, and we need to do a walk around town."

For Levi. He was her reason for being here. She had to remember that.

Tyler brushed some hair back from her face. A beat passed, where he looked into the depths of her eyes and seemed to find everything. The hesitation. The battle that raged. Then, finally... "Okay, honey."

He was letting her go without forcing her to share her secrets. The relief almost whooshed from her chest.

CHAPTER 10

"*Y*our home is beautiful."

Tyler's gut spiraled in waves of heat at the way Emerson's eyes ran over his living room. He'd never cared what anyone thought of his home before, but with this woman, he did. He wanted her approval. He wanted her to like where he lived and feel comfortable in his sanctuary.

He cleared his throat as he dropped his keys on the kitchen island. "I'm glad you like it."

Each member of his team had received a large payout from the government after Project Arma. It meant they could invest in both their business and where they lived. His home was comfortable—two story, four bedrooms, and all his.

A photo on his mantel caught her attention. She moved closer and lifted it, a smile playing on her lips.

"Is this your mom?"

He walked up behind her, touching her hip and letting awareness skirt up his arm.

His mother's face glowed with happiness behind the glass. The familiar sadness settled in his heart. "Yeah."

"She's beautiful. And she must be strong to have raised you on her own."

Oh, she had been. Strong. Kind. Generous. She'd also been his entire family. "She made me into the man I am today."

"Do you see her often?"

He snuck a thumb beneath her shirt, grazing it over her skin, letting it soothe him. "She passed away. Mismanaged diabetes."

He hadn't mentioned that the other night because he hadn't wanted to put a dampener on the evening. Even saying it out loud now hurt like hell.

As his mother had gotten older, he'd always been the one to make sure she was on top of her medication and eating the right things. But he hadn't been able to do that when he'd been taken by Project Arma. And he knew from her medical reports that she'd struggled with his disappearance, both emotionally and physically. She'd stopped taking care of herself.

Emerson watched him, a frown deepening on her face. "I'm sorry."

People had told him the pain of losing a loved one dulled with time. That wasn't his experience. But then, maybe it was because he allowed rivers of guilt and anger to block his acceptance of what had happened. In his mind, the second he'd been taken, those assholes had killed his mother.

Tyler let himself swim in Emerson's brown eyes for a moment, forcing the anger down. "She would have loved you. She was always on me about finding a woman who made me smile for no other reason than she was in the room."

That was Emerson. Even now, when he was feeling the pain of his mother's absence, he wasn't completely taken with his grief. Because he could feel Emerson's warm skin. Smell her floral scent.

"If she was anything like you, I think I would have loved her too."

"She was a better person than me."

She tilted her head. "She sounds like she was an incredible

woman. But then, that's not a surprise, because she raised an incredible son."

His gut twisted, then he lowered his head and kissed her. It was the second kiss of the day, and it wasn't nearly enough.

She hesitated, only for a moment, then she leaned into him, a low moan slipping from her lips.

Fuck...this woman could bring him to his knees. She made him want to hold her tighter, kiss her longer, and fear the moment their connection ended.

Her lips separated and he slid his tongue inside her mouth. She tasted of peppermint blended with sweetness. It was intoxicating. Addictive. And he wanted more.

Without stopping or opening his eyes, he took the framed picture from her fingers and set it back on the mantel. Then he lifted her body against his, fusing them together.

Her hands swept from his cheeks to around his neck.

They stayed like that for endless minutes. It wasn't enough, but he had a feeling nothing would be. When she pushed at his chest, he called on all his damn willpower to lift his head. To separate from her.

Her lips were red, her eyes sparkling amber. "I shouldn't be kissing you, Tyler Morgan."

Again, the hesitation from her combined with words that made no sense. Because in his mind, there was nothing they should be doing more.

"Why not?" he questioned, the question becoming more important with each touch.

She stared at him intently, then her thumb grazed his bottom lip before she dropped her hand. "We haven't known each other for very long."

"Is that all it is?"

Her pupils dilated. No. There was more to it than that. But her lips remained sealed.

With a sigh, he slowly slid her down his body onto the floor.

Shit, even that was torture—her soft curves grazing his hardness. He took a much-needed step back. It didn't help.

"I'm just going to have a shower and change. Feel free to grab anything you want from the kitchen. I won't be long."

She nodded, her bottom lip disappearing between her teeth.

He bit back a curse. This was going to be the coldest shower of his life.

~

NEAT. Tyler was very neat. It was a surprise, even though it probably shouldn't have been. Military guys were usually tidy, weren't they? Maybe she'd just been hoping he was a slob. Grabbing at anything that might be a turnoff, because God, she needed one. *Something* to make him a little less perfect.

He'd been gone for fifteen minutes, and in that time, she'd worked out how to use his very big and very impressive coffee machine. Every device in the man's home seemed to be top of the line.

She sipped her coffee before setting it on the island and returning to the photo of his mother. She'd hated hearing the pain in Tyler's voice when he talked about her. He'd loved her. And she'd left him earlier than she should have.

It was a pain Emerson was familiar with. Pixie had become her mother, and she missed her every day. But at the same time, a part of her was glad that the woman's suffering was over. She'd hated losing her son. Having him disappear and remain out of her reach. She'd already mourned her son's declining mental health before that.

When a knock came at the door, Emerson frowned, glanced toward the stairs, then back to the front of the house. Slowly, she moved forward.

She was about to look through the peephole when a warm hand touched her shoulder.

She spun, lips separated on a gasp before she saw Tyler. "I didn't even hear you come down the stairs."

He grinned. "What can I say? I'm good."

Yeah. He was. Especially for such a big guy. She swallowed at the smell of his clean, crisp scent. At the fresh shirt that strained against his thick chest muscles and biceps.

She tilted her head toward the door. "I was just going to check to see who's here."

He leaned over her shoulder, his arm sliding around her waist as he looked through the peephole.

Her pulse jumped. *Calm the hell down, Emerson.*

A small smile tugged at his lips, and he pulled the door open.

She frowned at the sight of her Airbnb host, Mrs. Henry, standing on the other side of the door.

"Hello, dear." She smiled at Emerson before turning to Tyler. "Tyler, would you come look at the HVAC system in my crawl space again? It's doing that thing where it just refuses to turn on like last time."

Wait... "You live on this street?" Emerson asked, surprised.

"Right next door." The older woman tilted her head. "Tyler didn't tell you?"

Ah, no. And he'd been at the cabin when Mrs. Henry had stopped by the other day with an electrician to check out the fuse box.

He shrugged and pressed a hand to the small of her back as they stepped outside. "It didn't come up."

They crossed the front yard to Mrs. Henry's home. The older woman didn't seem surprised to find Emerson at his house, but then, she'd seen them together at the cabin.

They stopped at the side of her home, and Emerson's throat closed at the sight of the entrance to the small crawl space.

"Now, I've already popped my head in there and turned on the light for you, but when I look at the system, I may as well be looking at a manual written in Japanese. I have no idea."

"Not a problem, Mrs. Henry." Tyler faced her, and she wasn't sure what he saw, but it made his features crease into worry. "Hey. You okay?"

She swallowed. "Yes, of course. I just... I'm nervous for you crawling into that space. It's really small."

"I'll be okay." He watched her for another beat, definitely seeing more than he should, then he kissed her forehead. "I won't be long. Stay close so I can see your legs."

She nodded, relieved when he didn't push or ask any more questions. Tyler gave her hip a little squeeze before disappearing.

Mrs. Henry stepped closer. "The day that boy moved in next door, my life got easier. He helps me with everything."

She forced herself to turn away from the crawl space and smile at the older woman. Mrs. Henry was in her mid-sixties and had a motherly kindness about her. "I can imagine. He's certainly been helping me with some stuff."

Concern flickered in the woman's eyes. "Is everything okay?"

"It's..." Not okay? Messy? "Complicated." Yeah, that word fit well.

"Oh. If there's anything I can do to help, let me know. I make a pumpkin pie that turns even the hardest days around."

The woman was so sweet. "Thank you." And wouldn't it be nice if pumpkin pie could fix her problems? A girl could dream.

They'd only been standing there a few minutes when the familiar tingle danced on the back of her neck. Her gaze shifted to the street. Was Levi here? Watching?

She'd just opened her mouth to call Tyler when he appeared from the crawl space. "It should work now. It was the same switch as last time."

The tingle disappeared. Levi was gone.

"Oh, you're a lifesaver," Mrs. Henry gushed.

Tyler moved toward Emerson, his warm hand slipping around her waist. "Everything okay?"

She blew out a long breath and nodded. "Yes."

CHAPTER 11

"Dark or milk chocolate?"

She studied the two bars of chocolate in Tyler's hands, noting the hint of a smile playing at his lips. They were standing in the grocery store, and she wasn't going to lie, it was a tough decision. "Younger me would have said milk. But now that I'm nearing forty, I'm definitely in the dark camp."

His lips twitched. "I'd hardly consider thirty-four to be 'nearly forty.'"

"Ah, well, my creaking bones would say otherwise. And I'm certainly closer to forty than you."

This time, it wasn't a twitch of his lips. It was a full grin, dimples and all. And man, it was a force. "Luckily, I find your maturity sexy as hell."

Her heart stuttered with so much force it rendered her silent. Then he winked, setting her heart off on a full gallop. God, the universe liked to torture her. Or, less the universe and more this man.

With a sharp inhale, she moved forward. Their day had consisted of a long walk around town—now that her ankle was feeling up to it—a longer stop at The Grind, followed by an afternoon of working at Blue Halo. She hadn't quite finished her commissioned piece, but she was close. It was taking her longer than usual, mostly because of all her distractions.

Now they were grocery shopping. It was so...domestic. And it was making her feel everything she *should not* be feeling. But then, they'd already kissed this morning—twice. At this point, she was steering a sinking ship.

He hadn't asked about her reaction to the crawl space at Mrs. Henry's house. She wasn't surprised though. If there was anything she'd learned about Tyler Morgan, it was that he was good at knowing when she wanted to talk about something and when she didn't. And good at not asking too many questions. She was almost certain that was because he wanted her to offer the answers herself. And she wanted to. Lord, she wanted to bare her soul to this man.

"Okay, next big question," Tyler said once she was beside him again. "Chili peppers in your chili con carne, or no chili peppers?"

That was an easy one. "Definitely chili peppers. I'm a 'how hot can you make it' kind of girl."

She expected laughter or some form of humor to play across his face. Maybe a witty retort. So the intensity in his blue eyes and the deepening of his voice almost had her stumbling.

"Guess we'll make it hot, then."

Jesus. Send help.

He held her gaze for a beat longer than he should have, then touched a hand to the small of her back as they walked to the end of the aisle.

Screwed. She was so screwed.

They'd just stepped out of the aisle when prickles on the back of her neck came for the second time that day. Only now, it was more intense. It was accompanied by the hairs on her arms standing on end. The thumping of her heart.

She stopped. He was close.

Tyler's eyes flashed to her in question, but she continued to scan the store, searching for Levi's brown eyes.

"Emerson?"

"He's here," she whispered, finally looking at him.

The change in him was instant. His features tightened. He lowered the basket and reached for something at his waist with the other.

A woman shouted.

Levi walked out of another aisle, gun in both hands, pointed right at them.

Cold sweat drenched her skin.

No. Not them. Tyler.

More screams echoed throughout the store. The pounding sound of people running to get out or hide behind counters. Tyler shifted his body to cover her fully. Emerson remained still. So still, she felt stuck. Unable to move forward or back.

Tyler tried to speak. "Levi—"

"Shut up." Levi stepped in a wide arc to meet her gaze. "Come with me, Emerson. I'll keep you safe."

His left hand released the pistol, and he touched his shoulder. The same shoulder he'd been scratching at the bus station. Like it was itchy or uncomfortable.

"Levi…" She stepped forward, but Tyler's hand whipped out across her body, keeping her in place.

"Don't touch her!" Levi shouted.

She jumped at the vicious anger and aggression in his voice. At the way his fingers twitched on the gun.

"I'm not here to hurt you *or* her, Levi." Tyler's voice was quiet as he inched forward. "I'm here to help." His hand slowly moved behind him. He slipped his phone from his pocket and pressed something. Perhaps to alert his team… Then his hand hovered over something else. The concealed tranquilizer?

Levi's chest heaved with his uneven breaths. "You're lying. You're working with *him*."

"Who's him?" Tyler sounded so soothing and calm. It was the voice an adult would use with a child when they were having a meltdown.

"You know who *he* is! Commander James Hylar."

Her brows creased. Her brother knew that man was dead. Everyone did. When news about Project Arma had broken in the media, so had details about the commander's death.

Another small step forward from Tyler. "Hylar's dead—"

"Stop. *Lying!*"

Her heart cracked at the pain in her stepbrother's voice, at the anxiety and fear she heard behind the words.

"He's alive!" Levi pressed. "And his men are everywhere. I know you're one of them!"

Tyler shook his head. He was blocking her body again. "Some very good friends of mine in Texas killed him themselves. They listened as his heart stopped in his chest."

Again, Levi touched his shoulder. His eyes shut for a second but flashed open the moment Tyler stepped forward. "I just want my sister. Give her to me and I'll leave."

"I can't do that, Levi."

Movement caught her eye from the door. A uniformed officer with a pistol.

No...

The click of the officer thumbing off the safety was loud in the shop—and the second it sounded, Levi turned and fired.

The officer fell to the floor, blood blooming on his chest.

Emerson's heart stopped.

Tyler shot his tranquilizer gun, but Levi ducked faster than her eyes could track. The second he did, Tyler flew forward just as quickly, grabbing Levi's wrist and shoving the pistol's muzzle up toward the roof. Another bullet fired.

People screamed even louder and ran for the door. Emerson raced toward the fallen officer and dropped beside him.

Oh God, there was so much blood!

His eyes were half-closed, his breaths rattling in his chest.

"Hey, stay with me!" she cried as she pressed her hand to his bloody wound.

A woman who'd been working behind a counter crawled toward them. "I've called the paramedics!"

Emerson nodded and searched for Tyler and Levi. Her heart squeezed. They were on the floor, Tyler on top. Levi spun them, throwing a punch. Tyler dodged, then quickly rolled them again.

Fear for both men caused her world to slow and panic to bubble in her chest. Each was as fierce and dangerous as the other.

The officer coughed, and she looked back down to see blood splutter from his mouth. Levi had done this. Levi had hurt this man. The knowledge was like a bullet to her own flesh.

She applied more pressure to the wound.

Had he shot others? Killed them? People he'd deemed a threat?

She swallowed her nausea, and when a loud grunt sounded, she looked over to see Tyler grabbing his side. Levi jumped to his feet and lunged for the gun.

Emerson moved without thought. She dove on top of Tyler, covering his body with her own.

"*Levi, no!*"

Her stepbrother's gaze clashed with hers. Something flashed over his face—confusion mixed with rage.

Tyler quickly stood, lifting her easily and tugging her behind his body.

Liam and Jason flew into the store, one from the entrance, the other from the back, heading straight for them.

Levi took off, smashing through a huge front window and racing into the night.

ANGER AND FRUSTRATION thrummed through Tyler's veins as the paramedic applied a bandage to his stomach. He'd taken a knife to his gut. But he didn't care about that. It was superficial and would heal within a few days. What bothered him was that, for the second time, Levi had been literally in his grasp, but he hadn't been able to capture the guy—because he was trying to detain him without injury.

Thanks to his failure, someone else had been injured instead. The officer had been taken to the hospital. He'd lost a lot of blood, and paramedics hadn't been able to confirm whether he'd survive the night.

Emerson wrapped her arms around herself. His gaze had barely left her since the incident. Meanwhile, since giving a statement to the police, she'd been stuck in her own head.

The rest of his team had arrived minutes after Levi fled, and now everyone had gone home except Jason and Liam. They'd remained in case Levi returned. He hadn't.

When the paramedic was finally done, Tyler stood and walked over to Emerson. He slid an arm around her shoulders, his voice soft as he asked, "Are you okay?"

She nodded too quickly, glancing at his stomach, then back to his face. "Yes. Are you?"

Lie. She wasn't okay. He didn't need his enhanced abilities to hear that. "Just a scratch, honey." He looked up at Jason and Liam. "Thanks, guys. I'll see you tomorrow."

They both nodded. Liam, of course, wasn't actually going home. He was going to tail them back to Tyler's house. Neither Emerson nor Tyler were staying at her Airbnb tonight. Not after Levi had made it clear he wanted to take his stepsister. Tyler's home had more security. It was safer.

He guided her toward his car and waited until they were driving to touch her knee. "Still with me?"

She nodded, but there was no part of him that believed it. Not that he blamed her. She'd watched her stepbrother shoot someone, knife Tyler in the gut, then run away through a plate glass window. It was a shitshow all round—of *course* she was stuck in her own head.

His muscles thrummed with tension as he shot a glance into the rearview mirror. Liam was just visible in the distance. Knowing there was backup close by relaxed him. Marginally.

When they reached his place, he parked in the garage. He was around to her side before she got out of the car.

She stopped when they reached his living room. "Is it okay if I have a shower, then just go to bed? I'm exhausted."

She *looked* exhausted. But he knew it was more emotional than physical. He stepped closer, tucking a lock of hair behind her ear. "You sure you're okay?"

"You should stop asking me that. You're the one who got stabbed." Her face turned down, like she was staring at his waist.

"I told you, it's just a scratch."

She shook her head like she didn't believe him. "Do you think…"

When she stopped, he gently caressed her cheek with his thumb. "What is it, honey?"

"Do you think that officer will be okay?"

Tyler wanted to lie. He wanted to tell her the guy would be fine. But the bullet had hit too close to the heart for him to be able to give her any reassurance. "I'm not sure."

Pain flashed across her face. And maybe guilt, too. She stepped out of his reach.

With a sigh, he led her up the stairs and into the bathroom connected to his room. Once she had a towel and one of his shirts to sleep in, he left her.

The second he was back downstairs, he pulled out his phone and called Liam, who answered on the first ring.

"Hey."

Tyler checked the lock on the back door. "All clear out there?"

"All clear, but I'm gonna stay out here until around two, then Aidan's gonna take over."

God, he was so grateful for his team. "Thank you."

"You got it. Call if you need anything."

He hung up and spent the next few minutes confirming that all entry points were locked and the house alarmed. He grabbed something quick to eat, even though he wasn't hungry. When the shower turned off, he took some food upstairs to the bedroom. She'd probably tell him she didn't want to eat, but he'd still offer.

He was beside the bed, removing his shirt, when she stepped into the room, hair damp around her shoulders, his shirt drowning her.

Desire slammed into his gut. And something else. Something darker. More possessive. Because he liked looking at this woman in his clothing...and he almost didn't get the chance. She could've been taken from him tonight. And it made everything in him scream *his*.

Emerson didn't meet his eyes. She was staring at the bandage on his torso.

Slowly, she stepped forward until she was in front of him. Then, just like she'd done with the bruise last night, she grazed his stomach. And even though her fingers slid over the bandage, he swore he felt skin against skin.

So many emotions flickered over her face that he couldn't tell what she was thinking.

Gently, he cupped her cheek. "What's going on in that head of yours?"

Her brows creased, but she didn't take her eyes off his stomach. "It just kind of hit me tonight... Maybe I can't save him."

There was so much anguish in her voice, like the very thought of failure killed something inside her. It fucking tore at him.

"Hey." He put some pressure on her chin. It took her a moment, but finally, her eyes rose. "He's suffering from a mental illness. He needs help. And we're going to get him that help. After that, it will be up to him to get better."

Her frown deepened, and she looked away. "There are things I haven't told you."

"What haven't you told me?"

He needed to know. The reason for her hesitation. The secrets in her eyes.

Her hands moved over his chest, slowly, like she was familiarizing herself with him. Every muscle in his body tightened. Instead of answering his question, she inched closer and pressed a kiss to his bandage. And again, despite the thin material of the dressing, her lips burned him. Singed his very skin.

"I'm so sorry he stabbed you."

That wasn't an answer to his question. "Emerson..."

She looked up, her gaze filled with so much emotion. "I need you to be okay."

"I am. But I didn't like you putting yourself between me and that weapon today." He would have nightmares about that. Of her shielding him from a bullet with her body.

"I was trying to protect you."

"That's not your job. It's mine."

She took a deep breath, her chest rising and falling. The next words tumbled from her lips in a whisper. "Kiss me, Tyler."

He needed answers. But that was a request he couldn't say no to. He simply didn't have the strength.

Without hesitation, he lowered his head and kissed the beautiful woman in his arms, needing the reminder that she was here...and she was his.

CHAPTER 12

*E*verything inside Emerson stopped. Her breaths. Her thoughts. Even her heart felt like it paused in its steady beat.

Tyler was kissing her, and for once, no part of her hesitated. She didn't think about stepping away. About forcing the dance in her belly to pause or doing the right thing. All she could do, all she *wanted* to do, was lean into him. Let him soothe the chaos of her emotions tonight. The pain. The anguish. The guilt that she was asking good men to help someone they'd probably consider an enemy.

She threaded her fingers through his hair and tugged him closer. Held him so tight that she almost felt she could keep him in place if he tried to move away.

He didn't. His hands lowered to her ass, and he lifted her as if she weighed nothing, letting her wrap herself around him like that was exactly where she was meant to be.

And God, it felt that way.

Her lips parted and his tongue slid inside her mouth. She hummed at his masculine flavor. It was a taste she wanted to fall into and never get out of.

As his tongue danced with hers, the air around her moved. Then her back was against a wall. Her breasts pressed into his firm chest while her core hit his hard stomach.

Oh God…

She groaned as his lips moved down her cheek before settling on her neck and sucking.

"Tyler…" she breathed.

"Emerson." His voice was low and raspy, and it slithered inside her belly.

His hands went to the base of the shirt, which had gathered around her waist, and he tugged it over her head. She was naked underneath, so they were instantly skin against skin.

"You're so beautiful," he whispered against her neck.

The cold wall disappeared, then he lay her on a soft mattress. Instead of following her down, he stood by her feet, the muscles in his chest so thick he looked like a warrior. *Her* warrior.

He toed off his shoes, his strong fingers going to the button of his jeans. His gaze never left hers. Not while he pushed down his pants. Not when he stepped closer, a knee going to the mattress beside her leg. And that look in his eyes, the intoxicating mix of heat and desire and need…it made her breasts ache and toes curl.

Almost involuntarily, her gaze lowered once again to the bandage on his stomach.

Reality tried to splinter the fog of desire. The reality that his injury was Levi's doing, and in turn, *her* fault, and the possibility that it could have been worse.

But then Tyler's fingers glided up her thigh, his calluses rough against her smooth skin. And suddenly she was back in the sensual fog. Back in a world where Tyler was all that existed.

His lips pressed to her belly, and they felt like silk, soft and smooth. As he peppered kisses up to her ribs, her breathing shortened, her skin tingling wherever he touched. She arched into him, wanting more. Needing it.

When his mouth reached her chest, her throat closed. He

cupped both her breasts and took one hard bud between his lips. Air rushed into her lungs on a gasp. And when he sucked, her cry tore through the room.

She grabbed his shoulders, trying to anchor herself.

The combination of his weight, his hands cupping her, and now his tongue thrumming her nipple was a perfect storm of ecstasy. She ached for him.

She threaded her fingers through his hair, her chest rising and falling quickly.

He switched to her other breast. Now she didn't just ache, she throbbed. And in this moment, her heart beat for him. Only him.

After what felt like endless minutes of torture, he finally drew up and his mouth returned to hers. Their tongues once again tangled. She pressed her hands to his chest, wanting him on his back. With an arm around her waist, he rolled them, his mouth never leaving hers. She ground herself against his hardness, feeling him thicken at her core.

He growled, his hands going to her hips, fingers digging into her flesh. She wanted to drive him as crazy as he drove her. Push him right to the brink of insanity. She kissed him like this was her only chance. Like this was all she'd ever get, so she had to take and give everything.

His hand moved between their bodies and stopped at her core. When he grazed her slit, she trembled. A full-body tremble that rolled through every limb and organ.

He swiped again. Same reaction.

"So damn responsive," he murmured, his heated exhale whispering across her skin.

She gripped his shoulders as he continued to massage her clit. Then he reached farther down and touched a finger to her entrance.

Her belly burned, air halting in her lungs. Slowly, he pushed inside her.

She gasped, her head trying to lift, but he cupped her cheek and brought her back to him, his tongue melding with hers once again. He thrust his finger, his thumb moving to her clit and stroking.

Her breaths shortened, her heart pounding in her chest. Pressure began to build, an undeniable throb she couldn't stop.

She grasped his neck and tore her lips away before pressing her temple to his. "I need you, Tyler."

"You have me." One more sweet kiss.

Her pulse thumped.

She reached between their bodies, slipped a hand inside his briefs, and wrapped her fingers around him. His eyes scrunched, his thick muscles tensing so hard she swore they doubled in size. She moved her hand, exploring his length. He thickened in her grip, a growl moving from his chest, cutting through the air.

She learned what he liked, enjoying the masculine sounds that seemed to tear from somewhere deep inside him.

Too soon, long fingers wrapped around her wrist, stopping her.

Then he spun them again, his beautiful weight pressing her into the mattress. He removed the last thread of his clothing and reached for something in the nightstand.

She took the foil from his fingers, tore it open, and rolled the condom onto him, stroking him from tip to base then back again. Another rumble of his chest.

The second she was done, he settled between her thighs. But instead of sliding straight into her, he gently brushed some hair from her face and looked at her in the way he aways did. Like he saw everything. Like she was his, and he was hers, and there was nothing either of them could do to stop it.

"Mine," he whispered, reading her mind.

The word should've made her panic. At any other moment, she was sure it would have. But in this perfect moment, while she lay trapped beneath a man she wanted more than anything else in the world, all she could think was—*yes*. She was his, without question.

So she whispered the word she knew she might regret tomorrow. "Yours."

He threaded his fingers through hers and pressed her hands to the mattress. Then he kissed her, his tongue nudging her lips apart, while he slowly slid inside her body.

White-hot fire rippled through her. He stretched her in the best way. He didn't move immediately, instead making love to her mouth while her muscles grew used to his size.

Finally, he lifted his hips and thrust back in. Holy Jesus, it felt like nothing else. He thrust again, igniting more of the same. As he continued to move, his tongue worked hers. He reached for her breast, kneaded and pinched.

Every part of her was on fire. A fire he'd set ablaze and continued to feed.

She tugged her mouth from his and cried out. But his lips didn't leave her. They trailed down her cheek and behind her ear, sucking.

Her body was in overdrive, consumed by him. She dug her fingers into his shoulder, almost breaking skin.

She was so close.

His breath brushed her ear, then he whispered, "Fucking gorgeous. *And all mine.*"

Her back arched and her world exploded.

⌇

DESIRE. Want. Need. It was all there in an intoxicating mix, and it burned through Tyler as Emerson's muscles pulsed around him.

Fuck, who was this woman to do what she did to him? She made every vibrant, colorful image in his head gray and blur. All but the image of her. She was his only light.

He lifted his head and watched her body bow and her eyes

shut tightly. She didn't hold back. She broke in front of him, and she was beautiful. So damn beautiful he wanted to capture this moment in the palm of his hand and make damn sure he never lost it.

He continued to thrust, her breast heavy in his palm. His head dipped, teeth nipping her bottom lip. Her soft whimpers splintered through the quiet, skewering his heart.

Blood roared between his ears. And all too soon, his body tensed and he shattered. His growl was long and deep. He continued to thrust until he had nothing left. Until she owned all of him, even the pieces he hadn't known existed.

Then, finally, he stilled.

Her heart beat loud in his ears and her breaths were rough. He lifted a hand, and with the pad of his thumb, grazed her bottom lip. "You're incredible, Emerson Charles."

So incredible, he had no idea how he'd survived all these years without knowing she existed. There was no possible way he could fight this. Go back to the way things were.

Her eyes softened, and her small hand clutched his much larger one. She lifted it and pressed a kiss to the inside of his wrist before saying the same words that had just played in his head.

"I don't think I can fight this anymore."

His eyes flared. His. She was *his*.

With one final press of his lips to hers, he slid out of her and tugged her into his side as he settled onto the mattress.

This was it. This was everything his brothers had spoken about. The love that hit you out of nowhere. And the knowledge that nothing could possibly match it...or ever be the same again.

CHAPTER 13

*T*yler kept a hand on Emerson's thigh the entire drive to her place. Things had changed between them. Shifted. He'd felt this pull to her since the moment he'd first laid eyes on her, but after last night, it was stronger. And the fear he felt for her because of her brother was now tenfold.

The way Levi had looked at her in the grocery store played on a loop in his head. With wild possession. Like she *belonged* to him —and he wouldn't stop until he had her.

Blake followed close behind them, but Tyler still had this knot in his gut.

He flicked a quick glance her way.

She'd woken in his arms, a smile on her face. He'd almost expected the new day to bring back that flicker of hesitation he always saw in her. The wave of uncertainty. But the smile hadn't wavered all morning. Not until they'd climbed into the car. That's when the worried frown returned to her face.

What was she thinking about? Her brother? The injured police officer? Or did it have something to do with the secrets she still kept inside her, wrapped so tightly she didn't dare let the world see? Her words from the previous night came back.

There are things I haven't told you.

After what had passed between them last night, would she finally let him in fully?

He gave her leg a little squeeze. "Everything okay over there?"

She gave a small start and faced him. His words must have pulled her out of whatever deep thoughts she'd been caught in.

"I'm just worried about him." She covered his hand with her own, tracing a scar that ran near his thumb. "Where has he been sleeping? How has he been feeding himself?"

Both were good questions. "He didn't look homeless or malnourished yesterday." Scruffy? Yes. But his clothes weren't dirty, and he appeared to be well fed.

"How'd you get this scar?" she asked.

The topic change was abrupt, but he went with it. "During a fight in the compound. Liam and I were sparring with knives, and he nicked me."

Her tracing paused. "Did you spar with any of the guards?"

"We did. Less so at the end of our stay there. I think they started to fear us and what we could do."

She gave a slow nod.

"Did Levi?" Tyler asked, curious about the man's time in the project. Was it similar to his? Different? Was he part of a team?

It was a moment before she answered, and he just knew she was turning the question over in her head and trying to figure out the best way to carefully arrange her words. "He only stayed with us for a month after the project shut down, and he didn't talk to me about what happened in there. I think he was concerned for our safety. Over those few weeks, I watched as his mental health deteriorated. It happened so fast... I asked him to talk to someone. He said no. I've rarely seen him or had a proper conversation with him since."

She went back to stroking his hand.

He squeezed her thigh again, understanding why Levi had trouble adapting. He'd lived through Project Arma as well, and he *still* found everything that happened hard to believe. "I still think about those guards—wish I'd had the chance to end them when they were within easy reach. People who can witness the suffering of good men and ignore it..." He shook his head. "They deserve a special place in hell."

There was a small tensing of her muscles beneath his hand, and when he looked at her, it was to see her brows slashed together. It took a moment for her to respond. "My ex-husband was obsessed with the study of human behavior. He loved to learn about what motivated people to act the way they did. He said all human behavior has a reason, and that reason aligns with a person's experiences and belief systems. So, then, certain behaviors are usually indicators of issues and traumas."

She lifted a shoulder, finally looking over at him. "I'm not saying that trauma makes certain behaviors right or okay, just that...I wonder what those people working on the project had to go through to get to a place where ignoring the suffering of inno- cent men became possible."

He'd never really considered the lives of the men before they'd landed in Hylar's hands. Maybe because a lot of people in the world had it tough, but not everyone used it as an excuse to hurt others.

And the men working for Arma had stolen his last moments with his mother. Possibly even indirectly caused her death. Certainly, by keeping him hostage, they'd contributed to the pain she'd endured *before* her death.

That was an agony he'd carry forever.

So, giving forgiveness to men who neither asked for nor deserved it? No. All he could offer in terms of kindness was a quick death.

Emerson probably didn't want to hear his thoughts on the matter, though. So instead, he smiled gently and rubbed his hand over her knee. "Are you trying to make me a better person or something?"

The first real smile since they'd climbed into the car touched her lips. "Not possible."

When they reached the cabin, Tyler kept her close as they walked up to the door. He continuously scanned the woods around them, almost expecting her stepbrother to be there. Waiting.

When he unlocked the door, Emerson started forward, but he moved an arm around her body, touching her hip, halting her. Then he listened. For movement. Heartbeats. Breaths. There was only silence.

"It's clear." He lowered his hand.

She blew out a loud breath. "I was so sure there'd be some kind of note or something. I'm not sure if I'm relieved or not."

When they reached the living room, he tugged her into his chest, loving how she softened against him and fit so perfectly. Every time he touched her, any resistance to what they had melted away. "Let's go with relief. We'll find him regardless."

She ran her hands over the planes of his chest, and when her bottom lip disappeared between her teeth, he growled before crashing his mouth onto hers.

The kiss was raw and uninhibited. It was everything he needed it to be after last night. Their tongues melded, and both their hearts pounded loudly in his ears. When they finally separated, her grin almost undid him.

"I like you," she hummed.

Like? He was way beyond that. "You *own* me."

The heat in her eyes turned to fire, but in the depths of the fire there was something else. Something he didn't want to name.

Before he could question it, she stepped away. "I'm going to have a quick shower, put on some fresh clothes, then pack some stuff."

"Need any help?"

She shoved his chest lightly. "Absolutely not. We'd never leave this place."

She wasn't wrong.

With a final smile, she disappeared into the bathroom. The second she was gone, he whipped out his phone.

Blake answered immediately. "Hey."

Tyler moved over to the window, spotting Blake's car not far from his. "All clear out there?"

There was the sound of wind over the line. "Just parked. Not a person in sight."

"Shit. I want him away from her, but I also want—"

"Him caught. I know, brother. I'm with you on that one."

He blew out a breath and ran a hand through his hair. "I appreciate the backup."

"You got it. Before you go, there's something else," Blake said, his voice somber.

His gut clenched. "What?"

"The officer from the grocery store survived the night, but he's got a bad infection from the wound. Things aren't looking good."

Jesus. He scrubbed a hand over his face. If he didn't pull through, Emerson would be devastated that her stepbrother had killed someone.

"Thanks for letting me know, Blake."

As he hung up, his gaze caught on the open door to the spare bedroom. Her art room. He could just make out a painting on her easel.

Without thought, he moved into the room. His gaze scanned the painting. It was an elderly couple in a loving embrace. Probably the commissioned piece she'd been working on. The expressions on their faces…love. Devotion. Loyalty.

She was good. The image had heart. She'd captured so much in her intricate lines and shadows.

His gaze swung to the nearby dresser, where she was storing most of her paint supplies. He lifted a half-finished piece. A heated breath hissed from his mouth.

Another man and woman, obviously younger, her back pressed to his front. His fingers circled her wrists in a possessive hold. As Tyler traced those fingers with his eyes, he could almost feel Emerson's skin beneath his own fingertips. The woman's chin touched her chest, while the man's rested on her head. Neither of them had faces yet, but something inside him knew this was her and him. And they looked as right together in the painting as they felt in real life.

He was still smiling when he nudged it aside to see the painting that sat beneath this one.

Levi.

He ran his gaze over her stepbrother's face, noting the small scar beside his eye and shaggy hair...but when he reached Levi's chest, the smile faded.

Something dark burned in his gut. Like acid. Poison.

The small logo on his shirt was one Tyler remembered well. One that was permanently ingrained in his memory. Men had worn them at the Project Arma compound.

But not prisoners.

He looked through the door to the empty living room. The secrets. The hesitation. Her question about redemption during their first meeting...it all finally made sense.

Her brother hadn't been a prisoner at Project Arma. He'd been a guard.

CHAPTER 14

*E*merson tipped her head up into the spray of water. She wanted to be happy. Hell, after last night, she wanted to smile from ear to ear. But everything that came before her night with Tyler weighed too heavily on her heart.

Levi had held a gun on Tyler. *Shot* a police officer. She shouldn't be falling for a man in the middle of what could only be described as a hot mess.

And on top of that…she was *still* keeping a secret from him. It was like a gray cloud hanging over their relationship. And it would continue to darken as long as she kept it from him.

It was time to trust Tyler. Tell him the truth and pray like hell that the man would still work with her to get Levi the help he needed.

She closed her eyes. Levi had done bad things. She wasn't disagreeing with that. But he'd been so deep in his suffering when Hylar had recruited him. That was *why* Hylar had recruited him. Because Levi had been trained, deadly and vulnerable. The perfect combination.

Tyler would listen. But when he did, would he see things the way she did? She knew he wasn't inclined to forgive, and she couldn't judge that because she didn't know what it was like to have had years stolen from her.

Yes, she'd had a rough upbringing. Her father had been pure evil. And here she was, asking Tyler to forgive one of the men who'd wronged him, when she'd never really forgiven the man who'd wronged *her*.

But the difference was, she'd seen goodness in Levi. And she had to believe that if he was in his right mind, he would regret his fateful decision.

With a deep breath, she turned off the water and stepped out of the shower.

She was going to tell Tyler. Today. She had to. Her feelings were too strong to avoid it any longer.

Quickly, she dried off and stepped into the bedroom, where she pulled on some tight black jeans and an oversized red turtleneck sweater. It didn't take her long to pack her bag. She'd only brought one with her from Vermont, beyond her painting supplies.

Bag in hand, she left her room. Tyler stood by the window in the living room, his back toward her. She took a few steps forward, then paused when he didn't turn. And not just that…the way he stood seemed wrong. Too straight. Too rigid.

"Ty?"

Again, he didn't turn right away, and when he did, he wasn't wearing the smile he had earlier. None of the softness or affection was in his expression anymore. In fact, for the first time, his face was completely devoid of emotion. All emotion.

Worry skittered through her belly. She took two steps closer. "Hey. Are you okay?"

For a moment, his gaze just moved between her eyes, almost like he was searching for something.

The worry deepened, and fear began to gnaw at her insides. Something was very wrong.

When he finally spoke, his voice was hard. "I saw the painting, Emerson."

Confusion marred her brow. "Painting?"

She racked her brain to think of which he could be talking about. It couldn't be the commissioned piece. Maybe the one she'd started the other night of her and Tyler?

"The painting of Levi," he said before she could ask. He took a small step closer. Why did that step feel more like a prowl?

"Levi?" She scrambled to think of what she'd painted. She'd done so many of her stepbrother over the last year.

"He was wearing the uniform Hylar made all his guards wear."

Realization hit her like a ton of bricks. It was so heavy on her shoulders, her knees felt weak and her chest breathless.

He knew.

"I was going to tell you," she whispered.

"When?"

"Today." At least she could give him that small bit of truth.

He watched her closely. Probably making sure it *was* the truth. "What if last night hadn't happened? Would you still have told me?"

She opened her mouth, searched for words, begged herself to find them, but she didn't. She'd told herself she would tell him. But in the past, every time she'd considered it, nerves had stolen her words.

She wanted to say yes. God, she wanted that more than she wanted her next breath. But maybe that would be a lie.

"I think I would." It was the best she could offer.

His jaw clenched, and he turned away. As if looking at her was too painful. Like he regretted every moment that had led to this one.

Her heart pounded in her chest. In pain. In fear that she was losing him when she'd only just found him.

"I'm sorry." Her voice was barely a whisper. "I was just so

scared that if you learned the truth, you'd want to find and kill him, instead of getting him help."

"So instead, you lied to me," he said quietly. The quiet was almost worse than if he'd yelled. "Asked me to save someone who knew the guys and I were being held against our wills and did nothing to help us or prevent it from happening."

It wasn't a question, yet he wanted her answer. Her confirmation.

The conversation with Levi flew back into her head, like a shout she couldn't deafen.

"You told Rowan that innocent men are suffering. Are you hurting people, Levi?"

"There are no lengths I wouldn't go to, to make sure others don't go through the hell that was Iraq. If that means a few good men are sacrificed so that many others live, then that's just what has to happen."

"He knew."

Tyler's features changed. Steeled. He became a man she almost wanted to step away from. A man she knew could pose a deadly threat.

She ignored the fear and moved in front of him, reaching for his hand. He whipped it away as if she'd burned him.

"Was he in his right mind when he worked for Hylar?"

She gnawed at her bottom lip. "He was suffering. He had PTSD. He was struggling with adjusting to civilian life. Struggling with the fact he'd killed his teammates. And Hylar took advantage of his mental state once he was out of the military."

There was a small softening of his eyes, but it was so tiny, she might have made it up in her mind. Created it out of sheer desperation.

At his long silence, a wild panic spread through her chest like cancer, and she couldn't get enough air. Her hand twitched to touch him. Break through this new wall that had just erected. "He's my stepbrother—and he needs *help*."

Tyler ran his hands over his face and turned away again.

Tears pressed to her eyes. "If we don't fight for and protect the people we love, then what is even the point of living?" She wrapped her arms around herself, fingers digging into her waist. "He protected me when no one else did. He made sure I was okay. And now I'm all he has."

She hadn't shared that part of her life with him yet. The darkness. The evil that had almost ended her. Was it too late now?

Tyler abruptly turned toward the door. "I need to go."

Her heart cracked. Still, she whispered, "I'm sorry."

He stopped, his fingers around the doorknob. "I wish you'd been honest with me from the beginning, Emerson."

"If I had...would Levi have been safe with you?"

He remained silent and so still she almost questioned if he was breathing.

Did his silence mean no?

Her heart thudded. "Is he safe *now*?"

Tyler's entire back tensed, and suddenly he looked ten feet tall. "Blake's watching the house. You're protected."

Then he left. And his avoidance of the question was the only answer she needed. Her life might be safe—but Levi's wasn't.

CHAPTER 15

*T*yler hit the bag so hard, it surged back with the force. He was in the Blue Halo workout room. He wasn't sure if he was hitting the heavy bag out of rage or frustration or the deep hurt that ran through his chest. Probably a mix of all three. A perfect fucking cocktail of chaos.

He hit the bag harder. Again, it flew and shook.

Emerson had intentionally withheld the truth. Asked him to help a man she *knew* he considered an enemy. To *save* him.

He hit the bag three more times, not caring that he was on the verge of splitting the damn thing in two.

He'd known she was hiding something, but this...this was so much bigger than he'd thought.

His foot connected with the bag next.

Footsteps sounded in the hall, then stopped outside the door. It opened. He turned his head to see Logan lean a shoulder on the doorframe.

For the first time in hours, Tyler's fists dropped. He tugged the gloves from his hands.

"How are you doing?" Logan asked.

Tyler had notified his entire team about Levi the second he'd left Emerson's house. Even typing the words into his phone had been damn painful.

"I've been better." He threw the gloves into a box full of others in the corner.

"Wanna talk about it?"

Did he? Could he even articulate the fucking emotions swirling in his gut stealing his ability to breathe and damn near function? "I lost my mother when we were in there."

"You did," Logan said quietly.

"She died not knowing what happened to me. Whether I was dead or alive." His jaw ticked. "My disappearance killed her. I didn't need to be with her to know that."

Plenty of others had told him that his mother had never recovered from his disappearance—her medical team, her friends and neighbors. It was why she'd stopped taking care of herself. Why she'd stopped eating properly and taking her medication like she was supposed to.

"I'm sorry, Ty."

He shook his head. "I've been trying to help a man who knew what was happening and could have done something to end it. I could have killed him in those woods, then again in the grocery store. I didn't for *her*. Because she let me believe he was a prisoner. Because she told me he was worth saving." Every word made her betrayal more real.

"You're right," Logan agreed. "She shouldn't have let us believe a lie."

He grabbed his water and emptied half the bottle. Even that tasted like acid on his tongue.

"But that's not even what has me feeling like I have a hollow fucking hole in my chest." He swallowed. "Levi had PTSD. I understand that. And I understand how Hylar would have preyed on his vulnerability. What I can't wrap my head around is that she didn't trust me enough to tell me vital information, *especially* after we…" He couldn't even *think* about their night in his bed. "I had to find out through a damn painting of hers."

Trust. She didn't trust him. And that realization sat the heaviest inside him.

"You're right again." Logan straightened. "Trust is important. But we all know that when there's a lot at stake, and putting your faith in the wrong person can end in devastation, trust can take a bit longer to build."

Tyler ran a hand through his hair. "I don't know *what* the hell to think."

Her deception burned through his veins. They'd slept together. He'd claimed her. All the while, she'd been keeping a secret from him that she knew would have destructive consequences.

"We also need to remember," Logan continued, "it was a huge risk for her to come here and ask for our help. She must have been extremely desperate." He paused. "I wonder if what happened between Levi and her father has something to do with her loyalty."

It had everything to do with her loyalty. He didn't need her confirmation to know that. But, fuck, he wished he knew more about the incident. He should have pressed her for information. Did her fear of the dark and small spaces have something to do with all of it?

Of course it did.

"Has she told you about that?' Logan asked.

"I didn't ask." Stupid. He'd been so blindsided by her deceit, he hadn't stuck around to ask questions.

Logan's shoulder lifted. "So ask."

Tyler ran a hand through his hair. He could have done a lot of things differently. Even been more patient when she was trying to explain this morning. But he'd been standing in that cabin feeling so damn connected to her that finding the painting, having the evidence of her lie right in front of him… God, she may as well have dug her hand into his chest and ripped out his heart.

"You forgave Grace after what she did," he said quietly.

It wasn't a question, but it kind of was. Grace had revealed facts about Project Arma to a reporter. That was literally how everyone in the world had learned their secret.

Logan hadn't told his family about what he'd been through, but thanks to Grace's revelations and the ensuing media frenzy, they'd found out. It made his friends' lives difficult, and the lives of their families.

Logan nodded. "I did."

"Was it easy? Moving past that?"

"Before I knew her, I had a lot of anger toward her for what she'd done. Then we grew closer. I learned her story, learned what had driven her to do what she did." Logan's muscles visibly bunched, and Tyler's also went hard.

Grace's background involved sex traffickers and running for her life. Hiding for years. That woman had been through hell.

"I learned," Logan said quietly, "that good people are sometimes pushed into doing bad things."

Fuck.

He was right.

Tyler should have listened to her. He should have asked more questions. Regardless of whatever was going on with her stepbrother, Emerson wasn't a bad or cruel person. He knew evil, and she wasn't it.

He blew out a long breath. "Thanks, Logan."

"Let me know if you need a sparring partner."

Oh, he'd definitely be needing that. But the second his friend disappeared, he grabbed his shit. He needed a shower, then he'd figure out what the hell he was going to say to Emerson.

∾

EMERSON'S FEET beat against the uneven dirt path. Wind whipped across her face, and the sounds of the forest pierced her ears.

She wasn't a big runner, but right now, she needed to move. Get out of the house and exhaust her body until that look on Tyler's face scrubbed clean from her mind.

Shock. Hurt. Disappointment. It had all been there, mixed to create a perfect storm that spelled the end of them.

She'd tried painting. She'd even worked on the piece she'd started of her and Tyler. The piece with him standing at her back, his fingers holding her wrists. She'd wanted to wait to do their faces. There was a lot of complexity involved in capturing a person's unique expression. The emotion driving them in the moment she was trying to recreate.

She'd waited because she wanted to capture love. Affection. She'd wanted to wait until their feelings for each other grew.

And they'd started to. For a brief, fleeting moment. Until the truth had destroyed their progress.

So instead of love, and instead of the alternative—what she'd seen on his face this morning—she'd painted shadows across Tyler's face. Deep, dark shadows that reminded her of the sky before a storm.

While she'd riddled *her* features with pain—a vivid agony that dulled her amber eyes and tugged the corners of her lips down.

So, yeah…painting hadn't helped.

She moved her feet faster, letting the burn of her lungs compete with the pain in her heart. Callum was behind her somewhere, watching her. Although, while her breathing was heavy and her footsteps loud, he was completely silent.

A part of her wished she could press rewind on this awful day. Return to where they'd been this morning. In a fog of love.

Well, love for *her*.

She sucked in air. She should have told him earlier. Why hadn't she told him earlier? But she knew the answer to that.

Fear.

Christ, she hated how much this hurt. She hated that she'd fallen for a man she *told* herself not to fall for.

She rounded a tree, pumping her arms even though her body cried to stop, her lungs burning and her previously sprained ankle now aching.

Maybe others would have stopped trying to save Levi long ago. Maybe after he'd decided to work for Project Arma. Or when he'd gone missing. But Emerson couldn't do that. She couldn't stop. The memory of him protecting her in their youth, and others of him pulling her out of that dark closet. Keeping her awful secret when he was only a child himself. He'd been the first person in her life to ever save her. And now she was all he had.

That couldn't be for no reason.

She increased her speed again, welcoming the pain cascading throughout her body.

Levi had been desperate to chase away his demons. Find meaning in what had become a meaningless world. Hylar had known that, and he'd promised things he had no business promising.

The air was roughly sawing in and out of her chest when a hand touched her shoulder.

"Hey. Slow down."

Callum's gentle words pulled her out of her hazy pain, and she finally allowed her feet to slow, then stop. She was panting hard, her chest tight like it was bound.

Callum stepped closer, a supportive hand on her upper back. "Breathe. In…and out."

He took deep breaths, and she matched them until finally, she was back to semi-normal. Her heart still beat fast, and sweat beaded her forehead, but her breathing was easier.

"Thank you." She scrubbed a hand over her face, feeling its dampness. "I don't run often, but I needed to get out of the house and…"

"Exhaust yourself?" He finished when she couldn't.

"Yeah."

"I get it. I do that too. Or try to…"

At least it wasn't just her.

He tilted his chin back toward the house. "Come on."

She walked beside him but was very aware of his gaze on her, as if he thought she might pass out. Which wasn't an unfounded concern. She'd been so deep in her own head, she'd pushed herself too hard.

She snuck a peak at Callum from beneath her lashes. She'd expected him and every other man on the team to be angry with her. The man would know who Levi was by now, so she'd just assumed the entire team would look at her with distrust.

But he didn't.

They were silent the entire way back to the cabin. Every so often, he'd help her over a log or touch the small of her back in support. Sweet. Callum was very sweet.

He entered the house behind her, making the small space feel even tinier. Callum was the tallest on the team, which said something, because Tyler and all the others were huge. He had intelligent light brown eyes and almost honey-colored hair. Handsome. And dangerous, of course.

She moved over to the fridge and opened the door. "Would you like a drink?" She certainly needed one. Her throat was so dry it felt like sandpaper.

"Sure."

"I have juice, sparkling or still water, or I could make you a coffee, but it would just be instant."

"Still water would be great."

"You got it." She grabbed two bottles from the fridge and handed one to him.

He uncapped it and drank some before he spoke. "Are you okay?"

She took a small sip, turning the question over in her mind. She wasn't. But she didn't feel deserving of his sympathy.

"I was planning on telling him today." Her words were quiet, like she expected him not to believe her. "I hate that he found out the way he did. I didn't get a chance to explain anything."

Callum was silent for a moment, but he did the same thing Tyler did. Gave her that concentrated look, where she could almost feel him digging around and pulling out all her secrets.

"Tyler feels a lot of anger about losing his mother while he was away," Callum finally said. "She died six months after he was taken due to complications with her diabetes."

Her heart thudded. "And if he'd been around, he could have made sure it was managed well."

"Yeah. He was an only child, and he and his mom were close."

His inability to accept that anyone involved in Project Arma might be worthy of saving finally made sense. Because no one had cared enough to save *him*, and in turn, his mother.

Levi could have done that. He could have let authorities know the second he'd learned what was happening. He didn't.

It hit her then—Tyler was never going to forgive Levi. How could he? No one could give him that time back with his mother. Stolen time. In Tyler's mind, Levi might not have kidnapped and drugged him, but he was equally to blame.

Nausea swelled in her belly.

Callum's brow furrowed. He straightened and stepped toward her. "Hey. It'll be okay."

No. It wouldn't. Because she had to choose. Tyler or Levi. She couldn't have both. It was a realization that almost made her knees buckle.

She was all Levi had. So as much as she wanted to choose Tyler, to beg the man for forgiveness, tell him that her heart belonged to him...that would seal Levi's fate.

She forced a small smile she didn't feel. "Of course it will." She wet her lips. "I have a commissioned piece I need to mail. Would we be able to go into town?"

Callum opened his mouth to respond, then his gaze rose

above her head. His expression changed. Hardened. And something dangerous took over. "Stay here."

He reached for the tranquilizer on his holster.

"Callum?"

"I'll be back in a second." He stepped out of the house and pulled the door closed behind him.

Her heart jolted painfully. She swallowed and closed her eyes, saying a little prayer that no one got hurt. She was just opening them when she heard it. The patter of feet on the front deck. Her throat closed. She ran forward and looked through the peephole.

Levi's back was visible for a split second, then he was moving so fast, he was a blur, running from the house and into the trees. Callum followed but stopped not far from the house, gun aimed and ready.

She swallowed, opening the door, and immediately saw the folded piece of paper on the deck.

Goose bumps erupted on her arms. Slowly, she bent down and, with trembling fingers, picked up and unfolded the piece of paper to see Levi's scribbled handwriting.

I will do whatever it takes to keep you safe, Emerson. Last chance. Leave, or I'll kill any man I have to.

Fear like nothing she'd ever experienced coursed through her body, turning her skin to ice.

Callum remained in her yard, tranq gun aimed toward the woods.

So that was it. If Tyler didn't find Levi and make him pay for his crimes, Levi would find and kill Tyler and his friends.

There was no scenario where staying in Cradle Mountain kept the two men she loved safe.

CHAPTER 16

*E*merson nervously tapped the passenger window frame with her fingers as Callum rounded the car and slid into the driver's seat. She was nervous but trying like hell to calm her racing heart.

The commissioned piece was on its way to its new owner. Callum had gotten a call as she was finishing her transaction, and he'd stepped outside the small facility. She'd taken advantage of his moment of distraction and quickly used the ATM next door, withdrawing as much money as she could.

The handbag at her feet was almost empty. The cash and her phone were both in her pocket. The bag was just for show. Part of the plan she'd frantically scrambled to come up with.

Escaping Callum's watchful gaze wouldn't be easy. But this would work. It had to.

Before they'd left the Airbnb, she'd sent a text message to Mrs. Henry. She hated involving the older woman, but she had no one else. She'd also texted Rowan. Her ex-husband would help her.

Thank God for both of them. There was no way she could have done this on her own.

She wasn't thinking long term. The here and now was critical.

If she left, Levi would follow. And she needed that to happen. Because Levi killing Tyler and his friends, or Tyler and his team capturing and doing God knew what to Levi...

Nope, those outcomes didn't work for her. She couldn't live with herself if anyone died.

The scenery out the window changed without Emerson really seeing a thing beyond movement. She had to focus on the plan and not on the fact that she was leaving Tyler. God, he'd stolen into her heart so quickly. And she would likely never see him again.

She closed her eyes and begged her mind to accept that reality.

"Hey."

Her eyes popped open at Callum's gentle word. She swung her head around to look at him. He'd pulled out of the parking lot.

"You okay?" he asked.

She swallowed. Time to set the last piece of her plan into action. "I haven't really eaten today. Any chance we can grab some food?"

He nodded. "The Grind is just down—"

"Actually, could we stop at the other café? The one down the road, Brown Bird? You guys are always at The Grind, and I don't really feel up to running into anyone today."

He'd probably assume she was talking about Tyler, but she meant *all* the guys. Plus, she was sure Jason had security-proofed The Grind. She'd been to the other café. Knew there was a window in the bathroom above the basin, near the ceiling...and it had been ajar during her visit, proof that she could open it easily enough.

His eyes softened. "Sure. But we can never breathe a word of this to Courtney."

He smiled at her, and a flood of guilt riddled her chest. "Deal."

She nibbled her bottom lip as Callum pulled onto the street

with the café. Nerves trickled her spine, and thoughts of Tyler once again tried to change her mind. She didn't let them.

Once Callum was parked, she grabbed her handbag and climbed out of the car. He stepped into the café first, his gaze sweeping the shop, no doubt taking in every person, before heading toward the back corner booth.

He sat with his back to the wall. When he placed his phone on the table, she shot a quick look at the time. Two minutes. That's how long she had until Mrs. Henry got there.

She lifted the menu, trying to appear like she was reading.

A waitress stopped at their table, her gaze brushing over Callum with interest. "Hi, I'm Kasey. What can I get you both?"

She didn't even catch what Callum said. A buzzing had started in her ears. Fear that maybe this wouldn't work.

The waitress's attention turned to her. She read the first item on the list. "A cobb salad, please."

Emerson waited until the woman left the table before looking at Callum. "I might just pop into the bathroom."

He nodded.

Strategically, she left her bag on the bench seat. Because women didn't run without their purses, right?

She gave him another smile, then with legs that weren't quite steady, she pushed up from the booth and beelined for the bathroom. The second she was inside, the air whooshed from her chest.

The window was ajar, just like last time. And not only that, but the bathroom was empty.

Quickly, she climbed onto the sink and grabbed the windowsill. She had to move fast. Callum wouldn't wait for long before he came looking for her. She had to be gone by then.

The screen unlatched easily, and she pulled it out. The second she set it down, she hoisted herself up and through, then dropped to the ground with a quiet thud. Slight pain shot up her legs, but she ignored it and ran to the end of the alley.

Another exhale of relief left her lips when she spotted Mrs. Henry's red car on the side of the street, idling. Emerson slid into the passenger side. Right away, the woman pulled from the curb.

"Are you okay, dear?"

She'd told Mrs. Henry she needed to get out of town quickly. That it was a life-or-death situation, and if Tyler found out the reason, he'd be in danger. None of it was a lie.

"I am now." She touched Mrs. Henry's arm. "Thank you so much."

"Of course. I grabbed your bag from the cabin like you asked. Are you sure you want me to take you to Economy Car Rentals and not the police?"

"Yes. Getting out of town is the best option right now."

Worry flickered over the woman's face, but she nodded.

Before Emerson could talk herself out of it, she whipped out her phone and typed in the text she'd been wanting to send all day. A text she'd held off on because it would alert Tyler that she was leaving.

But now, before she disappeared, she needed to tell him...

I'm sorry it didn't end the way we were hoping, Tyler. I'll always wish things could have been different. I'd like to cancel the contract to locate and bring in Levi. Thank you for the time you put into the search. And thank you for giving me a part of yourself, even if only for a short amount of time. I'll take that with me and cherish it forever. Em x

She hesitated for several agonizing minutes...then hit send.

Once that was done, she switched the cell off. She had no idea if he could trace her location when it was on, and she couldn't take the chance.

Thank God Rowan had organized the car and accommodations for her. The hotel was a couple of hours away. And even though driving away from Tyler would kill her, it would be worse if she stayed and something happened to him, or he did something she could never forgive.

STEVE WAS SPEAKING to the team through a video call, but Tyler could barely concentrate. He kept glancing at his damn phone, his fingers twitching to pick it up and text Emerson. Call her. *Anything* to connect with her. He'd expected to do so before now, but this meeting was last minute.

"The incident was in Hailey, Idaho."

Tyler dragged his attention back to Steve, his brows creasing. "That's close to us."

"Really close," Steve agreed. "And the timeline doesn't fit his MO. It's only been four days since the last victims were found."

"So he's accelerating his timeline," Blake said quietly. "Why?"

Steve scrubbed a hand through his hair. "My question too."

Jason leaned forward. "Tell us about the victims."

"Victim one was nineteen-year-old Chloe Jarvis. She was charged with hitting and killing three pedestrians with a car, including an infant. She was given three years' probation instead of jail time. Victim two was her older sister. Only, she didn't die in the fire."

There was a small moment of surprised silence before Flynn spoke. "So she can tell us about the people who took her?"

"Unfortunately, not. Or not at the moment, at least. She was running, possibly in shock or fear, when she stepped straight onto a road and was hit by a GMC Sierra. She's in intensive care."

Tyler cursed under his breath.

"How were they kidnapped?" Liam asked.

"Chloe was taken from inside her home. No neighbors heard or saw anything. But there was blood on the floor, probably from the laceration we found on her head." Steve shuffled through papers. "Her sister, Lauren, who's currently in intensive care, was leaving her retail job. Never made it to her car. But when the local community was made aware of the missing women, a man came forward and said he saw a guy with his arm around a woman's waist, walking to a white sedan in the parking lot of her workplace. The day and time matches. He said the woman was leaning heavily on the man. When Lauren was found, she had drugs in her system."

So they had two leads. The woman, if she woke up, and the witness.

"Just a sedan?" Blake asked.

Steve sighed. "He didn't get a plate number, or the make or model."

Damn.

Liam tapped keys on his laptop. "What did he look like?"

"Witness claims it was too dark to distinguish features and the guy was wearing a baseball cap. Body wise, he was about six feet and slim. He believes the guy was younger, though. Suggested mid-twenties."

Which gave them almost nothing. Tyler ran a frustrated hand through his hair.

"So that's the only evidence we have until Lauren wakes up?" Jason asked.

"No. There was also skin found under Chloe's fingernails."

Tyler leaned forward. "She scratched him?"

"Yes. So we have DNA, we just don't know who it belongs to."

That was better than nothing.

"Strange that he's so close," Liam said, almost talking to himself.

Really strange.

"If you give us the witness's address, we can go talk to him."

The guys started talking details, how they'd best be able to help, but Tyler's attention once again drew to his phone. He needed to talk to Emerson.

He swallowed, then spent the next ten minutes trying like hell to concentrate. He was tapping his fingers on the table when his phone vibrated with a text message.

A message from Emerson.

He clicked into it.

I'm sorry it didn't end the way we were hoping, Tyler. I'll always wish things could have been different. I'd like to cancel the contract to locate and bring in Levi. Thank you for the time you put into the search. And thank you for giving me a part of yourself, even if only for a short amount of time. I'll take that with me and cherish it forever. Em x

Unease trickled down his spine. Cancel the contract? He quickly read it again, his gaze catching on five particular words.

I'll take that with me.

Take it with her where? Was she planning to leave?

He pushed to his feet, ignoring the way the guys shot curious glances his way. He was about to call Emerson when his phone rang.

Callum.

Dread crawled through his stomach.

Something was wrong.

He answered the call, putting it on speaker so his team and Steve could hear. "Tell me you have eyes on Emerson, Callum."

"We stopped at Brown Bird for lunch, and she snuck out the bathroom window."

His blood iced in his veins.

"I've checked the streets," Callum continued, guilt and anxiety riddling his voice. "I couldn't find her. I'm in a shop across the road now, the owner's offered his CCTV footage from the front of his store. It has street coverage. We're searching it now."

Tyler's chest rippled in frustration and fear.

"If she got into a car, give me the plates and I'll run it through the system to find the owner," Steve said from the screen.

The next couple minutes felt like a lifetime. His body itched to go. Move. Find her.

There was the muffled sound of Callum talking to someone else. Three minutes later and he spoke again. "Got it. She got into a red Honda Civic."

Callum recited plate numbers, but the second he heard the description, Tyler's muscles had stiffened. Steve started typing, but he didn't need to. Tyler already knew who owned the car.

"Glenda Henry," Steve and Tyler said at the same time.

Tyler cursed. "She's my neighbor and Emerson's Airbnb host. I'm going to call her now."

The second Callum hung up, Tyler tried Mrs. Henry. The call went to voice mail. *Dammit.*

He was moving before he could stop himself. Out of the office and down the stairs. Footsteps of his team sounded behind him. As he ran, he called Emerson's number. He was pretty sure she wouldn't answer, but he had to try. He needed to hear her voice. He needed assurance that she was okay.

Straight to voice mail.

He ran faster. He had to find her. His gut told him if he didn't, he wouldn't like the outcome.

CHAPTER 17

*T*yler slammed his foot on the brake outside Mrs. Henry's house. Liam and Blake sat in the car with him. They'd called Mrs. Henry again, but still no answer.

She was their best chance of locating Emerson. Too many minutes had already passed since she'd left the café. He needed to know where she was, and he needed to know *now*.

Mrs. Henry was just walking from her car in the drive to her front door when he and his friends climbed out of his vehicle.

She paused, her eyes widening as she looked at him, lips parted. "Tyler."

Liam and Blake trailed him as he jogged to the older woman. "Where is she?"

"Tyler...she asked me not to tell anyone. She said if I did, you'd be in danger. Actually, she said *everyone* would be in danger."

Oh, Emerson.

Liam moved a little closer to Mrs. Henry's front door. When he turned back to Tyler, he shook his head. Dammit, the house was empty.

He gently grasped Mrs. Henry's arm. "Right now, *she's* in danger. I need to find her before that danger finds her first."

The woman's brows knitted. She was obviously loyal to Emerson. Had probably wondered if she was running from an abusive ex or something.

His voice lowered, a thread of desperation tangling with his words. *"Please*, Mrs. Henry. You know Emerson's safe with us."

Her gaze flicked between his eyes once more before she sighed. "I dropped her at Economy Car Rentals. She said she already had one booked."

He took two big steps back. "Thank you." Then he turned and ran. The guys followed close behind. Liam drove this time, while Tyler whipped out his phone. Callum answered immediately.

"What did you find out?" Callum asked.

"She booked a car at Economy Car Rentals."

"Hang on, I might be able to get into their system." There was rapid typing in the background. A beat passed. "Got in, but there's no booking from Emerson."

Air hissed between his teeth. He wanted to throw his fucking fist through the window. Had she booked with someone else's name?

"Hang on."

Hope flared in Tyler's chest.

"There was a last-minute booking placed today by a Rowan Perez..."

Her ex-husband. "What type of car did she take?"

"I can do better than the type. They have GPS on all their vehicles, and I can tell you her exact location. She's heading south, currently about twenty miles past Bellevue."

Liam sped up.

"Thank you," Tyler breathed.

Blake clasped Tyler's shoulder from the backseat. "We'll get to her."

Yeah, but would they reach her in time? There was a good

chance her stepbrother had been on her tail since the moment she left...and the guy wasn't even close to stable.

$\sim$

EMERSON DROPPED her bag beside the bed. Rowan had booked her a room at the Twin Falls Grand Suites. She'd made good time, driving faster than she should have, ignoring too many road rules. She was only about two hours from Cradle Mountain, but she was exhausted, both mentally and emotionally. Every mile further from Tyler had felt worse. Wrong. Like she was driving away from the only place she was meant to be.

She tugged her phone from her pocket. She should leave it off. That was the smartest thing to do. But she couldn't. Too much of her needed to feel connected to him, even if it was just through a text.

She switched it on. No texts. Just a single call that she knew would've gone straight to voice mail...but no message, either. Why did that make her feel worse?

She knew the answer. Because she desperately wanted the momentary connection that a text or voice message would provide.

There was also another emotion running through her, though...unease. He would be searching for her. She already knew him too well to think otherwise. Whether out of guilt or obligation didn't matter. Did the lack of a message mean he'd already gotten some clues as to where she was?

Her dry throat ached as she looked out the north-facing window.

She was just about to push the phone back into her pocket when a call from Rowan came through. Dropping to the edge of the bed, she pressed the cell to her ear.

"Hey."

"Did you get to the hotel okay?"

The fancy duvet cover was soft beneath her fingertips. She'd asked him to book her a cheap motel. He'd done the opposite, instead booking a multistory hotel, full of staff and plenty of rooms. There was even some kind of big function taking place downstairs in one of the ballrooms.

None of that mattered, though. She just needed somewhere to rest briefly because she'd known leaving Tyler would be draining. She'd leave before the sun came up and endure a full day of driving tomorrow.

"I did. I'll get a few hours of sleep and then drive through the day to get to San Francisco." She had a better chance of lying low in a big city like that for a short while.

"That's a big drive, Emerson. How long is it?"

"About ten to twelve hours. But I'll drive straight through and try to cut the time down."

Rowan sighed. "Emerson—"

"I know. But a city will make it harder for Ty to find me." Her heart rebelled against those words. "I'll be okay."

There was a short pause. "You sound sad. Because you're worried about Levi? Or because you had to leave Tyler?"

She scrunched her eyes closed at the sound of his name. At someone else voicing her fears out loud. "Both. I need them *both* to be okay."

There was a heavy pause. "Are you certain you've made the right decision? Levi's made his bed. He signed up for the project and did nothing when innocent people were being hurt. God, Em...you even told me he shot a cop the other night. Did the officer survive?"

"He's in intensive care."

Or at least, he was when she'd woken and asked. She'd been too scared to ask for an update before running from Callum.

"And honestly, no, I don't think I made the right decision, because I don't think the right decision exists. Tyler hates everyone who willingly took part in Project Arma. He's confirmed that more than once, and his friend told me why today." She shook her head at the memory. "If Levi's within his grasp, he won't let him escape a third time. He may even kill him."

He hadn't told her that, but he hadn't promised her that her brother was safe with him either. She couldn't take the risk.

"And Levi…" Her eyes closed. "He thinks Tyler's the bad guy. Which means as long as Tyler's close to me, he isn't safe. Neither of them are."

And the thought of either of them dying because of her? No. Her heart couldn't handle that.

She could almost hear Rowan's brain processing what she'd said before he spoke. "I commend the way you love people so deeply, Emerson. But you need to remember, Levi isn't the same man who protected you against your father all those years ago."

"Because of what he's gone through. Because of his mental health. He has no one else. When I had no one, he was there. And I believe that Hylar took advantage of a vulnerable man."

"Have you ever wondered what he's done while he's been missing? Everything you don't know about? Who he's possibly hurt?"

The question left a sour taste in her mouth and almost made her feel like one of Rowan's case studies. "I can't do this right now," she decided abruptly. "I'm tired and hungry. I have to go."

She hung up before her ex-husband could respond.

A knock sounded at the door, and she jumped, her heart thumping. Would Tyler knock? Or would he just beat down the door?

With slow steps, she crossed the room. Panic swirled through her chest, but she pushed it down and looked through the peephole. The air rushed out of her when she saw a man in a hotel uniform standing on the other side.

She pulled the door open a crack, leaving the safety chain engaged. "Yes?"

"Sorry, ma'am, but the car you registered at check-in has its lights left on in the front parking lot."

Dammit. She'd been so frazzled...was still so frazzled. "Oh. Okay. Thank you. I'll run down and turn them off."

As soon as he left, she grabbed her keys and exited the room. She felt on edge the entire walk down the hall. Like someone was going to jump out at her at any second.

Stop it, Emerson, she chastised herself. *You're fine.*

Yeah, maybe if she repeated that to herself enough times, she'd believe it.

She got into the empty elevator and pressed the button for the ground floor. When it stopped, the doors opened and she was about to step out—when she saw him.

Tyler.

Her throat closed.

He was just walking into the hotel foyer, Blake and Liam close behind him.

With trembling fingers, she stabbed at a random floor, then hit the Close button three times.

She looked back across the lobby just as Tyler's gaze clashed with hers.

In that second, time stood still. He was all she saw. And the way he looked at her stole her breath. It stole everything. He didn't try to catch the elevator...but there was steel in his eyes. A promise that she wouldn't get away.

The doors snapped shut. The connection broke.

She scanned the small space like the beige walls might provide a new plan. A desperate exit strategy. Sweat beaded her forehead, and her hands grew clammy.

He'd found her. *How* he'd found her, and so damn fast, she wasn't sure. But it didn't matter. She had to accept he was here now and figure out how to leave unnoticed. And not just from him. He'd brought his team.

Oh Jesus. Her mind was a mess. She couldn't think. She could barely breathe. Exhaustion fogged her brain.

The doors opened and she ran. She didn't know what floor she was on or where she was going. She just sprinted, her feet pounding down the carpeted hall toward an exit sign.

Halfway to the stairwell, the tingle chilled the back of her neck.

Levi was here.

No. Not now...

Something wrapped around her waist. Before she could comprehend what was happening, she was tugged off her feet. Air whipped around her. Then they were moving down the dark stairwell.

Music permeated the air when they reached a landing. They must be close to that function on the ground floor. He carried her out of the stairwell, the walls blurring around her again, then he stepped into a small room.

The second they were inside, she was enclosed in darkness.

CHAPTER 18

$\mathcal{E}$ merson was in the elevator, frantically pushing buttons even as she met Tyler's gaze. His chest tightened and a buzz filled his ears. He wouldn't make it to the elevator in time, but he'd found her. So instead of rushing forward, he waited for the doors to close, then he watched the numbers, legs twitching to go. The second they stopped, he took off running.

Third floor.

Liam followed him. Blake would stay behind and guard the exit. The other guys from the team wouldn't be far behind to surround the hotel. He couldn't let her slip away.

He moved up the stairs so quickly, air cooled his face. Liam pounded up behind him, and they burst through the door nearly side by side.

The hallway was empty.

Fuck. Had she stayed in the elevator? Stopped on the third floor to throw him off?

They'd already hacked the booking system and knew her room was on the fifth floor. Had she gone back there?

Finding the elevator bank, he watched impatiently again as the numbers climbed to the tenth floor.

"Go," Tyler said quickly to Liam.

Heartbeats and voices sounded from behind closed doors. Dozens of them in the rooms lining the hall. A part of him wanted to knock down each damn door, but it would take too long.

He grabbed his phone. Blake answered before a single ring had finished.

"She's not in the hallway on three," Tyler said before Blake could get a word in. "I need you to access hotel surveillance."

"I'm on it."

Voices sounded. He was talking to hotel staff. If they didn't allow him to see the footage, Callum would be here soon to hack into the system.

PANIC FLOODED EMERSON. The dark engulfed her. Like a blanket over her face, suffocating.

"Give me your phone, Emerson. I'll turn the flashlight on."

Levi's words were like white noise seeping through the cracks of her panicked fog.

Breathe. She needed to breathe.

She closed her eyes and tried to get air in. A curse sounded, then a hand touched the pocket of her jeans. A second later, there was light.

Some of the panic eased, but not all of it. The room was still too small.

"I'm sorry. I know you don't like cramped or dark spaces."

She tried to focus on the room around her. There were mops. A broom. Paper towels.

It was a supply closet. And by the sound of the booming music, the function she'd seen earlier was in the room beside them. She was back on the ground floor.

She blinked, forcing her eyes to focus on the man in front of her.

Another layer of terror receded and, in its place...an ache in her chest. For her stepbrother, with wide, almost wild eyes. So different from the clear gaze she used to see when she was younger.

"Levi. What are you doing?" Her voice trembled, but she was glad to get the words out.

"I saw you escape out that window. I knew you must have realized the same thing I have. That they're all with *him*. Against us." He took a step closer.

Her muscles twitched to step back, but there was nowhere to go in this tiny room. She tried to remind herself that this was her brother, but that brought little comfort when a near stranger stared back at her.

"I ran because I didn't want you hurting them, or them hurting *you*." Despite this new apprehension, she touched his arm, trying to bring back the Levi she remembered. "They're good men, Levi. I don't want you to destroy each other. You need to leave here. Run."

His brows slashed together. "You really still believe that?" He shook his head, almost in disbelief. "I'm not leaving without you. I'll protect you, just like I always have. But we need to get out. This place will be crawling with them soon."

Her mind scrambled to figure out what to do while coping with the lack of light and space around her. "Okay. Fine. If it'll get you to leave them alone, I'll go with you."

"First, I need you to cut the chip out of my shoulder."

Her breath caught, unease coiling in her belly. "Chip?"

"Hylar tagged all of his test subjects and guards. He said it was a way to control us, but I'm sure it tracks us too. It must be how they found me here. I need you to cut mine out."

Her knees wobbled. *Cut it out?*

He produced a knife. The blood drained from her head, leaving her dizzy. *Oh God.* It was huge, more like a hunting knife than anything else.

She lifted her hands in a defensive gesture, the size of the room suddenly the last thing on her mind. "Levi, I'm not cutting into your shoulder!"

"I've tried cutting it out myself but I can't." He stepped closer. "You *have* to do this, Em. Otherwise, we'll never be free."

He pressed the knife into her hand.

A frantic, insane idea came to her. One she hated with every fiber of her being, but dammit, she had no good ones.

"Okay." Her voice was so quiet it was barely a whisper. "I need to swap places with you."

Her heart ticked with relief when he didn't question her, just swapped so her back was to the door. He turned and pulled his shirt over his head. She gasped at the sight of the jagged scars that riddled his shoulder.

Jesus. He really *had* to tried to cut it out.

"We need to be quick, Emerson."

She smothered her shock and took a deep breath, feeling sick at what she was about to do. *Oh God.*

"Ready?" she whispered.

"Do it."

She steeled her spine—and stabbed him.

But not in the shoulder. She stabbed Levi's outer thigh.

He cried out, immediately grabbing at the wound.

She spun and tore the door open, running into the hall, then darting right, toward the loud event.

People were everywhere. Talking. Eating. Dancing. She moved straight into the dense crowd, trying to hide amongst the people. She didn't dare look behind her, just kept walking forward. When several loud gasps sounded from behind her, she knew Levi had entered the room. But she didn't stop.

A couple was just stepping inside a set of sliding glass doors, and Emerson slid through the opening before the door could fully close. She turned her head in time to see Levi running toward her.

Her heart leapt into her throat. Without looking where she was going, she bolted across the patio.

A voice boomed from her right.

Liam...?

A car slammed into her.

Pain exploded through her side. Her feet didn't touch the pavement. Then she hit the ground, her head slamming against concrete.

Everything buzzed. She felt someone's presence. Then a tentative touch on her shoulder. "Emerson...?"

Definitely Liam.

Another voice. Something on her cheek. A warm, gentle hand. Familiar fingers.

"Emerson!"

Tyler.

The buzz started to fade, and the world returned around her. The sound of fast footsteps moving away. Dozens of distressed voices. Maybe from the party full of people. Maybe the car driver.

"Ty..." Her head pounded and her body ached like nothing she'd ever felt.

Hands slipped behind her back and under her knees. She groaned at the careful movement.

"I'm sorry, baby."

More footsteps. Then Blake's voice. "Where's Logan?"

"He went after Levi when he ran," Liam said, also from close by.

She leaned her head into Tyler's chest. Her eyelids were heavy, her mind foggy, darkness threatening to close in on her.

"Go after them," Tyler said to someone, his voice a rumble against her cheek.

"I'll drive you both to the hospital," Liam said quickly.

With the steady thump of Tyler's heart against her ear, she allowed herself to relax.

Then, Tyler's whispered words. "You're safe."

Finally, she let the darkness close in on her.

CHAPTER 19

*T*he beeping was like a hammer in her head, hitting her skull in a steady, never-ending rhythm. There were other sounds too. The click of heels hitting hard floor. Whispers of voices at a distance. And there was a smell…a clean disinfectant type of smell. It reminded Emerson of the endless days she'd sat beside Levi in the hospital while he healed from the damage her father had done.

She stretched her fingers, frowning when she felt warmth encasing her right hand. Not just warmth. Strength. Hard, thick fingers.

"Em?"

Her heart gave one giant thump against her ribs. One she knew so well. The kind she only felt for one man.

Slowly, she peeled her eyes open. Sun shone into the room from a large window, hitting a tired, worried-looking Tyler.

"Tyler."

"Yeah, honey. I'm here."

His deep, familiar voice hummed through her system, forcing every part of her to attention. Memories trickled through her mind. Of escaping Callum's watchful gaze. Slipping away from

Cradle Mountain. Everything after that was a gray blur...but leaving this man, she remembered.

And even though she'd just run from him, having him here, beside her...it felt good. Safe.

Right.

She tried to sit up, but the second she moved, pain rippled through her skull and her side, causing her to groan.

Tyler cursed, pressing a gentle hand to her shoulder to keep her down. "Careful. You have a concussion and some pretty extensive bruising. Nothing's broken though, thank God. The car had been driving slow enough that the injuries are minor."

Car?

Flashes of what happened at the hotel finally came back to her. Levi. Stabbing Levi in the thigh. Running into headlights.

Her gaze flew up to Tyler's. "I stabbed Levi with a knife. Is he here?"

Tyler's jaw clenched, and she knew the answer before he gave it.

"No. He ran. Liam was closest, but he chose to go to you instead of giving chase. By the time Logan went after him, it was already too late."

Disappointment dropped like a weight in her stomach. Disappointment that he was still on his own. Still so scared and angry and confused. And God, now he was wounded too. But there was also a small flicker of relief.

That he was still alive. That no one else had been shot...or worse.

The stroke of Tyler's thumb on her hand brought her attention back to him.

"Emerson. We need to talk about why you ran...and Levi."

Anxiety cramped her belly, but she remained silent.

Another swipe of his thumb. "I understand protecting the people we love. And when you asked if your brother was safe with me yesterday morning, I was still processing the new information and didn't give you the assurance you needed. So I think I also understand why you ran."

Some of the panic in her chest dulled. He understood...but did he understand everything?

It took a couple breaths before she could answer. "Callum told me about your mother. How you blame Project Arma and everyone involved for losing her."

Pain flashed over his face. And anger.

"My mother was an amazing woman," he said softly. "My father left her when I was a few months old, and she worked three jobs to make sure I was fed and had a roof over my head. She sacrificed for me, and she was my best friend."

Grief was like lightning in her belly. She glanced down at their entwined hands, almost unable to meet his eyes. "If Levi had acted differently, if he'd let someone know what was going on, you might have gotten out in time to save her."

The stroke on her hand was now a comforting, gentle rhythm. "Hylar was smart and strategic. He chose people he knew would be loyal to him. People who were angry or disillusioned or broken. He told them exactly what they needed to hear. And if things had ever changed for Levi, if he'd ever considered betraying Hylar, the man would have known it, and Levi would be dead."

Her stomach rolled at the thought.

"But what you said in the car the other day was right. Nothing is black and white. Behavior, and why people choose to do what they do, is more complicated than that. Levi had PTSD. I understand the condition. It's too common in the military for me not to. And maybe Hylar knew and took advantage. It's likely. But regardless, you love him...so I'm going to try to help him. For you."

Those words...that promise... It was all she'd ever wanted.

And something she now realized might not be possible. Though she still had to try.

Ignoring the ache in her head and limbs, she pushed herself up again.

"Emerson."

She ignored his growled warning and the way his hand touched her shoulder, as if not sure whether to help her sit or guide her back down to the bed. She leaned into his chest and rested her head against his heart.

"Thank you, Tyler. You have no idea what that means to me."

Instantly, his arms came around her, gently pulling her closer. And she felt it all. Familiarity. Safety. Home.

This man had become home.

"I'm sorry I didn't tell you the truth from the beginning," she whispered. She hated that the start of their relationship hadn't been built on honesty.

"I understand why you did what you did." He pressed a kiss to her head. "But I need you to promise me something."

She lifted her head and looked at him. Her hands remained on his chest. "Anything."

"*Never* run from me again." He smoothed some hair away from her face. "I need you within arm's reach. I need to be able to protect you. The fear I experienced when I learned you were gone..."

Pain tormented his eyes, causing guilt to streak through her.

"I won't. I promise." She had no reason to now. And more than that, she didn't think she'd be capable of leaving him again.

A knock sounded at the door.

"Come in," Tyler said quietly.

Liam, Blake, Logan, Jason, and Callum stepped into the room. She almost didn't want to look at Callum. Was he angry with her for escaping him?

She forced herself to look into the big man's eyes.

He didn't look happy, but he didn't look angry either. "We're okay, Em."

The air rushed from her chest. "Still. I'm sorry."

Liam clutched Callum's shoulder. "Maybe our friend here needs to brush up on his bodyguard skills."

Callum shoved him away with a snort.

"We ready to get out of here?" Logan asked.

The guys nodded.

She frowned and looked back at Tyler. "How'd you get in here, anyway? Isn't there usually a family-only rule?"

One side of his mouth lifted slightly. "I told them you were my wife."

Callum scoffed. "Wishful thinking."

The guys laughed. All except Tyler, whose eyes heated as they looked at her. "Damn straight it is."

TYLER LET the steady beat of Emerson's heart calm the storm in his chest. She'd fallen asleep an hour ago and had been sleeping ever since. They were almost home, and it couldn't be soon enough. He wanted her in his house with its high-tech security system. In his bed with his arms around her.

The lights of the car behind him—Blake, Jason, and Liam—glowed in the rearview mirror. Logan and Callum drove in front. He wasn't taking any chances. Levi had attempted to take her twice now. And he'd try again.

Everything in him tightened and iced at the thought of last night. He'd gotten there just in time to see her body hit the pavement.

Breath hissed from his lips. His whole world had stopped.

Never again. He'd never allow the man to touch her. Not unless he was absolutely certain she was safe. She was too important to him. Losing her, seeing her almost die, put everything in keen perspective.

He loved her. So he either had to be the support she needed or accept that she'd run from him again.

It wasn't a hard choice.

Levi was tremendously fast. If they ever saw him again, they needed to be faster. He'd slipped away from them too many damn times. It was enough. *Beyond* enough.

Her breathing shifted, shortened. He looked across the seats to see her eyelids scrunch tight, then slowly lift.

"Hey there, Amber Eyes."

The second she met his gaze, her frown eased and her expression softened. "Sorry, did I fall asleep?"

"I'm glad you did." And she needed a hell of a lot more of it. "Your pain medication's in the middle console." He reached down and handed her the small bottle.

He waited until she'd taken a pill before resting his hand on her thigh and squeezing. She covered his hand with her own, stroking the pad of her thumb over his skin.

Fuck, he felt that stroke deep inside.

He cleared his throat. He needed to ask her something. It was something he'd been planning to bring up later, but he couldn't hold back the question any longer.

"Yesterday, at your cabin...you said he almost died saving your life." The muscles beneath his fingers tightened. "Is that when he ended up in the hospital and your dad was shot?"

Her throat bobbed. "Yes."

"Was that also the first time your father tried to hurt *you?*"

There was a heavy moment of pause. Like she was collecting her thoughts. Trying to think of the best way to word what she needed to say, maybe to soften the blow.

In the end, her reply was simple.

"No."

His grip tightened on the steering wheel. He'd suspected as much, but hearing it out loud was worse. "Will you tell me about him?"

It might kill him, but he needed to know.

She stared at his hand on her thigh as she spoke. "My mother

144

died just after giving birth to me. There were complications and she lost too much blood." His chest ached at the pain in her voice. "I wish I could say my dad did the best he could after that, but he didn't. He blamed me for her death. I think he hated me for it."

Jesus. How any person could hate a child, he had no idea. "I'm sorry."

She traced the veins on his hand, running her fingers over him so softly he almost didn't feel it. "He was an awful father. I could never do anything right. I felt like all I had to do was breathe too loudly for him to want to punish me."

Tyler's throat tried to close. "How did he punish you?"

"He was violent. He hit me a lot. Kicked me. Sometimes he'd throw me into walls."

An anger like Tyler had never known exploded in his chest. If the man wasn't already dead, he'd kill Emerson's father himself.

"Then after he hurt me," she continued, "he'd lock me in my closet for hours. Sometimes days. I hated that more than his fists. It was so dark and tiny in there."

"That's why you hate small, dark spaces," he said quietly.

She nodded. "It got better when he met Pixie. They had this whirlwind romance and married within a couple of months of meeting. She and Levi moved in after the wedding. My father never hurt me in front of her. In fact...some days, I could even convince myself he'd started to love me."

Tyler amended his previous thought. He wouldn't have just killed her father. He would have torn the asshole apart.

"She was a shift worker," Emerson continued. "There were some evenings when she wasn't home. Levi was close to my age, but he was always out with sport practices and games, so there was still opportunity for my father to do plenty of damage."

"Until Levi found out," he said quietly.

"He saw the bruises on my arms." Tyler heard her heart speed up. "I was so scared he'd tell Pixie and she'd leave my father. Leave *me*. And it would go back to how it used to be. I denied it at first. Then one day, he got home early from practice and heard me crying in my closet. He jimmied the lock and let me out. I told him everything, then begged him not to tell his mother."

Tyler gave her thigh another squeeze.

"He agreed. Very reluctantly. But he made his mother take me to his sporting events after that. He did everything he could to make sure I wasn't alone with my father. I felt so safe when I was with Levi, even though he was only a year older than me."

"I'm glad you had him."

Another tick of her heart. "On that terrible day…Levi had to stay late after school. I think my father and Pixie had had a fight that morning, because I remember hearing their shouts. My father was so angry. After school, I was in the kitchen and I dropped a glass. I still remember the sound of it shattering and my heart stopping."

Again, her heartbeat sped up. Again, he tightened his fingers around her thigh, wanting to remind her she was safe.

"My father entered the room and did that thing where he got really close and towered over me, but something seemed different that time. His eyes were darker. And I just knew, whatever was about to happen would be worse than anything before."

She paused, her breathing slightly labored.

"He punched me. He didn't try to avoid my face like he usually did. I didn't even hit the ground before he grabbed me and threw me into the living room. I landed hard on the coffee table, then fell to the floor."

Jesus. It was getting hard for Tyler to keep his rage in check.

"I'd never been so scared as when I watched him cross that room. He looked ready to kill. Then the door opened and Levi stepped inside. My father didn't even care. He lifted his fist—but Levi raced across the room and stood in front of me. Told my father to leave me alone. There was no fear in his voice at all. My father told him to move…and he said no."

She swallowed once. Twice. "It was like my father was

completely blinded by rage, because he hit Levi. Instead of staying down, Levi got back up and stood in front of me again. My dad shouted at him to move, and when he still refused, he hit him harder...

"And he got back up and stood in front of me *again.*"

A quiet sob escaped her throat, and it made his entire chest hurt.

"I was screaming at my father to leave him alone. Every time Levi got up, it just enraged him further. But neither of them would stop. Eventually, Levi couldn't get up, and my father *still* didn't stop. I ran out of there as fast as I could to get a neighbor."

She paused, turning toward the side window.

"What happened next, Em?" He had to know all the details, even if it killed him.

"I told my neighbor my dad was killing Levi. The guy grabbed his gun and ran over. He shouted at my father to stop, and when he didn't...he shot him. I thought he and Levi were both dead."

Her voice hiccupped.

"Pixie was frantic when she got to the hospital. And so was I. Worried that Levi was gone. That Pixie would leave me. All of it. But she never left my side."

Her heart started to calm.

"My father made it to the hospital but died shortly after. I didn't speak for days after that. I couldn't. I just felt so guilty and traumatized. It's why the police report wasn't entirely correct. By the time I was ready to talk to the police, Levi was awake and had already given a statement. He said *he* broke the glass and my father started beating him. He was just a kid himself, so I think...I think he did it so I wouldn't have to relive that part."

Tyler shook his head, thinking of the suffering Levi had endured. First at the hands of his stepfather, then after what happened during his military service.

"Pixie didn't blink, she adopted me, moved me and Levi to another home, and loved me like I was her own. They both did."

"I'm glad you had them. Both of them." So damn glad. He wished he could've met her stepmother.

"Thank you. Levi saved my life that day, and in return, he almost lost his."

He heard her unspoken words. Not only did she love him. She felt indebted to him. And now, finally, he understood why. "We're not deserting him. We're going to do everything we can to help."

"Thank you."

CHAPTER 20

"*H*er bruises and scrapes healing up okay?"

At Blake's question, Tyler's gaze swept across The Grind and landed on Emerson. She sat at the other end of the bar with Grace, Willow, and Mila—Willow and Blake's daughter—all of them chatting with Courtney on the other side of the counter. Emerson wore a long-sleeved shirt so her injuries couldn't be seen, but he knew they were there...and every time he saw them, he felt that same black rage.

"They're better, although it's only been four days. They shouldn't have happened at all. I hate that we couldn't get to her in time."

Logan pressed a hand to his shoulder. "We got there as fast as we could, and now she's here, with us, safe."

Didn't make it easier.

"Steve hasn't been in contact again?" He needed to change the subject, although his gaze kept returning to Emerson and the windows. Searching. Making sure Levi wasn't around.

Logan blew out a breath. "He has. But only to vent about there being no more clues as to what's going on."

Tyler looked across the room to see Mila wriggle her hand

149

out of Willow's and run toward them. She jumped into Blake's arms. He caught her, then dipped her back to tickle her neck with his mouth, causing her to giggle.

The kid was five and too damn cute.

"Daddy, stop, we're in public!"

Tyler and Logan laughed at that.

Mila turned to look at Tyler then leaned toward him to whisper, "I met Emerson. I like her."

His grin widened. It felt good. Smiles had been few and far between this week. "Does she have your stamp of approval?"

"She does. She likes painting, like me. She said we could paint together sometime. I could paint her, and she could paint me!"

The thought of Emerson spending time with Mila instantly put ideas in his head about her spending time with kids they could make together.

His chest tightened.

Logan said something to Mila, then kissed her cheek, but Tyler's attention had moved to Emerson again. It was crazy that he hadn't known the woman for long, yet the idea of creating a family with her didn't scare him. The opposite.

"No, I am not fifty percent sugar. Daddy says I'm all love."

Logan laughed at Mila's words just as the door to the shop opened and Callum stepped inside. He stopped beside them and ruffled Mila's hair. "Hey, kiddo."

"Have you gotten taller?" She squinted her eyes like that would help her figure it out.

"Nope, I've always been a monster."

Mila laughed. "You're not a monster. Monsters are green."

"Yeah, he's a bit green," Logan said, getting a shove in the shoulder from Callum.

"Did you come from Blue Halo?" Tyler asked.

"Actually, I just stopped at the library to return a book."

Tyler's brows shot up, and he saw similar expressions on his friends' faces.

"The library?" Blake finally asked.

"Yep."

"Daddy took me to the library last week," Mila said excitedly. "We borrowed *Ice Cream Soup*. What did you borrow?"

"You wouldn't like what I borrowed. It's a thriller."

She scrunched her little nose. "What's a thriller?"

"Something you might read when you're older," Blake said before Callum could.

"Since when do you read?" Tyler asked.

"Since always. I've just recently gotten back into it. Got my butt chewed out today by my favorite librarian because I folded the book into my pocket and it was bent when I gave it back to her."

Interesting. "Is this librarian good-looking?"

Callum grinned.

Yes, clearly she was.

"Wouldn't say no to a date. Not that she'll be asking. My very existence seems to annoy her. Unfortunately for her, I'm a fast reader."

Tyler smiled. Callum hadn't dated since they'd moved to Cradle Mountain. Could this be an end to that drought?

When he looked across the room yet again and saw the flicker of Emerson's brows, he straightened. She was due to take her pain medication. Even though four days had passed since her concussion, she was still getting headaches.

"I'm going to take Emerson back to the office."

He moved across the coffee shop and slipped an arm around her waist. Immediately, she leaned into him.

Courtney grinned. "Hey, Ty, guess what we're planning?"

He almost groaned. "Do I want to know?"

"A girls' night. It will involve drinks. Dancing. And letting all our worries slip away in an alcohol-induced fog."

Nope. He didn't want to know. "I don't think that's a good idea."

Grace lifted a shoulder. "If the whole team's there, I would argue that nowhere would be safer."

He wasn't agreeing to anything right now. Not when Emerson was recently concussed. "Time to go."

"I'll see you ladies later," Emerson said softly.

Then she let him lead her out, and he continually scanned the area as they walked.

~

EMERSON TILTED her head to the side. Her painting was missing something. She'd been working on it since they'd gotten back from The Grind, and it was almost finished.

She blocked out the sound of a ringing phone from somewhere in the office, the quiet voices and hard footsteps, and studied her work with a critical eye—

The eyes. They were open, but she wanted them closed. She wanted the body language to speak for them.

She touched her brush to her palette. She was redoing the canvas of her and Tyler. This time painting it the way she'd originally intended. With light and love and the promise of a future.

He had his arms around her middle now, holding her, while she held his forearms and leaned against him, her head back. Rays of light hit them both in just the right way. She'd drawn herself in a flowy dress and him in a white button-down, his jeans rolled at the ankles. And beneath their feet was water from the background ocean.

She spent endless minutes changing the eyes. Once she was finished, she sat back.

And there it was. Peace.

That's what she felt when she looked at this. Peace and love and trust. The closing of the eyes had given them both trust. In each other. A trust that, a few days ago, hadn't existed. It was all there in the way she held his arms and leaned into his embrace. In the way his lips pressed to the top of her head in a gentle kiss.

A smile was just tugging at her lips when thick arms wrapped around her waist, much like they did in the painting.

She sighed and leaned back into the familiar body. "Hey."

"I missed you."

She chuckled. "You came in an hour ago."

"Too. Long," Tyler growled. When he nibbled on her neck, she hummed. "Your painting's beautiful," he said softly against her ear.

She looked back at it, her heart thudding at the emotion that rose to the surface. She loved it. She loved all her paintings, but something told her this was going to be a favorite. "I painted it before, but I painted it wrong. This one's better."

A lot better.

She stood and turned in his arms. "Did you get some work done?"

"Yes. But I still hate that you're here. You should be at home, resting."

"I feel fine. And I don't want your world to stop for me."

"You've done more than stop my world, Em. You've set it on a completely new trajectory."

Her lips tugged up. "A good trajectory?"

His head lowered and his breath brushed over her lips as he spoke. "The best."

Then the man swooped, his mouth crashing onto hers. She groaned and leaned closer as their tongues melded.

God, a kiss from this man was like nothing else. Each and every time, she felt like she was floating. Like at the simple touch of his lips, she became weightless, completely at his mercy.

When his head finally lifted, she wanted to groan. Or maybe she did, because Tyler chuckled.

"I need to get you home."

Hm. Didn't sound like a good enough reason to halt the kiss. She grumbled out an "okay, fine" that made him laugh again.

She spent the next ten minutes cleaning her paintbrushes. She'd leave the painting there overnight to dry, then tomorrow, that was going up on a wall. Tyler didn't get a choice. Not that she thought he'd object.

The other offices were dark. Everyone else had already left. He flipped the light switch off in the room she'd been using before slipping his hand into hers and leading her toward the front door. He'd just touched the handle when he stopped, his brows tugging together.

A sliver of unease trickled down her spine. "Everything okay?"

"Someone's walking up the stairs."

Her lips parted, but before she could say anything, Tyler ushered her around the reception desk and gently pushed her down. She lowered to her knees and hid. Tyler moved away, but not before she caught sight of him pulling his gun from its holster.

Her heart thudded against her ribs, her breaths moving quickly.

Who was it? Levi? No, it couldn't be. She didn't feel the familiar tingle she got on the back of her neck anytime he was close.

The door opened.

There was a man's quick gasp—then she heard a voice she wasn't expecting.

She stood up to see Rowan standing at the door, his mouth open as he stared down the barrel of Tyler's pistol.

CHAPTER 21

*E*merson accepted the warm mug of coffee from Tyler. They'd returned to Tyler's home to talk. Rowan sat at the opposite end of the couch from her.

Tyler's fingers grazed hers. It felt good.

"I couldn't *not* come and check on you after you ended up in a hospital, Emerson," Rowan said, recapturing her attention. "I needed to know you were okay."

She shook her head. "Rowan, you're busy. You absolutely did not need to drive out here."

"I *did*. One second you're safely in your hotel, and minutes later, you've been hit by a car? Come on! We may not be married anymore, but I still care about you."

Her features softened. The man had been a good friend for years, but an even better one throughout the last several months, and particularly, the last week. "It was just a concussion and a few scratches. I'm okay." *Thanks to Tyler.*

Tyler pressed a kiss to the top of her head. "I'm just going to do a quick workout in the gym. Call if you need me."

She nodded, appreciating that he was giving them some

privacy. He'd given very little away about how he was feeling since Rowan's unexpected arrival.

She stared after him as he left the room.

The second he was out of sight, Rowan leaned forward and lowered his voice. "I wanted to make sure everything was okay with Tyler, too. It was only a few days ago that you ran from the guy. Then he went after you. And now you're staying with him?"

She knew what Rowan was asking. Was she staying with Tyler voluntarily, or was he keeping her here? She would hope that would be obvious with the way she looked at him. But maybe it wasn't. She also knew Tyler would be able to hear their conversation. She didn't care about that. In fact, she *wanted* him to hear.

"Rowan, you already know I ran because I was scared of what he'd do to Levi when he found him, and I was just as scared of what Levi would do to *Tyler*. At the time, I truly thought it was the only way I could protect them both. But things are different now. I know Tyler won't hurt Levi. And I'm trusting him and his team to be able to keep *themselves* safe."

The second part was a bit harder, because it felt totally out of her and Tyler's control. But she couldn't run again. Not only because she physically wouldn't be able to get away from Tyler's watchful eyes—ha, like the guy would give her an inch of space— but because she loved him. She felt drawn to him in a way she'd never felt drawn to another soul. So she'd accepted she was here to stay.

Rowan studied her eyes, as if watching for signs she wasn't telling the truth. He wouldn't find any.

Finally, her ex-husband nodded decisively, as he often did. "That's good. I was really worried." He sipped his coffee. "So... where have you settled on Levi? Will he be locked up when he's caught?"

She flinched at the way Rowan said "locked up." There was a time in the recent past when the two men had been friends.

"Actually, I'm hoping he'll be evaluated and they'll realize he's not in his right mind, and he gets psychiatric care."

She knew he shouldn't be around the public, not in his current condition. But he also shouldn't just be locked up.

Rowan was quiet for a moment, clearly weighing his words carefully, then he set his coffee on the table. "I'm a bit concerned that you're basing your entire foundation of his innocence on your belief that he's suffering from psychosis."

"That's because he is. He believes Hylar, a dead man, is still alive. He believes that everyone around him is an enemy and working for a project that's already been shut down. Hell, he even told me he has a chip in his shoulder!"

Memories of her brother begging her to cut the chip out made a shudder race up her spine.

Rowan gave her a look of surprise. "Emerson, the men from Project Arma *did* get chipped."

She shook her head. "No. Just the prisoners." That's what the various reports had said. She'd done so much research, she knew almost every detail that had ever been published.

"Did they even check the guards?"

She opened her mouth to answer, but stopped.

She didn't actually know.

Rowan shuffled closer. "I just want you to really consider where you're putting your allegiance. You're a good person through and through, yet you're fighting for a killer."

"He's not a killer," she breathed.

"He shot an officer. Is the man out of intensive care yet?"

Again, she didn't have an answer.

"I've said this before and I'll say it again," Rowan continued. "You have to ask yourself—if he shot this officer without even blinking, how many others has he shot, maybe even killed, that we don't know about? And without a medical diagnosis, you can't plead his insanity."

She swallowed around the lump stuck in her throat. "Rowan, I appreciate that you're worried…but we're not married anymore. Where I put my allegiance, and who I fight for, is not your concern."

He blew out a long breath, like he was both surprised and disappointed by her answer. "I'm not saying any of this to upset you. I think you know that. I'm saying it because I don't want to see you sacrificing your ethics and morals for a man who might not deserve it, just because you love him."

"I do love him. And I *know* him. That's why I continue to believe that, if he was in his right mind, he wouldn't hurt another soul. It's also why I continue to fight for him. My ethics and morals are the very things that won't let me give up on him so easily."

Now, Rowan looked at her like she'd given the wrong answer on an easy test question. He put his hands up and stood, and she rose also. "Okay. I can see you've made up your mind. And I really *did* come to see for myself that you're all right, Em. I didn't mean to push. I'll go for now, but I booked a room for a few days. I'll call you before I leave and hopefully see you again. Maybe dinner?"

She nodded noncommittally and walked Rowan to the door. The second he was out, she locked and alarmed the house. Then she pressed her head to the wood.

Nothing he'd said was wrong, yet it *felt* wrong. Levi *had* shot someone without blinking. Without pause or hesitation. And that did hurt. Hell, her heart ached for the policeman and his family.

Had her brother truly hurt or possibly killed others that she didn't know about?

She already knew the answer. Yes. It was possible.

But it wasn't possible that he was in his right mind. That was something she refused to believe.

∾

"I DO LOVE HIM. And I *know* him. That's why I continue to believe that, if he was in his right mind, he wouldn't hurt another soul. It's also why I continue to fight for him. My ethics and morals are the very things that won't let me give up on him so easily."

Tyler paused his workout on the heavy bag. There was conviction in her words, but there was also something else. Guilt? Pain? Because Rowan had mentioned the officer Levi had shot? Because she was starting to question whether her love for her brother was clouding her judgment?

He listened to their final words and heard as the door closed with a click behind Rowan. One of his brothers was watching the house today. It was the only reason he was allowing her to open the door when danger was out there.

Why Rowan cared so damn much about trying to convince his ex-wife that her brother wasn't the victim she thought he was, Tyler had no idea. Yes, they were friends. Yes, she trusted him, and he'd helped her when asked, booking the car and hotel. That immediate support was the only reason Tyler had allowed the man into his house.

He waited, listening for her footsteps. They didn't come right away. Instead, there was a moment of silence. Everything quiet, bar her heavy sigh.

Cursing under his breath, he wrenched his gloves from his hands and stepped toward the door but stopped when her footfalls finally sounded in the hall. Then she was in the doorway, her eyes as sad as her voice had been while talking to Rowan.

"You okay, Em?"

She crossed her arms over her chest in a defensive gesture. "Do you have an update on the officer?"

He gave a slow nod. "Still in intensive care."

Tears shone in her eyes, but they didn't fall. "Levi shot an innocent man."

"Because he was confused."

"Was he?" She shook her head. "I don't even know anymore. I

don't know if the trauma of my past and the way Levi saved me are making me blind to his faults. Maybe I *want* him to be mentally ill. I *need* him to be, because that absolves him of at least part of the blame from his crimes."

Tyler reached her in three strides and slipped his arms around her waist. When she didn't look at him, he lowered his head, touching his temple to hers.

"Hey."

It took a moment, but she finally lifted her face.

"I don't think love blinds us. We see the flaws in the people we love. The sickness. The mistakes." Her brows twitched at his words. "We just fight like hell to get them to a better place."

"All I've ever wanted since he disappeared was to get him help. I know he's dangerous. I know he shouldn't be out in the world right now. But I don't want him to be locked up and his mental health ignored. He'll only get worse. And then I'll lose him completely."

She touched her head to his chest, and he tightened his arms.

"I know, baby."

"Rowan made me feel like I was sacrificing my principles for Levi. Like loving him is a weakness."

"Love is never a weakness." How could it be? He loved this woman, and that love only made him stronger. It made him want to fight like hell to make sure she was safe from danger both in reality and in her head.

Her gaze lifted to his shoulder. "Do you think the guards were microchipped too?"

Anger sliced through him at the memory of those chips. "It's highly likely. They were a means to control us, and I'm sure Hylar would have wanted a backup plan in case his men turned on him." His thumb slipped beneath the material of her shirt and stroked her skin. So damn soft.

She reached up and cupped his cheek. Fuck, but he wanted to lean into that touch. "Thank you. You have more reason than

Rowan to question my loyalty to my brother. Yet, here you are, helping me."

"Because your battles are my battles. We're in this together. You and me." He'd go to war for this woman.

Something flashed through her eyes—a mixture of relief and gratitude and…something else. Something soft and sensual.

"You and me," she said quietly.

Heat spiraled through him, and before he could stop himself, he lifted her off her feet, pressed her to the wall, and kissed her.

And damn, but it felt good to have her in his arms. Her lips moved against his, and when they parted slightly, he plunged his tongue inside.

This woman owned him. She took every part of him that had been unclaimed. She destroyed any part that had been unsure.

Hers. He was all hers. He wanted to memorize the feel of her against him. The taste of her on his tongue. So in the small slips of time when she wasn't near, he had instant recall.

It wasn't until they were out of breath and panting, forced to separate, that she touched her forehead to his once again and spoke. "Thank you, Tyler Morgan. For making the hard moments a little bit easier."

CHAPTER 22

Tyler watched Emerson from across the bar. He hadn't stopped watching her since they got here. She wore a tight beige dress that hugged her curves like a second skin and showed way too much creamy leg. He liked it. A lot.

What he *didn't* like were the looks she was getting from other men.

A group in the far corner, in particular, had been looking at not only Emerson but all the women. A bunch of rough-looking guys. Tyler was keeping a damn close eye on them, as well.

The only reason he'd allowed her to come out tonight was because his entire team was here. And Emerson needed a night out. He just wanted the woman happy.

He cradled his beer as he sat in a booth near the back deck. Flynn, Aidan, and Callum sat around him, while Logan and Liam stood at a bar table near the entrance, beers in hand. Jason and Blake stood near the back entrance, also at a tall bar table.

All exit doors were covered, yet no one watching would look at them and know they were each on full alert.

"You doing okay over there, Ty?"

Tyler dragged his gaze back to his friends at Flynn's question. "I don't like not knowing Levi's location."

The guy was too unstable.

Aidan leaned across the table. "There are eight of us and one of him. She's safe tonight."

On a practical level, he understood that. Didn't stop the unease from coiling in his stomach and eating away at him.

"I can't lose her," he said quietly. He watched as she threw back her head and laughed at something one of the women said. "I've never felt like this before. Like the idea of losing her..."

"Means losing yourself," Flynn finished, an intensity in both his voice and eyes. "I know that feeling well, my friend."

Aidan sipped his beer as he looked over at his own woman. "When Cassie was in Salt Lake City, every day was a battle. When you've found your person, but they're out of your reach, you don't ever feel whole." His gaze shifted back to Tyler. "Exactly why we won't allow you to lose her."

"We've got your back *and* hers," Callum finished.

"Thank you." He was so damn grateful to have them. He'd lost his mother while he'd been at Project Arma, true, but he'd gained seven best friends. Men he considered brothers. Men he'd step in front of a bullet to protect.

When he saw Callum smiling at two women he'd never seen before, Tyler had to ask. "Someone caught your eye, buddy?"

Callum grinned wider as he looked back at them. "Fiona, the librarian who hates me, is over there."

Tyler glanced in the direction Callum indicated to see a brunette and a blonde, both in heels and short dresses. He only had to wonder for a second which woman might be Fiona before the brunette swung a look their way. Her gaze caught Callum's, and when he winked at her, she rolled her eyes and looked back to her friend.

Callum laughed under his breath. "I put the last book I

borrowed in my duffel bag, and the cover folded over. I folded it back, but she noticed the crease. Told me I was a book murderer."

Flynn lifted his beer to his mouth. "Well, it's certainly sounding like you're not taking care of her books."

"It's just a *book*. It's no reflection on how I take care of women." He grinned again, his gaze shooting back to her.

"Bring her by," Aidan said. "I'll fill her head with a bunch of great stories about you."

Callum smirked. "I don't think so."

Tyler's smile broadened. His friend had that look in his eyes. It was one Tyler had seen before. It said that Callum wasn't going to give up.

The woman had no hope.

Now that he'd met Emerson, he knew exactly what falling in love could do to you. It pulled you apart, then put you back together exactly the way you were meant to be.

He wanted to tell Emerson he loved her. The words had been right there on the tip of his tongue three nights ago, when he'd had her pressed against the wall in his home gym. But she'd been too upset about her brother. When he told her he loved her, he wanted to be the only thing on her mind. He wanted her to hear his words and have the two of them be the only things that existed in that moment.

When he saw Emerson move to the dance floor with the women, he straightened. She started to sway her hips, and heat tinged with desire whipped through his body.

Fuck, she made him want her so bad.

When he saw the guys in the corner watching too, he stood.

So did they—and the other men were closer.

When one of the guys reached her—and actually touched her ass—Tyler saw red. He flew across the room, intent on claiming what was his.

❀

It was taking everything in Emerson not to stare at Tyler. Not to glue her gaze to the man like he was the only person in the bar.

The women surrounded her—all partners of the men from Blue Halo. Grace, Courtney, Cassie, and Carina. Even Willow had gotten a sitter for Mila so she could join them.

They were all great. Welcoming, friendly, funny. She was on her second Blue Lagoon cocktail and hadn't stopped laughing all night. She sipped the sugary drink, listening as Carina shared a story about her failed attempt at breakfast in bed.

"The eggs were soggy, the coffee cold, and I even managed to burn the toast." Carina shook her head. "I swear, it was the worst attempt at spoiling the man, yet he ate it all with a smile on his face." She grinned. "Then he thanked me in a way that made me want to bring him soggy eggs every morning of the week."

They all laughed.

"I had a very similar dinner experience with overcooked, dry chicken and undercooked, hard potatoes," Grace said, shaking her head. "Logan ate everything I put on the table."

"That's love," Cassie sung, sipping her own drink.

Emerson's gaze once again flashed to Tyler. Did he love her? She wanted to share how she felt about *him*, but God, she was nervous. Nervous he wouldn't say it back. That he'd tell her it was too soon.

She took a big gulp of her cocktail as she turned back to the women.

Courtney nudged her shoulder. "Good, right?"

"Dangerous." It was deceptively sweet, but by the feel of her head, she was sure it was packed with alcohol.

"Eh. Who wants to play it safe when we have super-soldiers who can carry us home?"

She chuckled. The idea of Tyler carrying her out of here and slipping her into bed didn't sound terrible. Especially if he slipped in with her.

She looked at him again, her eyes softening. It was only

Courtney's chuckle that pulled her attention back to the women. No, correction, not just Courtney's chuckle. They were all staring at her with big grins on their faces.

"Is that how I look at Flynn?" Carina asked.

Grace lifted her wine to her lips. "Oh yeah."

"Why wouldn't you, though?" Cassie asked, humor in her eyes. "Those men deserve to be stared at."

Courtney shook her head. "No, they deserve to be plastered on billboards for the world to see."

"I'd line up to see those," Emerson said, running her finger over the rim of the glass.

"You doing okay, what with everything that's happening with your brother?" Cassie asked tentatively.

Emerson's smile dimmed. "Honestly? I'm not sure. I want to talk to him." And not in a small, dark closet while running from Tyler and on the verge of a panic attack. Really talk to him. See if she could get through his paranoia. "I need to know if there's any part of the old Levi still left."

Until then, she could only hope and pray that there was.

When she looked up, she wasn't sure what she expected to see. Judgment? Disgust that Emerson still cared for a man who'd worked for Project Arma?

She saw none of that. The only emotion staring back at her from the women around the table was sympathy.

"You will," Courtney finally said.

She wasn't so sure. Some days it felt like she was asking for a miracle. Because catching Levi felt awfully close to catching a drop of water in the ocean.

"You're all so kind," she said softly. "And Tyler...God, he's just been amazing. Standing by me, even though I want to help a man who indirectly hurt him."

Cassie squeezed her hand. "Not all situations are so simple, especially when the heart is involved. I would know. Aidan and I were together. But, to save my sister, I married another man six months after Aidan was taken."

Her eyes widened.

Cassie smiled. "It's a long, complicated story, but Aidan and I never stopped loving each other. Eventually, we found our way back together and he forgave me."

That did sound like a long story.

Grace leaned forward. "I revealed the big secret of Project Arma to a journalist. It's because of *me* that everyone in the world knows what they can do and what they went through. I did it because I was put in a situation where, if I didn't, I would have been in a lot of danger. Logan forgave me."

The women nodded.

"These men aren't only dangerous," Cassie offered. "They're smart, and they protect the people they love with everything they have."

Love. Yet again, she wondered what Tyler was feeling. "Thank you for saying that."

Cassie lay a hand over hers. "Of course."

"Look." Courtney nodded at someone across the room. "Callum's been staring at that woman over there," she said, clearly trying to lighten the mood a bit. "He won't be far behind Tyler."

Emerson looked at Callum, then followed his gaze, and sure enough, he was watching a pretty brunette across the room.

Courtney winked and gulped the rest of her cocktail. "All right, it's dancing time!"

"I'm really not much of a dancer—"

"*Everyone* is a dancer." Courtney pulled her from the table. "Come on."

She took a last sip of her drink, a little more liquid courage, then allowed herself to be dragged to the dance floor. The second they got out there, the others started moving to the music like they were born to dance.

It was contagious. She moved her body with them, letting

herself forget the danger that surrounded her for a moment, getting lost in the music.

When her gaze moved around the room, she caught sight of Logan walking toward them, his eyes only for Grace. Jason was approaching from the opposite direction. Both men looked like forces to be reckoned with.

Suddenly, a hand grazed her ass.

She swung around to see a tall, scruffy-looking man standing behind her, a sleazy grin on his face. "Hey, baby. Wanna dance?"

She opened her mouth to tell the man no, but Tyler was there before she could, pushing between them, looking tall and fierce. Anger just about bounced off him.

He shoved the guy in the chest. "What the hell do you think you're doing?" There was a dangerous edge to his voice. Like he was daring the man to try something.

The guy frowned. "She yours?"

"Yeah. She's mine." He stepped closer. "And if I see you touch her again, I'll break your fucking hand."

The guy's jaw clenched, but he took a step back. "I didn't know."

"Well, how about you wait for permission to touch a woman's ass next time?"

Tyler took another step toward him, but she grabbed his arm.

The guy held up his hands in surrender. "Fine. Sorry." He walked away, but Tyler didn't turn around.

Her fingers tightened on his arm. "Hey."

Finally, he turned and looked at her. "Are you okay?"

"Yes." Because Tyler was here.

Some of the anger slipped from his face. Then his arms wrapped around her. When his head lowered, his warm breath brushed her neck. An earthy, masculine scent surrounded her.

"You're beautiful."

Her skin tingled all over at his whispered words, and her

tummy warmed at the intensity in his stare. The way he made her feel so much with a single look was staggering.

"I think he's gone now if you want to sit back down."

His lips brushed her ear. "Not a chance. Now that I have you, I'm not letting you go."

A shiver worked down her spine. Then his lips pressed against her neck. Her eyes shuttered, and she was sure she'd perish right there and then. Burn to the ground.

"Tyler…" she breathed.

His arms tightened around her waist. They swayed for so long, she forgot time and surroundings and reason. She forgot the worries that plagued her. She forgot everything but him. She let the strength of his hands and the sway of his body lull her away from reality. Every so often, she felt a kiss against the top of her head. A warm, familiar breath by her ear.

She snuggled further against his chest.

Eventually, his voice broke the sensual haze. "I need to get you home and do unspeakable things to you."

Her belly flopped. "I'm not opposed to unspeakable things." Not even a little bit.

His hand lowered to take hers. Courtney and Grace were dancing with their guys, while Cassie and Carina had gone to Aidan and Flynn.

Courtney lifted her head from Jason's chest. "Going home?"

Jason nuzzled her neck. "Hm, that doesn't sound like a terrible idea for us, either."

Courtney chuckled. "Well, come on then, big guy."

Emerson laughed as she moved off the dance floor, Tyler's hand around hers. She'd only taken a few steps toward the exit when she felt it. The familiar prickling on the back of her neck. The eyes on her.

She stopped, a chill sweeping over her skin.

Someone said her name, but it was like white noise. All she could focus on was that feeling. His proximity.

Her gaze flew around the room, searching.

Strong hands gripped her shoulders. Tyler's hands. She looked up, heart hammering, and whispered, "He's here."

Tyler's eyes narrowed. His gaze whipped around the room. She caught glimpses of his team standing taller. Alert.

Then a scream sounded, quickly followed by another, and some quieter cries. The music stopped. And finally, she found him.

Levi.

Coming out of the women's bathroom, gun to a woman's head.

The same woman Callum had been staring at all night.

CHAPTER 23

*F*ury was like a tidal wave inside Tyler. Levi had an innocent woman in his arms, pistol to her temple. A woman whose eyes were wide with fear, her face so pale he was worried she'd pass out.

The room had grown eerily quiet, although he could hear every single person's heartbeat thundering in their chests.

He stepped in front of Emerson and worked to keep his voice calm. "Let her go, Levi."

He caught sight of Callum off to the side. His eyes had turned black, and Tyler could almost see his friend's hands twitching to act. To save the terrified librarian. Problem was, if they moved even an inch, Levi could shoot the woman.

Tyler had to end this without any casualties.

Levi's eyes were steel, but there was a hint of shake in the hand holding the gun. Which wasn't fucking good or safe.

"I don't want to hurt her," he said quietly, eyes only for Tyler. "I just want my sister. Release her to me, and I won't kill this woman."

Fuck, he wished this room wasn't full of people. He stepped forward. "You know I can't do that."

The rim of the gun pressed harder into the librarian's head. Her eyes scrunched, and there was a collective gasp throughout the room.

"I know who you're working with. Who *all* of you are working with. Emerson isn't safe with you. Now release her! Or I shoot this lady in the head."

"You hurt her, and I murder you," Callum snarled with deadly quiet as he inched closer, his hand on his concealed Glock.

Levi met Emerson's gaze. "Come to me, Em. I'll keep us both safe."

Tyler's chest tightened. And when Emerson took a small step forward, his hand shot across her body, landing on her hip, keeping her in place. She wasn't going anywhere with him.

She turned to Tyler, her entire body shaking. "I have to," she whispered. "It's the only way no one gets hurt." There was real fear in her eyes. Fear for the woman in Levi's hold. Fear for Levi that someone would harm him.

He shook his head. "You're not going."

Emerson's eyes flicked between his. If she was trying to figure out if there was any give in him, she wouldn't find it. Not a single fucking shred.

Suddenly, a new voice boomed. The man who'd touched Emerson's ass. "Either let her go to the guy, or shoot his fucking brains out already!"

Tyler's gaze swung to the man, but before he could say anything, Emerson called out to her brother.

"Put the gun down, Levi. Please. She's innocent."

"So are you," he growled.

Again, she tried to inch forward. And again, Tyler stopped her, tugging her body half behind his.

"Shoot him!" the asshole hissed again.

Emerson spoke over him. "Just focus on me, Levi. It's just you and me right now." His eyes moved back to her, and there was a small softening in his expression. "You're my brother. And you've always been my protector. I love you, and I need you to listen to what I'm saying right now. I'm *safe*. These guys are *safe*. And *we all* want to help you. I need you to remember who I am and trust me. Release her and let us help you."

There was a small hesitation. Was he actually considering it?

"I do trust you. It's *them* I don't trust."

"Trust me to keep us safe, then. Because I know, with everything I am, that these men do not mean you harm. But they also can't let you kill an innocent woman." Her voice choked at the end, but she calmed herself.

She'd already witnessed her brother shoot a police officer, and that was still tearing her apart. If he ended up killing this woman right in front of her...in front of everyone...

"Remember when you saved me?" she almost whispered, knowing he'd hear. "My father would have killed me that day if it hadn't been for you. We both know that."

There was another flicker of emotion in his eyes. Love. It was there. Below the crazed, wild desperation. He really was doing all this because he thought it was necessary, to save his sister.

She inched forward, and this time Tyler didn't tug her back, but he kept hold of her arm. "Now it's my turn. Let me save you. *Trust me* to save you."

Levi's hold on the gun visibly loosened, his tense muscles relaxing slightly.

Her brother was listening. They might actually get out of this without any casualties.

"Put down the gun, Levi," Emerson begged, her calm voice at complete odds with the situation in front of them. "Let her go and let me help you."

The next beat of silence was loud. It was like everyone in the room was holding their breaths.

Levi's finger shifted away from the trigger.

Tyler was just loosening his hold on Emerson's arm when he

heard it. The rustle of movement from somewhere beside him. He turned to look.

The asshole who'd touched Emerson's ass was lifting a weapon.

It happened so fast, Tyler knew he didn't have time to stop it.

Still, he lunged. "No!"

Too late. The bullet fired before he slammed into the asshole and grabbed his gun. Tyler turned his head in time to see Levi hit the ground, blood instantly pooling behind his head.

EMERSON'S WORLD STOPPED. For a moment, she couldn't move. She felt like she wasn't in her own body. Like she was stuck in a nightmare, watching on in horror, unable to wake up.

Screams echoed in the room around her. Loud rumbles thundered. Heavy footsteps pounded the floor as people fled.

She stood there for another half a second before it finally computed.

Her brother had been shot. In the head.

With an agonized cry, she lunged forward. She made it only a few steps before Tyler's arms wrapped around her, halting her progress. Restraining her.

"Let me go!" She twisted in his arms, shoved at his chest. But his hold on her was absolute.

His lips touched her ear. "There's nothing you can do, Emerson. They've got him."

Half of Tyler's team was on the floor with Levi, but it wasn't enough. She needed to be there. Touching him. Helping him.

"I need to see if he's okay!" In her head, she knew he couldn't be. He'd been shot in the head, and there was so much blood. A crimson river she'd never be able to rid from her nightmares.

A loud sob cracked through the air, and it took her a moment to realize it came from her. Then her knees buckled, and she would have fallen if strong arms hadn't been around her waist.

"I can't…" She couldn't breathe. A pain like nothing she'd felt before burned through her like a wild flame. "I can't watch him die, Ty!"

Was he already gone? Had he already breathed his last breath?

Her heart squeezed like someone had wrapped a fist around it.

Tyler cupped her cheek. "Then look at me, Em. Focus on me."

She stared into his stormy blue eyes like he was a lifeline. Like he was the only thing keeping her from falling apart.

When paramedics and police arrived minutes later, Tyler's team took care of everything.

And when they wheeled Levi into an ambulance, the first flicker of hope filled her chest.

"They're taking him to a hospital, right?" They'd spent a few minutes working on him…and there was no blanket. They usually wheeled dead people out with a blanket covering the face, didn't they?

"They are," Tyler said softly as he led her to the car. He had an arm around her waist and shouldered a lot of her weight. Blake climbed into the ambulance with Levi.

Tyler drove fast, making it to the hospital at the same time as the ambulance. She tried to follow Levi, but a paramedic held up a hand.

"You can't come in here, ma'am."

"He needs a guard," Tyler said before the man could turn away from them.

Blake dipped his head. "I'll go."

The paramedic nodded. Blake had probably explained part of the situation in the ambulance. Then they disappeared.

She itched to follow. To force them to allow her to remain with Levi. But Tyler's arm around her waist calmed her enough to think rationally. She had to wait.

Tyler tugged her the other way. "Come on, honey. Let's go to the waiting area."

When they got there, she was surprised to see almost everyone in the room. All the women and most of the men. She knew a couple of the guys had stayed behind to help police at the bar. Through her haze, she'd also noticed Callum comforting the woman Levi had held hostage.

Her chest constricted at the memory.

She spotted Liam, who had a streak of blood on his cheek. He was talking to another paramedic. When the EMT walked away, Tyler led her to his teammate.

Liam focused his attention on her. "Levi was still breathing when they took him into the ambulance, and the paramedic said his blood pressure remained high. Both of those things mean he's getting oxygen to the brain."

Some of the devastation that had been crumbling her world around her dimmed. "So he's doing okay, considering..." She couldn't finish that sentence. Considering he'd been shot in the head. Considering he should be dead.

Liam's expression softened. "The bullet didn't hit him head-on. It traveled the length of the left side of his skull and went straight through."

"And that's...good?" She knew she sounded desperate, but that was because she was.

"All of that is good," Tyler said quietly.

She blew out a long breath and leaned into Tyler's side. She was exhausted, both mentally and physically, but she wouldn't be getting a second of sleep or leaving this place. Not until she knew whether or not her stepbrother was going to pull through.

CHAPTER 24

*T*yler's fists clenched as he walked the length of the waiting room. He checked on Emerson for what had to be the hundredth time. She was sitting with the women, watching the hall, waiting for a doctor or nurse to come talk to them.

Agony. It was all over her face.

A nurse passed, and Emerson straightened, but when the nurse didn't stop, her shoulders dropped.

What took place tonight shouldn't have happened. Any of it. An innocent woman shouldn't have had a gun pressed to her head. That scumbag shouldn't have shot Levi when he'd been about to lower his weapon. Hell, he could have missed and shot the woman!

The guy was in police custody now. Everyone had given their version of events, and Tyler could only hope the man paid for his stupid decision.

Jason entered the doors of the hospital. He'd just stepped out to call his sister, Sage. She was a doctor. Her partner, Mason, was like them, as were all his friends. She'd been that team's doctor for years, and she knew their altered DNA. If anyone could help Levi, it was her. Problem was, she lived in Marble Falls, Texas.

His friend stopped beside him. "Spoke to Sage. She and Mason already booked a flight and will be here early in the morning."

He gave a small nod. It was something.

Callum was the next to come through the door—and he didn't look happy.

"How's Fiona?" Logan asked before Tyler could.

Callum ran a hand through his hair. "Shaken, but all right. I wanted to stay with her, but she insisted she was okay and that I should go."

He seemed frustrated by that.

"I'm sorry, Cal," Tyler said quietly.

"We're seriously lucky she didn't get hurt."

He wasn't wrong. Between the gun pressed to her skull and the bullet that had hit Levi, they were damn close calls.

Callum's jaw tightened. "At least we have Levi. No one else will be hurt."

Liam blew out a breath. "There were demons in his eyes. That guy's as unstable as they come."

Tyler's attention returned to Emerson. Deep, dark circles shadowed her eyes. He moved across the room and crouched in front of her. "Hey. How are you doing?"

"No news is good news, right?"

He swiped some hair from her face. "Right. Do you need anything?"

She shook her head, her gaze sweeping across the waiting area. "People should go home, though. I feel bad having everyone here."

"Honey, we'll stay as long as you're here," Courtney said gently from beside her.

Emerson's eyes softened.

"Family for Levi Campbell?"

Emerson shot to her feet, and Tyler followed her as she moved over to the elderly doctor in a white surgical coat.

"I'm his sister. Is he okay?"

"For now, yes."

The air whooshed out of Emerson, and she leaned against Tyler heavily. He held her close.

"Fortunately, because of the velocity of the lower-caliber bullet and the fact it traveled along the left side of his brain, he's alive. If it had passed through the center or even a centimeter or two over, it would have been much worse, likely fatal."

Tyler's grip on her tightened. Luckily, the asshole in the bar hadn't been able to shoot worth a damn.

"Thank God," she breathed.

"Similarly, if the bullet had hit any deep structures, like the brain stem or the thalamus, he probably wouldn't be with us. They control breathing and heartbeat. The bullet also missed the major blood vessels that bring oxygen to areas of the brain where it's needed."

"So he'll be okay?" She sounded unsure, like she was scared to ask.

"The prognosis is good. The swelling is usually worse around day three, although with his altered DNA, he may heal faster. We just don't know *how* fast. Regardless, when it goes down, we'll be able to perform surgery to remove the damaged bone in his skull. A gunshot wound can also bring bacteria, so we'll want to be certain there are no infections before we install any plates."

It sounded like her brother was pretty damn lucky.

"Thank you," she said quietly. "Can I see him?"

Tyler's gut coiled. He wanted her to see her brother, but the man was still dangerous, bullet to the head or not.

"You can. He's on some medication so he can rest before surgery, and so that he doesn't..." He cleared his throat. "Doesn't escape. Police have also cuffed him to the bed."

Handcuffs wouldn't stop him. Unless they'd been specially made for his kind.

She gave a quick nod. "I understand."

"Usually, it's family only, but—"

"I'm her protection," Tyler interrupted. He was more than that. But he'd say whatever he had to say to remain with her.

The doctor nodded. "That's what I thought."

The doctor led them down the hall before stopping in front of a door where Blake and a couple of local police officers stood. His friend dipped his head as they passed.

Emerson stopped just inside the room. Her sharp inhale was loud. For a moment, she was still. He didn't push her to move closer. Instead, he stood quietly, hand on her back. A gentle reminder that he was here.

Eventually, she stepped forward, slowly drawing closer to her stepbrother. When she stopped beside him, she took hold of his hand. Levi had a bandage around his head and an IV in his hand, but other than that, he looked exactly the same.

"He was going to lower the gun," she whispered. "I saw it in his eyes. He trusted me to help him. If that guy had just waited another second…"

"I know, honey." He pressed a kiss to her head.

"But I don't know if he would have shot her before that. I want to believe it was just for show. Just a means to get me out of there. But the truth is…I don't know who he is anymore."

"He'll wake up and we'll find out."

"But what if he's beyond redemption? Beyond saving?"

She knew the answer to that. But she didn't want to hear it. "We'll tackle that when we get there. And I'll be with you the entire time."

She gave a slow nod, then leaned back into him, all the while never releasing Levi's hand.

~

EMERSON LET *tears fall onto Levi's chest. Endless tears that fell like a waterfall from her hollowed eyes. There were so many wires attached to his body. So much bruising on his skin.*

Because of her.

He was here, hurt, because of her. *Because of what her father had done to him for protecting her.*

She should be in this bed.

A sob released from her chest, and a new wave of tears fell. Desolation drowned her. She'd thought her father's fists and that closet he shoved her into were the worst things in the world. They weren't. This was. Watching another person suffer in her place.

Pain, she'd learned to deal with. Guilt, she had no idea how to navigate.

A hand touched her back. A small, warm hand. One she'd grown to know well over the last couple months. Only this time, she didn't want to look up. Because the woman would hate her now. How could she not?

"Darling." That voice...that soft, sweet voice. "Please. Will you look at me?"

Three more seconds. Three more breaths. Then, finally, she turned her head. Pixie's eyes were red rimmed, but there were no tears. Maybe she'd reached her quota and had no more to shed. Emerson was starting to believe she had no quota. That her tears were endless, like a river of guilt that just kept on flowing.

She opened her mouth to apologize. To tell the woman how awful she felt. But just like every other time she'd tried to speak in the last twenty-four hours, her voice never made it to air. So instead, a fresh wave of tears flooded her eyes.

Pixie didn't hesitate. She tugged her into her chest.

Emerson should pull away. She didn't deserve the affection. But she couldn't. Pixie was safety. She had been from the moment they met. Her softness. Her smell of peaches and sunflowers. And Emerson so desperately needed safety right now.

Pixie held her so tightly, and it was like the little pieces that had cracked and separated in Emerson were trying to slot back together.

"This is not your fault," Pixie said forcefully.

Wasn't it? Levi was here, unconscious, hurting, because he'd stepped in front of her father to protect her.

Like the woman had heard her thoughts, she pulled back and the softness disappeared from her features. "It's not." She said the words so vehemently that everything inside Emerson wanted to believe it. "I'm guessing that wasn't the first time your father hurt you. I wish you'd told me. But that doesn't make this your fault. It makes it his."

She tucked some hair behind Emerson's ear. The touch so soft, so gentle, Emerson wanted to lean into it.

"My son loves you," she continued quietly. "You're a true sister to him, just like you're a daughter to me. I taught him that we protect the people we love. And if he was hurt protecting you, then even if I'm devastated that he was injured, I am so proud of his bravery."

A fresh wave of tears coursed down Emerson's cheeks.

"I love you too," Pixie said softly. "And just like my son, I will do everything in my power to protect you."

No one had loved her before. It felt as unfamiliar to her as Levi's protection.

She dug her head into the woman's chest and let her arms become a sanctuary.

Her eyes flashed open, the hazy glow from the salt lamp the only light in the room.

For a moment, she just breathed, a familiar ache at the memory of her stepmother filling her chest. The first woman to ever show her love. And she'd kept her word. God, she and Levi had done nothing but care for Emerson and protect her for years after that. The second her father had died, Pixie had adopted her, always treating her like she was her own.

Her words flashed back into her head.

We protect the people we love.

Yet, she hadn't been able to protect Levi.

She turned her head, tracing Tyler's features with her eyes. He lay on his side, his arm curved around her torso as he slept.

God, he was beautiful. How the world had deemed her deserving of a man like him, she had no idea. But she wasn't letting go. She was holding onto him with both hands.

Her hand twitched to reach out. Touch him. Stroke his cheek. But she didn't. They'd spent so long at the hospital, he deserved sleep. It was early enough that the sun wasn't up yet, but she wouldn't be getting any more rest.

A small light flashed through the room. She dragged her gaze from Tyler and turned to grab her phone from the bedside table.

Rowan.

Hey, I'm so sorry about the other day. I can't leave knowing you're upset with me, especially after hearing about what happened at that bar. Can we go for a coffee? Chat?

She huffed out a long breath. She didn't feel like talking to him, but at the same time, they'd been friends for so long, and it would be good to at least clear the air before he left. Not today, but she'd find out when he was leaving and try to see him before then.

She went to slip out of bed, but the arm around her waist tightened, keeping her firmly in place.

"Where are you going?"

Wait…why didn't he sound sleepy? "When did you wake up?"

His eyes opened, and there, in the dim glow of the light he kept on for her, were those beautiful blues. Blue eyes that looked wide awake. "When you did."

Oh, the little phony. "Why didn't you open your eyes?"

"Because I like holding you." He swiped his thumb over her bare midsection. "And if you stayed where you were, why would I stop?"

Well, she liked him holding her, too.

"Something wake you up?" he asked gently.

She swallowed at the memory. "I just had a dream about the day Levi was in the hospital and Pixie came and talked to me."

"Will you tell me about her?"

She smiled. A genuine smile that seeped inside her and lifted her spirits. "Pixie was the most beautiful soul I've ever met. She was the kind of person who just does the right thing because it's what you should do. She used to make pancakes on the weekends and crank music so the three of us could dance around the kitchen. And she always said 'I love you' when she said goodbye. She said life's too unpredictable not to."

"She sounds like good person."

"The best." She traced her finger over Tyler's chest. "I was so sure she'd hate me after what my father did to Levi, but she didn't. Instead, she helped me heal and made me feel like I was hers."

Tyler pushed up onto his elbows. "She'd be proud of you."

Her brows twitched. "No. I haven't—"

"You *have*. You've done everything in your power to bring him to safety. You've sacrificed and maintained an unwavering loyalty to him." His voice lowered. "If she was here, she'd tell you the same thing. That this isn't your fault. That she loves you. And she's glad you're watching over him."

"Even if he doesn't deserve it?" She'd meant for those words to be a whisper in her head, but they slipped into existence.

"One thing at a time, Amber Eyes."

God...this man.

She looked at his lips, but he moved first, dropping his head and sealing his mouth to hers.

CHAPTER 25

*E*merson smiled as she opened the bathroom door to the smell of bacon drifting up the stairs. Tyler knew she loved the stuff, and it was exactly what she needed today.

The second visiting hours started, she was going to see Levi. Sage and her partner, Mason, had been able to get on an early flight, so they might already be at the hospital. And Emerson was keeping her fingers and toes crossed that the swelling had gone down already and the surgery on his skull could be performed soon. Then, they were one step closer to being able to talk to him. Have an actual conversation with the man and figure out how best to help him.

She pulled on a flowy, colorful dress and pulled her hair up into a high ponytail. She'd never been a makeup person—she touched her face and rubbed her eyes way too often for that.

She was just moving down the stairs when she heard Tyler speaking.

"She's awake?"

Emerson paused. Tyler sounded hopeful. Then...

"No, if Steve wants you down there for the questioning, you should go."

Go? Go where? She continued down the stairs, slower this time. At the kitchen, she paused again. Tyler held out his arm.

Smiling—of course he'd heard her coming—she moved forward and slid against his side.

He kissed her head in greeting before talking to whoever it was again. "Yeah, keep us updated." She was about to move out of his arms, but he snagged her wrist and pulled her back into him. "Hey. Where are you going?"

"Everything okay?" she asked quietly.

"We do some off-the-books work for the FBI. They have a case right now that no one can crack. It's doing everyone's head in. We might have something now, though."

She saw the stress lines beside his eyes and traced them with her finger. "I'm sorry. Want to talk about it?"

"You have enough going on, baby. You do *not* need to hear about this messed-up case."

Oh, she definitely felt like she had enough going on. Still, she hated that he had to shoulder an additional burden.

He lowered his head, nibbling on her ear. "I made you bacon."

A shudder rocked her spine. "I smelled it the second I got out of the shower."

In fact, she'd probably smelled it *in* the shower. Pixie had always joked that she'd smell bacon miles away in the middle of a snowstorm.

Emerson set the table while Tyler plated the food. The bagels caught her eye. If there was a second food she'd sell her left kidney for, it was most definitely bagels. It wasn't surprising that he'd noticed; she only ordered them nearly every time they went to The Grind.

"Better be careful making all my favorite foods," she said with a smile, grabbing a bagel for her plate. "I might come to expect this kind of treatment."

"If bagels and bacon put a smile on your face, I'll make them for breakfast, lunch, and dinner."

She laughed. "Well, then you'd have to roll me around because I'd be the size of a house."

"You'd still be the most beautiful woman in the room."

Oh, this man and his beautiful words. "Say sweet things like that, and I might come to expect *those* every day too."

"Good. You should expect me to say nice things and treat you the way you deserve to be treated," he said quietly, an intensity about his expression.

She swallowed, piling bacon onto her plate. A lot of bacon. Definitely too much. But then, could you have too much bacon?

Tyler spent every second of their meal making her smile and laugh when those should be the last things she felt like doing. He even shared a bit more about his mom. Their little traditions and the way they'd celebrate holidays. The woman sounded a lot like Pixie. Kind. Nurturing.

"I wish I could have met her," Emerson said quietly after she'd swallowed her last mouthful of food.

"She would have loved you."

The way he said it, the way he looked at her…it made something in her belly stir.

She took a big gulp of water to soothe her entirely too-dry throat. "We should clean up so we can get to the hospital."

"We should," he agreed, and yet, it was another few beats before he finally rose.

She was just slotting the last dish into the washer when Tyler's ringtone sliced through the room. She turned her head as he answered.

"Sage, how's he doing?"

Sage, the doctor. She must be with Levi already.

Tyler frowned. "Yes, we can come in now."

Her breath caught. Come in… Because something had happened?

~

TYLER COULD FEEL the nervous energy rolling off Emerson in waves as they stepped through the hospital doors. He lowered his head and whispered into her ear, "Relax."

"I can't."

His hand tightened around her waist.

Jason was guarding the room today, with Mason by his side. Tyler shook Mason's hand. "Good to see you, man. Thanks for getting to Cradle Mountain so quickly."

"Not a problem, Ty."

His hand returned to Emerson's waist. "This is Emerson Charles."

Mason dipped his chin. "Hi, Emerson."

"Hi."

"Sage is with Levi," Mason said, nodding toward the door.

They looked inside the room to see Sage by the bed, glasses on her nose and notes in front of her. Emerson looked from Levi to Sage as they walked in.

Sage glanced up and smiled. "Hi, Ty."

"Sage."

She held out her hand for Emerson. "Hi. I'm Dr. Sage Porter."

"Emerson. Thank you so much for getting here so quickly."

"Of course. Now, I've looked over Levi's charts and can see his bullet wound is healing really quickly, but then we expected that. All the guys with altered DNA heal from injuries at an astounding speed. He's already past the peak of the swelling, so I would say that by tomorrow morning, we should be able to perform the surgery he needs."

He heard Emerson's heart speed up. "And he'll wake up after that?"

"As long as everything goes to plan, yes."

Emerson sighed, almost deflating beside him.

"Also, I did a scan of his shoulder today and found he does have a chip embedded."

So the commander responsible for Project Arma had chipped

his guards as well as his prisoners. Asshole. Had he thought they would eventually desert him? Go against orders?

"I'll remove that before he leaves here," Sage said softly. "But... there's something else."

When a look of sympathy flashed in Sage's eyes, Tyler got a sinking feeling in his gut. Whatever the "something else" was, he knew Emerson wouldn't like it.

The doctor's gaze flicked to the notes. "I did a full panel on his blood and found drugs in his system."

Whatever he'd been expecting the woman to say, it wasn't that.

"Drugs?" Emerson asked quietly.

"Lysergic acid diethylamide, to be exact."

Tyler frowned. "LSD? The hallucinogenic?"

"That's the one. There was also a small unlabeled box of tablets in his pocket. When we test it, I'm fairly certain we'll find it's the same drug."

Emerson shook her head. "No. That can't be possible. He wouldn't do illegal drugs."

But even as she said the words, Tyler heard the doubt in her voice. Her brother had gone through a lot. He had issues, and not only was it possible he'd take illegal drugs, it might also explain his downward spiral and paranoia.

Sage gave Emerson an empathetic look. "I'm sorry, Emerson."

"So it *is* his fault," Emerson said, almost sounding like she was talking to herself.

"Em—"

"The reason he's not thinking logically, the reason he's hurt and killed people, is because he's *voluntarily* taking drugs. Even though he knows how dangerous he is already, between his PTSD and his altered DNA."

Her gaze flashed to her brother, but this time, in addition to the sadness, there was anger.

Before he could say anything to soothe her, Emerson spun

and quickly left the room. He shot an apologetic look Sage's way before going after her. He let her get halfway down the hall before grabbing her arm.

"Emerson—"

"I've been *fighting* for him!"

"I know."

"I left my home. I lied to you. I used all my savings to hire two different firms to find him!"

"Because you love him."

She shook her head. "Yet, he didn't love me or anyone else enough to fight for himself."

CHAPTER 26

*E*merson sank lower into the tub, letting the bubbles cover almost her entire body. Other than her head, her toes, and the hand holding the glass of red wine, she was completely submerged.

LSD. Levi had been taking *LSD*. Why? Out of all the drugs available that could have helped him with his pain, why choose a hallucinogenic? A drug that made him even more dangerous. Even more paranoid. Gave him reason to do unspeakable things.

She sank lower again, letting the bubbles hit her chin.

When the delusions were caused by past trauma, PTSD, his actions were somewhat forgivable. But now, knowing this? No. How could they be? From what she could tell, it was *his* fault he wasn't in his own mind.

She'd been through pain. She knew it intimately. And when people had offered to help her, she'd grabbed onto it with two hands. Why hadn't Levi done the same? She'd wanted to be there for him, and he knew it.

Anger and pain and hurt mixed together in her chest to create a dangerous, painful concoction.

She sipped her wine, the roller coaster of emotions from the last few weeks overwhelming her. This would have killed Pixie. Her son had always been a hero in her eyes. And he'd been Emerson's hero too...once upon a time.

Her phone buzzed from beside the bath. She set her wine down and swiped open the message from Rowan.

Are we still okay to meet tomorrow?

Argh, she'd completely forgotten. She did not feel up to talking to her ex-husband tomorrow. She'd texted to finally let him know about Levi's blood work, and almost right away he'd called. But she'd ignored that call.

Sorry, Rowan. I've got a lot going on right now. Call me when you get back to Vermont and we can talk.

She set the phone down and took another sip of wine. Drinking probably wasn't the best idea, considering her mood, but she was past caring. She'd tied her hair into a bun on top of her head, filled the biggest wineglass she could find and slid into the hot water, hoping her bad day would slip away with it. So far, it hadn't.

A year of searching for a man who didn't want to be found. Of trying to help a man who didn't want help. What was wrong with her?

She knew what was wrong with her. She loved her brother. She owed him. And not just him. Pixie, too.

She raised her arm out of the water to look at the scrapes. They were healing well, but a few of them would no doubt scar. Reminders of that terrible day at the hotel. Caused when she was running from Levi.

Gone. The brother she knew and loved was gone. She had to accept that. Even if it hurt. Even if it went against everything she'd believed since she was a kid.

A knock sounded at the door.

She set her wine on the side of the tub and sat up a bit. "Come in."

The door opened, and there he was. Tyler. Looking big and

sexy and worried. Some of the anger and hurt in her chest dimmed. She'd come to realize that looking at him was like medicine in itself.

He crouched beside the tub and grazed his fingers along the back of her neck. Her skin tingled, the fine hairs on her arms standing on end.

"Are you doing okay?" he asked in his deep, rumbly voice.

"Not really." She touched the crease between his brows. "You look worried."

"I am." Another stroke of her neck. "I can tell you're upset and angry."

She was definitely both those things. "I shouldn't be surprised. He hasn't been himself for a long time." She'd just told herself it wasn't his fault. That he'd been taken advantage of when he was in pain and now struggled with mental illness as a result. But the truth was, all of it had been conscious decisions made by him. He could have chosen differently at every step, but he hadn't.

"There still might be more to the story."

"What more could there be?" She frowned. "He chose not to get help for his PTSD. He chose to join Project Arma. Then he chose to take LSD, which gave him dangerous delusions."

He shifted his gaze between her eyes. "What can I do to help?"

She sat up, water sluicing down her body, and cupped his cheek. "You, Tyler Morgan, have done so much already. If I didn't have you, this news would have made me crumble. Heck, these last few weeks would have left me a miserable puddle on the ground."

His lips twitched, but his words were serious. "You're stronger than you think."

She grazed her thumb over his cheek. "I don't deserve you."

"I think it's the other way around, honey." He tilted his head. "Why would you say that?"

"Because you're beautiful and kind, and I've been asking you to help a man who hurt you." Guilt. That was another emotion she could add to the long list.

"You asked me to help your brother. And you love him."

She swallowed. "Does that make me a terrible person? That I love a man who can do all that he's done?"

"You don't love a bad person, Em. You love the man you remember."

She studied Tyler's eyes. Eyes she could easily get lost in. Then she moved closer and curved her hand around his neck. "I'm so grateful you came into my life."

"You have no idea, honey."

God, this man owned her heart. Not a little fraction of it. All of it. The little slivers that had never been touched by anyone before. The big chunks that thought they knew what love was but really had no clue.

"Can I tell you something?" she said quietly.

"Anything."

"When I was married to Rowan, I thought love was supposed to feel comfortable. I thought it was supposed to be easy and not hurt when there was distance between you, and that moments of boredom and the absence of any excitement was normal."

She swallowed, unable to look away from those bright blue eyes of his. They pierced her. Claimed her.

"But I was wrong. Love is supposed to be so much more than that. It's breathless. Short gasps of air because you can barely breathe when your heart's so full. Trembling fingers because each touch is so electric. And a deep hopefulness even in the darkest moments of despair."

That was what he gave to her. What he made her feel. Every. Single. Day.

His brow creased, emotion washing over his face.

She grazed his cheek once more. "I love you, Tyler Morgan. You make me breathless. You make my fingers tremble, and you give me hope when I should be completely hopeless."

His eyes flared with heat and need and...something else. Something she was almost too scared to name in case she was wrong.

"I watched my brothers fall in love," he said quietly. "I saw their lives change. And I wondered how that felt. Now I know."

Her breath cut off, her tummy doing a little flip.

His large, warm hand covered hers over his cheek. He turned his head and pressed his lips to her palm. The touch lingered, and she felt it as if he'd kissed her everywhere. "I love you too, Emerson Charles. I can't not."

CHAPTER 27

*E*merson's eyes deepened from amber to dark honey as her heart raced. The beats matched Tyler's. Because this woman had just said she loved him. And damn, those words hit him right in the chest. They were everything. *She* was everything.

She stared at him, tears just visible in her eyes. Then she whispered, "Kiss me."

And hell if those two simple words didn't destroy him. His mouth crashed onto hers, and when her lips parted, he slid his tongue between them.

She whimpered, and the sound set off an explosion of need inside him. Need for this woman. To keep her close. To claim her as his and give her everything he had, was, and would ever be.

He slid his hands into the tub, wrapping his arms around her and lifting her up. Water splashed against tiles and soaked into his shirt. He ignored it all. Nothing but Emerson and the way she fit so perfectly against him deserved his attention right now.

With one hand beneath her and the other around her neck, he kept the woman close, daring the universe to try to take her from him.

He moved out of the bathroom, his tongue tangling with hers.

Then, gently, he lay her on the bed, covering her body with his own.

When he lifted his head, it was to see her features soft, eyes hooded.

His. This woman was his. And she'd just admitted to loving him like he loved her.

Captivated, he kissed her cheek, then her neck. He trailed kisses down her warm, soft skin before stopping at her chest, where he cupped her beautiful breasts and sucked one perfect nipple between his lips.

The sounds she made, the moaning and the heavy breaths...*fuck*, they were like gas on the inferno burning inside him.

He flicked her nipple with his tongue, swiping the other with the pad of his thumb. He was rewarded with more of those sounds. They pierced the room like a knife, her back arching, her breast pushing farther into his mouth. *Yes.*

He switched his mouth to her other breast and sucked again. She writhed beneath him, her fingers in his hair. Pulling. Tugging.

He released her nipple with a pop, then trailed his mouth down her ribs and belly, until he reached her core. With a hand on each thigh, he widened them, then lowered his head.

When he swiped her clit slowly with his tongue, her entire body jolted, and her cry was loud in the otherwise quiet room. He swiped again. Same reaction.

Fuck, he loved how she responded to him. He wanted more.

He closed his lips around her bud and sucked. Emerson's body trembled. He wanted her to feel everything. To burn for him like he burned for her.

Alternating between sucking and nipping, he swirled his tongue in circular motions around her clit. And when she was panting, he touched a finger to her entrance.

"Tyler..." she gasped.

His name on her lips, in her breathy, desperate voice, sounded so damn right.

Slowly, he pushed inside her, his lips wrapping around her clit once again. Another cry. He worked her body like it was an instrument only he knew how to play, rolling her clit with his tongue and continuing a steady thrust of his finger.

Her body tensed and tightened around him. She was on the edge, and he was about to push her over, knowing she trusted him to catch her.

Without stopping or slowing, he reached a hand up her body and thumbed her nipple. That's when she snapped. When her piercing scream shattered the quiet of the room, and her walls closed around his finger.

He rose, sealing his lips to hers, catching the last of her cries in his mouth.

Her eyes opened slowly, and her gaze locked with his. "God, I love you."

"I was *made* to love you."

～

EVERY INCH of Emerson's body was trembling with aftershocks. He annihilated her. Took her to a place only he knew the path to.

Desperately, she grasped the hem of Tyler's shirt and tugged it over his head.

The second his chest was bare, she ran her fingers along his smooth skin. His muscles tensed and rippled beneath her touch. Then, slowly, she lifted her head and pressed a kiss to his shoulder. At the same time, her hands went to the button of his jeans. Her lips continued to glide across his heated skin, her breaths brushing his flesh.

The second his zipper was down, she reached inside his briefs and wrapped her fingers around him. His chest stopped moving, the muscles tensing and hardening around her. He caged her beneath him on the bed. And it was the only place she wanted to be.

Slowly, she moved her hand, stroking him, feeling him thicken in her grasp.

An almost choked growl tore out of him. It was deep and masculine and Tyler. All Tyler.

He threaded a hand through her hair and gently pulled her face back to him. His eyes were closed, his brows tugged together like he was in pain. Like she was the one torturing him, not the other way around. Instead of kissing her, he held her close, his temple touching hers.

His mouth finally dipped and pressed to hers. At first they shared short, light kisses. Almost mere grazes of the lips. He did that several more times before slipping his tongue into her mouth and tasting her.

The kiss turned possessive and breathless and made time stand still. Yet her hand kept moving. Kept exploring. Until his fingers closed around her wrist, and he pulled her away. He rose and leaned to the side, donning a condom before returning to her.

His eyes flared with heat as he settled between her thighs, nudged at her entrance. And even though the man had just made her shatter into tiny fragments with his finger and mouth, the need was alive in her again. Wanting. Begging for him to take her.

Slowly, he slid inside, his eyes never leaving hers. And God, it was everything.

When he was seated deep, she wrapped her legs around his waist, tugged him closer. He slipped a bit deeper, and she groaned at the fullness, while he growled.

"What do you do to me, Em?"

She tugged his head down and nipped his bottom lip. "The same thing you do to me, Ty."

His lips crashed to hers, and he kissed her with raw,

passionate need. Then he was moving, lifting his hips and pushing back inside her in hard, even thrusts.

Her breaths shortened, her skin burning for him all over. Every time he rocked forward, his chest brushed her nipples, adding an extra wave of sensation.

She lifted her hips on each thrust, impatient for their bodies to meet, needing him deeper. She wanted the heat within her to burn. The love mixed with need mixed with desperation to drown them both.

His lips tore from her mouth, and he trailed a line of kisses down her skin, only stopping when he reached a place on her neck that shivered when he touched it.

Her body shook with a violence she wasn't familiar with. He continued to suck and lick, his thrusts an even rhythm in beat with her pounding heart.

She clenched his shoulders, fingers digging into his skin.

She wanted more.

Emerson applied pressure to his chest, pushing him onto his back. Then she lifted her hips and dropped back down. Her breasts bounced as she took him, and Tyler's fingers clenched her hips.

An almost animalistic sound ripped from his chest. He cupped one breast as she moved. Rolled her nipple between his thumb and forefinger.

Her breath hissed from between her teeth. He did it again, the hand on her hip lifting her higher, lowering her faster.

Her body was so tight she could break at any second.

Another squeeze of her nipple. Then the hand on her hip shifted to her clit. He circled, and she screamed his name, red-hot pleasure pulsing through her limbs. She continued to thrust. Continued to ride him as the bright shades of color flashed behind her eyes.

His hands returned to her hips as he pounded into her from below. Then he shouted her name as he tensed and hardened.

When he stopped, all she could feel was the throbbing of his length inside her. The beat of his heart beneath her hand.

She dropped onto his chest. Immediately, his thick arms wrapped around her, holding her close. She didn't know how long they stayed like that, tangled together, neither of them willing to separate. She never wanted to leave. So instead of rising, instead of rolling away to his side, she let herself relax. Let the thumping of his heart, its soothing rhythm, remind her there was still good in the world. *He* was the good. And he was hers.

CHAPTER 28

*L*evi lay still in the hospital bed, recovering from yesterday's surgery to repair the bullet wound. This morning, Sage planned to extract the chip in his shoulder, and if everything went well, he should wake soon after.

It was nearing nine a.m., so not too early, but Tyler had been sitting here on guard duty since two. He'd wanted the overnight shift because that meant he could spend the rest of the day with Emerson.

Memories of waking with her cheek resting over his heart played through his mind. Of the gentle rise and fall of her chest. The way her hair had splayed over his shoulder.

Last night had been everything. It had been the two of them declaring not only their love but their futures together. Because hell yeah, he saw his future with the woman. He wanted it all. The marriage. The kids. The white picket fence.

His gut heated just thinking about it.

Emerson had become his world. And he knew even if she was angry with Levi now, she still loved him. Which meant Tyler needed to fight like hell for the guy to get some psychiatric care.

Yeah, he'd have to pay for his crimes. But there was definitely some PTSD there. Possibly other issues too.

He'd already seen Sage. She'd only gotten here about half an hour ago and was prepping for Levi's final surgery.

His phone buzzed from his pocket. Callum's name showed up on the screen. He was leaving his place now, which meant Tyler's shift was almost over and he could return to Emerson.

He was just pushing his cell back into his pocket when a nurse stepped into the room.

She smiled at him. "Hi, it's time to wheel Levi to the operating room and prep him for surgery."

He nodded. "Go ahead. I'll stay close."

The nurse unlocked the bed wheels and detached some cords, then pushed Levi's bed out of the room. Tyler followed her through the halls.

When they reached another door, she smiled at him again. "Hopefully, the surgery won't take long," she said, before wheeling Levi through.

There were other quiet voices in the room. The sound of moving equipment. But he didn't hear Sage's voice in there yet.

He stepped down the hall a few paces, moving back as another patient was wheeled past him, heading in the direction he'd come with Levi. Loud beeping and footsteps peppered the air from rooms up and down the hall.

His phone rang, and he pulled it out to see it was Liam. He'd gone to question the surviving victim in Steve's murder case, the one who'd escaped but ended up stepping in front of a moving truck.

"Hey, how'd the questioning go?"

"You thought the case was already as strange as it could get? Wait until you hear this. After being drugged, the woman woke up in an abandoned warehouse, tied to a chair, with electrodes attached to her skull."

What the *fuck*?

"A laptop sat on a table in front of her, and questions flashed on the screen."

"What kind of questions?"

"Her memory was a bit blurry on exact words, but she remembered them being 'who would you save' questions. A few including her sister. But wait until you hear how it ended."

Shit. Did he even want to know?

Yes. "Tell me."

"She was given a choice—go to a burning house where her older sister was trapped and attempt to save her. Or run."

Nothing about that made sense. Why? Why do any of it? Was it all just a game some sick bastard was playing?

"Do you think they were all given that choice and everyone else chose their loved one?"

"Yes." Liam's response was instant. "And I think it's clear that whoever's responsible, they intentionally keep from the victim the fact that their loved one is already dead, in a bid to lure them to the house."

Yeah, definitely a sick bastard. He opened his mouth to ask more questions, then spotted Sage walking down the hall. She frowned when she saw him, her steps faltering for a moment before she continued forward and stopped in front of him.

"I've got to go, Liam. Thanks for the update."

"You got it."

"Hey," Sage said, "I was just heading to Levi's room. What are you doing down here?"

Now Tyler frowned. "Why were you going to his room? The nurse just wheeled him in here for surgery." He nodded toward the door at the end of the hall.

The increased confusion on Sage's face made unease coil in his gut. Without hesitation, he quickly moved back to the door, shoved it open—and his lungs seized.

The room was empty. There was a small recording device on

the counter, playing sounds to make it seem like there were people working in the room.

His gaze stopped at the door on the opposite wall.

Fuck!

He raced across and pushed through. An empty hall.

And at the end of the hall, he could see the bright exit sign.

EMERSON OPENED HER EYES SLOWLY. Tyler's woodsy, crisp scent filled her lungs, even though she knew he wasn't there.

Still, she felt the other side of the bed just in case. Cold. He was doing an early shift at the hospital this morning. Or, as she more accurately described it, middle-of-the-night shift, because she hardly considered a two a.m. start proper hours for the living. Not for her, anyway.

She rolled onto her side, and her gaze caught on a piece of paper with a lily lying on top.

Her heart fluttered, her lips stretching into a smile. She loved lilies but was pretty sure she'd never told him. How had he known?

Stretching out her arm, she grabbed and lifted it to her nose. Yep. It smelled amazing.

She read the note.

Hope you had a good sleep, Amber Eyes. I'll be back around nine-thirty. Love you. Ty x

God. Loving Tyler was the best decision she'd ever made, and the easiest.

Or maybe it wasn't a decision. Maybe she'd had absolutely no choice in the matter at all. Yeah, that sounded more accurate.

She grabbed her phone, then lay back on the bed, her heart beating a notch faster than it should. Eight-fifteen. All right, time to get her lazy ass out of bed and make herself look presentable before Tyler got home.

With a sigh, she rose. When she stood under the stream of water in the shower, her mind switched over to Levi. Sage had said he might wake this afternoon. What would he be like when he woke up? Would she be able to have a conversation with him now that the LSD should have worn off? Would he tell them why he'd taken the drugs? God, she had so many questions. So many answers she needed.

Ten minutes later, she was pulling her shirt over her head when her phone buzzed.

Her brows twitched at the name. Rowan. He was leaving today, and she didn't feel sad about it. Not when every time she thought about him, she remembered their last conversation and how he made her feel about her love for Levi. She almost let it go to voice mail, but at the last second, exhaled a breath and answered.

"Everything okay, Rowan?"

Wind blew through the line. "Actually, no. I'm running late for my flight and was just on my way to the airport when I got a flat tire."

Sucky timing.

"I'd call road service," he continued. "But I couldn't find anything local."

"I wouldn't even know who they have providing road service here." She shot a glance at the clock on the nightstand. Still half an hour before Tyler finished. Plenty of time to run out and get back. "I can come help. Send me a pin of your location, and I'll be there in a few."

"You're a lifesaver! Thank you, Emerson. The rental company swapped my car out, so don't be surprised when you see a different one."

"Got it."

She hung up and jogged downstairs to tug on her running shoes. Maybe she'd pick up some food from The Grind on her way home. Surprise Tyler with breakfast for once. Sure, it wasn't home cooked, but it was the thought that counted, right? Of course, she'd also have to ask Courtney to make her a gigantic cup of iced coffee today. She had a feeling it was the only thing that might settle her nerves before talking to Levi.

She stepped out of the house to see Mrs. Henry next door, watering her lawn. She smiled at the other woman, then headed over to the fence. After Mrs. Henry had helped her give Callum the slip, she'd gone over there with a baked banana bread as a thank-you and sorry-for-getting-you-involved gift. Of course, the kind woman had been as gracious as ever.

"Morning, Mrs. Henry. You treat your grass well."

She grinned. "My lawn loves its early-morning hydration. Where are you off to?"

"My ex-husband has a flat tire. Unfortunately, he's not very mechanically inclined."

Mrs. Henry's brows rose. "Your ex-husband?"

"Yeah, he's been in town for a bit, but he's leaving today." Then, because she felt she should, she added, "It's a long, complicated story. Have a great day."

"You too, dear."

She slid into the rental car she was still using and put Rowan's location into her phone. Ten minutes.

She went slightly over the limit and made it in eight.

The long stretch of road was surrounded by trees. No houses or businesses nearby. Not even many other cars going by.

She pulled in behind him, surprised he wasn't out of the car waiting for her. She climbed out and walked to his vehicle. The driver's side tires were both fine. She rounded the car...only to find the other two fully inflated, as well.

Not only that, but Rowan wasn't in the car.

What the hell?

She frowned—and was just turning to head back to her own car when something stung her neck.

Emerson gasped at the prick to her flesh, her hand flying to her neck. Then her car started to move in front of her. Wait, no… it wasn't moving. It was her vision. The world was blurring and wavering before her eyes. She blinked rapidly, but it didn't help.

When she opened her mouth to speak, to call out for Rowan, her voice didn't work. Or maybe it did, and she was just too out of it to use it. She blinked again. One slow, sleepy blink that had her eyes barely opening. Suddenly, her legs could no longer hold her.

The day turned dark as she fell to the ground.

CHAPTER 29

The phone rang. Then it rang some more. Tyler cursed under his breath. Why wasn't she answering?

Callum and Mason watched him. Both men had arrived at the hospital just in time to view surveillance footage with him. Footage of the woman wheeling Levi outside, where a man had helped lift Levi into a white sedan. Callum was running the plates on the car while Tyler desperately tried to get in contact with Emerson. They'd also contacted Steve, who'd called in the nearest guys from the FBI as well as local police who should be there soon.

But there was something in his gut telling him to get to Emerson.

Tyler pulled the phone from his ear.

"Cameras?" Callum asked, looking up from his laptop.

He opened the app to his home security and rewound the footage on one of the outdoor cams until he saw Emerson stepping out of the house.

He frowned. She hadn't told him she was going anywhere. Her gaze caught on the house next door, and she smiled. Then, instead of walking straight to her rental in the drive, she veered in that direction.

Mrs. Henry.

He clicked out of the footage and called the older woman's number while he heard Callum on the phone with Flynn, who was at Blue Halo.

She answered on the second ring.

"Tyler, dear!"

"I need to know if Emerson told you where she was going this morning."

"Oh, um...yes, she did. She said she was changing a flat tire for her ex-husband."

That knowledge should've had the unease lessening inside him. So why was there still so much goddamn dread?

"Thank you, Mrs. Henry."

He hung up before the woman could say anything else, then called Rowan's number. He'd saved it into his phone as soon as he'd come to Cradle Mountain.

It was five rings in when he knew the guy wasn't going to answer.

"Fuck!" he shouted, not caring who heard.

"Got it," Callum said. He looked at Tyler. "We hacked the rental car GPS system again and got the location of her car."

"Send it to me," he yelled as he ran down the hall toward the exit.

His team would start working on locating the white sedan. Right now, Emerson was his priority. It wasn't normal for her to ignore his calls. And everything in him shouted that something was wrong.

He made it to her rental in half the time it should have taken and parked behind it. The second he reached her car, he knew she wasn't here. There were no sounds, no heartbeats from inside. Still, he checked the front, back, and trunk of the car. Empty.

His gaze ran over an array of prints on the side of the road. She'd parked behind another car. She'd rounded that vehicle, then...

His gaze found the second set of prints. A man's. He'd walked out of the woods.

Had she gotten into his car willingly? Or had he taken her?

A dangerous rhythm pulsed in his temple. Because even though he wanted it to be the first option, everything in Tyler told him it was the second.

SILENCE. It surrounded Emerson. But not the calm, safe kind of silence you woke up to in the morning. This silence felt heavy. Dangerous. It made her skin prickle and her stomach clench and convulse.

She scrunched her eyes shut. A few minutes had passed since she'd woken, but her eyelids felt so heavy, she hadn't tried to open them. It wasn't just her eyelids that felt heavy, though. Her entire body did. Her muscles ached and there was a dull throb in her head that pumped behind her eyes.

She squirmed. Whatever she was sitting on was hard. She tried to lift her arms, but something stopped her. Some sort of restraint around her wrists.

Terror stabbed at her chest, and slowly, she forced her eyes open.

Thin ropes. They held her wrists to the chair and, by the feel of it, her ankles too.

Panic flooded her. There was barely any light in here, wherever here was. Through a breathing exercise, she battled back the fear and after several tense minutes, finally glanced around.

She was in...an old barn? The ceiling was vaulted with wooden beams cutting across. The concrete floor beneath her was cracked and dirty like no one had maintained it in months, maybe years. There was a big sliding door that was currently closed, and windows high in the structure. But they were covered in so much dust it made seeing any light nearly impossible.

She looked back at the rope around her wrists and noticed extra cords.

Electrodes. They were taped to her chest.

The cords attached to the electrodes led to a table beside her. Two laptops. One that faced her, another turned away. The latter had cords attached to it. And not just cords from her chest, she finally realized. There were more. On her skull. Her forehead. She shook her head, able to feel them.

What the hell was this?

There was a second chair on the other side of the table. Was someone else coming?

Her chest heaved with the need for air, and sweat beaded her skin. She opened her mouth to scream for help when footsteps sounded from behind. Then a voice.

A familiar voice.

"Good to see you awake, Emerson."

Immense shock coiled in her belly, making nausea crawl up her throat.

No...

Rowan came to stand in front of her, his features completely devoid of emotion.

She gave the ties on her wrist a hard tug. "What the hell's going on, Rowan? Untie me! Now!"

"I'm afraid I can't do that. I need to ask you a few questions first."

She frowned. "Questions?"

This was a dream, right? A surreal dream where she'd turned her ex-husband into some psychotic creep who kidnapped and held people hostage?

"We're going to do an electroencephalography test. I've attached electrodes to your chest to monitor your heart rate and more to your head to record brain activity. The information will be sent directly to my laptop."

She shook her head, ignoring the ache in her skull. "I don't understand..."

Understatement of the damn century.

Rowan gave her a look that almost seemed sympathetic before crouching in front of her. "You're part of my study, Emerson. For years, I've found your loyalty to your stepbrother utterly fascinating. Eventually, an idea started to form in my head. What if I made *that* the subject of my PhD thesis?"

What the hell?

She almost didn't want to ask but knew she had to. "What if you made *what* the subject?"

She tried to think back, to remember what the topic of his thesis was. Surely he'd told her? He'd been working on it for so long, she should remember. But God...she couldn't. Had she never actually asked?

"I'm investigating the neuropsychology of emotional attachment and its impact on moral judgment."

The words tumbled around in her head, and she struggled to piece them together in a way that made sense. It was hard, when nothing about her current reality made *any* freaking sense.

Rowan stood. "You know what I realized almost immediately? It's not just you. So very many otherwise good, *ethical* people desert their values for loved ones. The way emotional attachment impacts our judgment is something I've become quite obsessed with over the last few years."

Jesus...

"Do you kidnap all your research participants?" she growled sarcastically.

"Yes."

One word that shook the very foundation of her world. Maybe the drugs had affected her more than she'd thought. Maybe this was a nightmare she couldn't wake up from. Because in what universe did her ex-husband admit to kidnapping people?

"Usually I don't show my face," he continued, like he didn't notice her mental breakdown, "but you're my last test subject, and I'm certain you would have figured out it was me, so there really wasn't any point in hiding."

He was a freaking mad scientist. How the hell hadn't she seen it?

An angry breath hissed from her lips. "You really think after kidnapping me and tying me to a damn chair, I'm going to answer a single goddamn question?"

His slow smile made the back of her neck prickle uncomfortably. "Yes. I believe you *will* answer my questions. All of them. If you want Levi to live, that is."

Her breath hitched. "You don't have Levi. He's in a hospital bed being watched by Tyler and his team from Blue Halo Security."

"Yeah, it appears they're not as good as they'd like people to believe. It wasn't hard to get your stepbrother. All I had to do was pay a nurse to sneak him out to a car and deliver him to my assistant."

"Your assistant?"

Rowan's expression turned fond. "He was my student. And he's a big fan of my work. When I told him what I had planned, of course he wanted to be a part of it. He's been quite the asset."

God, there were more sickos like Rowan?

"I can see you're disgusted, Emerson, which is a little surprising, considering how easily you're able to forgive your stepbrother's sins. But that's okay. You don't understand my vision. While I've always been working toward understanding people and the brain and the way we're programmed to work, you've been off painting your pretty little pictures."

Her hands clenched. He meant that while she was creating art, he was kidnapping innocent victims. She shook her head. "I still don't believe you have Levi. And I'm not answering a single question."

He sighed, as if she'd disappointed him. Then he pressed a few keys on the laptop facing her. A photo appeared on the screen.

Horror gripped her throat.

It was Levi, still in a hospital gown, tied and bound in the back of a car.

"Now," he continued. "I'm going to explain what will happen. If you play along, your brother has a chance to live."

A *chance*? She opened her mouth to tell Rowan he wasn't a killer but then snapped her lips shut. She had no idea *who* this man was or what he was capable of. He certainly wasn't the Rowan she'd thought she married. The man who'd been her friend and confidant for years.

"There are two parts to my data collection," he said, turning the laptop facing her and taking a seat on the other side of the table. He tapped a few keys. "For part one, dilemmas will be presented as a visual display on the laptop screen. Each dilemma will be presented as text, sometimes through one screen, sometimes multiple. Some questions will be accompanied by visual aids in the form of photos. You'll then be able to select the option and state whether you believe the situation to be appropriate or inappropriate."

Her mind scrambled to keep up with his words.

"As I've already mentioned, your brain activity and heart rate will be monitored during the test."

She opened her mouth again, not quite sure what she was going to say, but he kept talking.

"You'll have a maximum time limit of one minute to answer each question, then a fifteen-second break between questions for the hemodynamic response to return to baseline."

A few more keys were clicked on the laptop, then he spun it around. Words were in front of her, but she didn't read them. She couldn't. Shock and disbelief were still pumping through her veins. That she was here. That Rowan, *her* Rowan, was responsible.

And what did he plan to do after the test? Let her go so she could tell the world? Had he let others go?

Nausea coiled in her belly at the suspected answers of those questions.

If she didn't answer the questions, what would he do to Levi? What had he *already* done?

"Answer the question, Emerson. The longer you take, the less chance you have of saving your stepbrother."

She lifted her gaze to him, hoping to find…something. Maybe a scrap of humanity?

She saw nothing. Only a cold, clinical expression.

Emerson clenched her fists and looked at the words. Then she forced them to make sense. Bit by bit, they did.

You kill ten people to save one. Appropriate or not appropriate.

One long breath. "Inappropriate."

The next question popped up.

You kill one person to save ten. Appropriate or not appropriate.

Her brows twitched. She wasn't sure she was capable of killing *anyone*. But was it appropriate? Was the most moral choice whatever offered the greatest number of saved lives?

"Appropriate," she said quietly, not entirely certain it was, but it was the best answer she had in the moment.

You kill the ten because the one person is a physician who saves people from impoverished countries, and the ten people are convicted killers. Appropriate or not appropriate.

He was asking her if the value of the life or lives made a difference. She wasn't sure. And she wasn't God, so she shouldn't be making such a choice anyway.

She said the first word that came to mind. "Appropriate."

More ethical dilemmas were put in front of her, all very similar. About saving some but in the process, killing others. And the more questions she was faced with, the easier they were to answer.

Until, suddenly, the information changed to an image of a smiling family. She frowned. The man looked familiar.

The next screen held more text...

Dad of three. Husband. Police officer.

And the last screen...

This officer was murdered by a convicted killer. You can choose to save him or his killer. You choose his killer.

The question made her skin cool. She opened her mouth three times before answering.

"Inappropriate."

The next slide had her gasping. It was three men. One, the officer she'd just been shown—and two that she definitely recognized.

The men who'd been on Levi's team in the military. The men he'd shot, sending him into a downward spiral.

The screen changed to a photo of Levi. Her heart stopped.

Then the statement.

The men on screen one are known victims of the man on screen two. There may be more who are unknown.

Her heart cracked. Was this real? Had the officer Levi shot died? "Victim" could mean more than one thing. As far as she was aware, he was still in the hospital. Her heart started to ache in her chest.

The screen changed.

The killer's in one room. His victims are alive in the other. You only have time to open one door. The people in the other room die. You choose the murderer.

Tears pressed to her eyes. Presented as simply as this, the answer was obvious. But, like every other question, no one should have the choice to save or take a life.

Three heartbeats later, she answered.

"Inappropriate."

For a split second, she wondered what her brain showed him. That the question was harder than it should have been? That there was brain activity when there shouldn't be?

God, what did he expect? That the second a loved one did things they shouldn't, love for them stopped? It wasn't that simple!

"Well done, Emerson."

Her gaze swung to him. "Is it true? Did the officer die?"

"We're up to part two," he said, without answering her question.

She frowned, remembering what he'd said earlier. Two parts. But he'd never explained the second.

Rowan stood. "The second part is the behavioral section of the test."

The what?

"Rowan—"

He moved toward her, and her skin crawled when he began to remove the electrodes from her chest and skull. She didn't want this man anywhere near her.

It stung every time he pulled one off, but she barely felt it. "Rowan? What is part two?"

He removed the final electrode, then stepped toward the laptops. He closed both and slid everything into a bag before pulling two things out. A compass and a small piece of paper.

She opened her mouth to ask what they were for, but he spoke before she could.

"Escape quickly, and you might just be able to save Levi."

Wait—*what*?

"Rowan!"

He ignored her, turning and heading toward the barn door.

"Rowan, come back! Tell me where the hell Levi is!"

He didn't. He left the barn, then an eerie silence surrounded her.

CHAPTER 30

"Talk to me, Callum. Is he still on the move?" Tyler just about growled the words to his friend through the car's Bluetooth.

Callum had found that the white sedan holding Levi was stolen and the owner had a GPS tracker. Apparently, the guy'd had his car stolen before. It was their one small reprieve so far today.

The car was heading south, and Tyler was breaking every fucking traffic law to catch him.

"You're not far behind him, Ty."

His fingers tightened around the steering wheel, and he pushed the car to move faster. The anger was like hot lava in his gut, threatening to burn straight through him. Any calls to Emerson's phone were now going straight to voice mail. She was gone. Out of his reach. And it was tearing him to fucking shreds.

They'd checked Rowan's hotel room. Not only was he not there but he'd checked out and his rental car had been returned. So all Tyler could do was focus on catching the stolen vehicle that had driven away with Levi. *That* was their only source of answers right now.

They'd figured out the woman was an actual nurse at the hospital. His team had already paid her a visit with the police, but she didn't know anything. Just that she'd been offered enough money to make stealing a patient and losing her job worthwhile.

Suddenly, a car appeared in the distance.

A white sedan.

"I see him," he said quietly, pushing the accelerator to the floor.

He knew the second the asshole spotted him, because they sped up.

Too late, scumbag. I've got you.

His engine roared as trees whipped past his car. The second he was close enough, he swerved into the opposite lane, raced past the car, then swung back in front of them and stomped on the brakes.

Tyler braced for impact, expecting a massive hit.

Instead, the driver of the sedan swerved wildly off the road and hit a tree—hard.

Tyler pulled over and was out of his car in seconds. He tore the driver's door completely off its hinges and ripped the male driver from the vehicle.

The guy groaned, blood gushing from a wound on his head, as Tyler shoved him against the car. "What did you do with Levi Campbell?"

"Oh God...I'm bleeding! I need a hospital."

"You'll need a fucking hole in the ground if you don't answer my goddamn question." He pulled the man forward and slammed him into the car. "What did you do with Levi Campbell?"

When the guy just groaned again, Tyler grabbed his wrist and squeezed.

Bones snapped. The man howled.

"Fuck!" he shouted. "You broke my hand!"

"Next is your knee."

Stark fear widened the guy's eyes. "Fine, I'll tell you!"

Tyler loosened his grip, but only slightly.

The asshole coughed blood. "I'm Rowan's thesis assistant. I do whatever he tells me to do, usually taking one of his test subjects to a certain location."

Test subjects? What the hell was he—

"I never stab them, though," he added quickly, "and I never set the house on fire! That's always Rowan."

Tyler's entire world slowed.

Two people kidnapped, one stabbed. One in a burning house.

Fuck!

It was Steve's case.

"Where are they?" Tyler growled.

More blood ran from the guy's mouth. "F-fourteen East Fork Lane, in Hailey. But she'll be given a choice. She might not choose to save him…"

The choice…what the surviving victim had mentioned.

Emerson would choose to save Levi if she had a chance. There was no doubt in his mind.

A car pulled up behind him. Flynn. A second later, he was beside them.

"Call paramedics and the FBI," Tyler said, barely able to breathe. "We've found Steve's killers. And I know where Emerson and Levi are."

He ran back to his car, put the address into his GPS, and took off. The second he was on the road, he called his team.

"You get him?" Callum asked basically in unison with Steve, who was already on a call with the team.

"Yes. Levi's at fourteen East Fork Lane, Hailey. I'm about thirty minutes away."

But he planned to halve that.

"We're the same distance," Liam said quickly. "I'm leaving now. We'll hopefully get there the same time."

"I'll alert my guys to go there now," Steve added.

Tyler was grateful. He needed as much backup as possible in case there were any surprises.

"The guy who took Levi is Rowan Perez's thesis assistant," Tyler said quickly. "And they're the killers you've been hunting, Steve. Rowan stabs the victims and sets the house fires."

The guys swore violently over the line.

"Emerson doesn't have much time then," Blake said.

Tyler knew that, but every inch of him rebelled against the confirmation.

"What's the fucking subject of his thesis?" Tyler growled. It shouldn't matter at this point...but he needed to know.

"On it," Callum said. Typing sounded for two minutes that felt like two hours. Then his teammate cursed again.

Trepidation spidered throughout his gut. "Tell me."

"According to notes from the advisory committee, Rowan was kicked out of his PhD program for an 'unethical methodology' proposal."

He certainly hadn't told Emerson. As far as she knew, he was still working on his PhD. "What was the proposal?" Though with everything he knew about the victims, he could hazard a guess.

"His research topic was 'neuropsychology of emotional attachment and its impact on moral judgment.' It looks like he wanted to create real-world ethical dilemmas and observe behavior, but the details of what he was proposing were bad enough for them to ask him to leave the entire program."

"So he got kicked out but continued his research himself." Emerson said he lived and breathed his work, so it wasn't a surprise. If he felt it was important enough to study, getting kicked out of the program wouldn't have stopped him.

"From the scant details included with the notes, the innocent family members would be the test subjects. He'd ask them questions and record their brain activity as they answered. Then he'd give them a choice between saving themselves or attempting to save their loved ones in a burning house."

The ultimate moral dilemma.

"The sick fuck," Jason growled.

He pressed his foot harder to the accelerator.

Rowan would no doubt be at the burning house. He knew Emerson would choose her stepbrother—and there was no way he'd risk letting her survive. Not when she'd have likely worked out exactly who was responsible.

~

EMERSON TORE at the scratchy rope with her teeth. *Almost...there.*

She'd been at it for at least ten minutes. She was making progress, but it was slow. And with each minute that ticked by, her heart thudded harder.

Escape quickly, and you might just be able to save Levi.

What did that mean? What had he done to her stepbrother?

She groaned as she bit at the rope again. Her teeth and jaw ached, and her wrists were red and raw from trying to tug them free, but she didn't stop.

Another strand finally snapped, loosening the bind. She tugged her hand out. *Yes!* She reached over and undid the other side. Again, it took more time than she could afford, and her wrist was bleeding slightly by the time she slid it free. A minute later, her ankles were free.

Then she quickly grabbed the note.

The final part of my data collection, Emerson. Levi is bound on the second floor of a burning house. The home is two miles west. Alternatively, there's a highway two miles east. You can save him—or yourself. Choose.

Her lips parted, a mixture of shock and sickness and fury washing through her like a tidal wave. But there was also something else...

Agony. For Levi. That he'd been abducted from the hospital,

bound, and left in a burning house. Was it already too late to save him?

Didn't matter. And there wasn't a choice. Not really. There was no way she could live with herself if she didn't try to save her stepbrother.

She stepped forward and immediately her legs caved. God, whatever he'd drugged her with was still in her system and making her muscles weak.

She pushed to her feet and locked her knees. Anger pulsed in her temples. She *was* going to save Levi. Then she was going to make sure Rowan paid for his crimes.

Emerson forced one foot in front of the other, and when she reached the large barn door, she put her entire body weight into pushing it open.

The scent of pine and dirt permeated the air as Emerson stepped outside and turned west. The faster she moved, the more her head ached. She fell a dozen times, sometimes due to looking at the compass and not watching where she was going, sometimes because of the exhaustion in her limbs. Twigs and rocks tore at her hands and knees with each fall.

She ignored it all, and every time she pushed to her feet, she ran that much faster.

It felt like it was hours before the two-story home came into view.

Oh God. The flames were huge! From what she could tell, they raged throughout the bottom floor, hot and angry.

She hesitated. If she went in there, would she even make it out?

Images of Levi flashed into her mind.

She had to try.

With a quick inhale, she moved, running up the porch steps and shouldering open the door, which was already ajar.

Flames engulfed the living room and kitchen. They hadn't reached the stairs yet. She had a path.

Fear spiked in her chest at the thought of running up there. Of becoming trapped. But again, she ignored the worst-case scenario, and instead, pulled her shirt over her mouth and ran. She took the stairs two at a time to an empty landing. There were closed doors on either side of the space.

"Levi?" The second his name left her mouth, a cough racked her chest. The smoke was thick on the upper floor. It burned into her lungs with every breath.

No answer.

She opened the first door. An empty bathroom. She tried the second. An empty bedroom.

Where was he? She checked every room off the landing. When she reached the last one, she almost expected it to be empty as well. Had Rowan lied to her?

The door opened into an office.

And in the center of the office was Levi, tied to a chair.

She cried out at the sight of his ashen complexion and the stab wound in his chest. She ran over, kneeling in front of him and cupping his cheek. "Levi? Can you hear me?"

He didn't respond. Jesus, was his chest even moving?

She touched the vein in his neck. A pulse bumped her fingers, and she nearly fainted with relief. He was alive. But if he was unconscious, how the hell was she supposed to get him out? There was no way she could physically move him. She needed help.

She rushed back to the landing, coughing the entire time, but flames roaring up the steps blocked her. *No...*

They were stuck. Trapped on the second floor of a burning house.

Panic tried to swallow her whole, but she took a moment to stop. Think.

Windows.

She ran back to the office and tugged at the nearest one.

When it didn't budge, she pulled harder. Nothing. She had a sinking feeling Rowan had made sure they wouldn't open.

That son of a bitch.

Her next breath was all smoke. She coughed and spluttered before running into another room and closing the office door behind her to keep as much smoke out as possible. None of them were going to open, but she had to try. She yanked at a window in the nearest bedroom. Same thing.

With an angry growl, she tried windows in every room on the second floor, coughing harder and harder.

Rowan had trapped them.

In the hallway, she coughed so violently she almost fell. The smoke was too thick to breathe.

Panic swamped her again, but she ruthlessly shoved it down. There had to be a way out. Today was not the day she was going to die.

Focus.

Water.

In the bathroom, one towel hung from the rack. She grabbed it, took it to the shower, and ran the water until the material was soaked through and dripping.

She covered her face with the towel as she ran back to the office, forcing herself not to look at the flames climbing up to the landing.

The second she was in the office with Levi, she threw the door closed, rolled up the wet towel, and shoved it into the crack at the bottom of the door.

Her lungs spasmed as she struggled to breathe. A wave of dizziness hit, but she shook it off. She had to keep going. If nothing else, she had to just keep herself and Levi alive and pray someone nearby saw the flames.

The only way out was through the window. She scanned the room for something to break it with and found a bookend on a shelf. Yes! It was heavy. That was good. She took a few steps toward the window.

Her vision blurred and dizziness hit again. She had to grab the desk to keep herself upright. Right on cue, another cough crackled through her chest.

She waited a few precious heartbeats, getting her shuddering breaths under control, then took two steps, threw her arm forward, and smashed the bookend into the window.

The glass shattered—and a fresh breeze blew over her face. Thank God! She wasn't safe, but it was something.

Her relief was short-lived, as black dots edged her vision. Her breathing was too shallow.

Ignoring the way the window went fuzzy before her eyes and air rattled in her chest, she cleared the small shards around the frame with the bookend.

She stuck her head out to investigate the area—and found a man partially obscured by a huge pine tree about fifty yards from the house. He stood out like a sore thumb in the otherwise deserted area.

Rowan.

She screamed and ducked as a gunshot sounded. Another round of coughing hit. Her lungs seized. She couldn't get enough air! The darkness in her peripheral vision became a dark fog that blanketed everything.

Emerson tried to fight it off, tried to rise to her feet, but the darkness won—and it consumed her.

CHAPTER 31

Tyler was speeding down the long, curving dirt driveway when he heard the gunshot.

His heart nearly stopped. Because he knew that shot was aimed at Emerson.

He drove faster. When the house came into view ahead, nausea crawled up his throat.

Flames. They were big and wild, hot even from a distance, and they'd smashed out the bottom-floor windows. He noted a top-floor window was also smashed, but no flames came from that one.

He skidded to a stop outside the house. The second he threw the car into park, his windshield spiderwebbed from a bullet.

Jesus! He didn't have time for a fucking shooter. He needed to get to Emerson!

He grabbed his Glock and slid out the passenger side, staying low and using the vehicle as cover, assuming that he'd driven up between the shooter and the house. He poked his head up to scan the trees beside the house just as another shot rang out.

It hit the front quarter panel.

And now he knew where the asshole was.

He rose and fired back, just glimpsing Rowan as he disappeared behind a tree.

Tyler ran, moving like lightning across the yard and behind the tree before the asshole could even peek his head around for another look.

Rowan cried out in pain as he hit the ground, crushed by Tyler's weight.

He heard another car pull up at the house. Liam or Blake—it had to be one of them. Both men had been close behind.

Rowan cursed and bucked wildly. Tyler slid an arm around his neck and squeezed, a millisecond from snapping it when Liam was suddenly behind him. He clenched his shoulder hard.

"Go. I'll stay with him."

With a growl and more self-restraint than he even knew he possessed, Tyler released Rowan and raced back to the house. He zeroed in on that upstairs window. The lower sash of the double-hung window was the only one with broken glass on the second floor, the upper sash still intact. And although there was black smoke coming out now, there were still no flames.

Emerson had broken that window. He knew it in his gut.

So where was she?

He took several big steps backward before running full tilt toward the house. He scaled the wall, getting three steps in against the siding before lunging for the edge of the window.

Hot flames raged below. He ignored the heat, pulling himself up and throwing his body into the house. Tiny shards of glass cut into his skin. He barely registered the pain.

Emerson and Levi. They were both in the room—and both unconscious.

The sight of Emerson, lying so still on the ground, made sickly panic surge throughout his system. The fire was too goddamn loud for him to hear a heartbeat. He dropped beside her and touched the pulse in her neck. Sluggish thuds beat at the pads of his fingers.

Alive. Thank God!

He tugged her into his arms and stood. She didn't stir.

He looked out the window to see Blake had arrived. He stood below, far too close to the flames, arms outstretched and ready to catch Emerson. *Fuck*, he hated dropping her out a goddamn window.

But he trusted his friend.

He hefted her easily and eased his torso out the window, leaning as far away from the house as possible—then he let her go.

Blake caught her easily.

Still, she didn't stir.

When Blake moved away from the structure, Tyler smashed the top half of the window, pane and sash, clearing as much glass as possible. Then he turned and went to Levi. Thick blood coated his hospital gown from the knife wound in his gut. As he had with Emerson, Tyler checked for a pulse. And again, there was a faint beat.

He broke the thin ropes restraining Levi's wrists and feet. If the man had woken, he would have escaped them easily.

Tyler threw him over his shoulder and stood. He moved to the window, climbed carefully to a crouch on the sill, and dropped to the ground.

Then he raced over to where Blake had placed Emerson on the grass, far enough away from the house that they were safe for now. He lay Levi beside her. In the distance, he could just make out the sound of sirens.

He cupped his woman's cheek. "Emerson! Can you hear me?"

When she remained unconscious, blood roared between his ears even as he gasped out a sob. He lowered his head, touched his lips to her temple. "I need you to come back to me, Emerson. I love you too damn much to lose you!"

∾

EMERSON FELT HIS PRESENCE. It had been there since she'd woken. Tyler. But she didn't want to open her eyes. Even though they were closed, they stung like hell. She couldn't imagine how much worse it might be if she opened them. On top of that, every time she swallowed, her throat burned.

She remembered everything. Rowan's call for help. The electrodes. The questions. The fire...

She needed to open her eyes and find out if anyone else was hurt. If Levi had gotten out.

At the thought of her stepbrother, her next inhalation was more of a gasp. Her chest suddenly tightened, and a painful cough caused her body to convulse.

Immediately, a hand touched her shoulder. A warm hand. A familiar hand.

"Emerson?"

The coughing slowly ceased.

That voice. A voice that was so comforting and loved. But it sounded so worried. She didn't like hearing the worry.

Slowly, she forced her eyes open. As suspected, the sting turned into a burn, and moisture instantly gathered in her eyes. She blinked three times before the tears cleared and he came into focus.

The worry in his voice matched that on his face.

"Hey." The second the scratchy word left her lips, another cough ripped through her, making her raw chest hurt even worse.

Tyler cursed. He carefully removed the oxygen mask from her mouth and nose, then placed a straw at her lips. She took a sip of water. Even that burned her throat, but the cool liquid still felt incredible.

When the straw disappeared and he looked at her again, she saw it wasn't just worry on his face. There was guilt and anger and...helplessness?

"I'm okay," she whispered, ignoring the pain at speaking. She touched the back of his hand.

His jaw clenched, his hand turning and fingers wrapping around hers.

She opened her mouth to ask the question she knew she had to ask. She almost didn't want to. Was almost too scared. But she needed to know. "Is Levi...?"

"He's alive."

The air rushed from her chest on a sigh, prompting another round of painful coughs. Still, she closed her eyes in relief. Yes, she knew Levi healed quickly, but he'd been so still in that chair, and his heart had beat so faintly.

"We got him here in time," Tyler continued. "If he was a normal man, he wouldn't have made it. He lost a lot of blood, but he's doing better now."

Thank God. She turned her head and looked toward the hall, not wanting to ask the *next* question, either. She was certain she already knew the answer.

"It was Rowan shooting at the house, wasn't it?"

Tyler's eyes narrowed and darkened. "Yes."

Of course. It wasn't enough that he'd kidnapped her. Kidnapped and stabbed her stepbrother before trapping them both in a burning building. He also had lie in wait, ready to shoot her in case she managed to find a way out. To kill her before she could tell the world what he'd done.

"I don't understand what happened to him. He's an *academic*. Not..." A murderer? Deranged psychopath? "The Rowan in that barn wasn't the Rowan I remember."

Tyler swiped the pad of his thumb over the back of her hand. "Turns out, he was the case we were helping the FBI with. You and Levi weren't the first victims. He's responsible for several deaths. He and his assistant will pay for their crimes."

Nausea crawled up her throat. Her ex-husband had planned

to kill her and her stepbrother. And he'd killed others. It was like a sickening nightmare she couldn't wake up from.

"Did you know the topic of his thesis?" Tyler asked.

"No. Not until he told me in that barn." She still couldn't believe it. She should have asked. Why hadn't she asked? "It took him a long time to come up with his research topic. Years. He was on a high when he finally did."

"He was kicked out of the PhD program for proposing unethical methodology tests. He wanted to create real-life ethical dilemmas involving people with emotional attachments."

The questions from inside the barn flashed into her mind. "He took me to this old, abandoned-looking barn. He attached electrodes to my head and chest and asked me utilitarianism-type questions. He was fascinated by the entire philosophy...the idea that the correct moral action is whatever offers the greatest happiness for the biggest number of people."

She recalled Rowan explaining that to her during their years of marriage. More than once. And how the philosophy was fundamentally flawed, in his opinion.

"The last few questions involved Levi. I guess that was the emotional attachment part. They weren't so black and white and easy to answer."

She gasped, swinging her gaze back to Tyler. "The police officer. Did he die?"

Her heart pounded as she waited for his answer. If the implication of that question was true, if the cop died...then she truly couldn't save Levi. The law wasn't kind to people who killed police officers.

Tyler stroked her hand again. "He's alive. He went home to his family yesterday morning."

Her eyes closed in relief. Alive. Levi hadn't killed him.

All too soon, her anger ignited. That asshole had let her believe the officer was dead to manipulate his test parameters.

She wanted to *kill* him. She wanted to make him feel every ounce of the guilt and pain he'd made *her* feel.

She shook her head, trying and failing to regain control of her emotions. "I was *married* to him. He was my husband for years. And he tried to kill me and Levi! He killed others."

An ache weaved its insidious web throughout her chest.

"I know, baby."

A knock came at the door.

Tyler kept his gaze on her. "That's Liam and Callum. They went to the station and helped the FBI question Rowan. Do you want to know what they have to say?"

Did she?

It didn't matter if she wanted to. She had to know.

She nodded. Tyler called them in, and a second later, Liam and Callum stepped into the room, neither man looking happy.

"Glad to see you awake," Callum said.

Liam nodded his agreement.

"Did you get everything you needed out of Rowan?" Tyler asked.

Callum's gaze flicked back to Tyler. "After a bit of pressure, he admitted to pretty much everything. He took responsibility for all the previous victims."

Emerson worked to control her breathing. "How many has he killed?"

"There were five previous pairs of victims," Tyler said quietly. "Only one woman chose to run instead of saving her loved one. She survived."

Five couples with one survivor? So he'd murdered nine people before trying to kill her and Levi.

Jesus, this didn't feel real. Any of it.

Liam ran a hand through his hair. "He said he did it all in the name of research. That the end justified the means, and the understanding of emotional attachment in connection to moral integrity would go a long way in the field of neuropsychology. He doesn't regret his actions at all."

Callum shoved a hand into his pocket, his sympathetic gaze locked on Emerson. "There's something else. He admitted to being in constant communication with Levi since he disappeared shortly after Project Arma was shut down."

Shock spiked through her limbs. "What?"

"Rowan said he wanted to see just how far your loyalty went. He always saw you as patient X. His first and last. He provided Levi with the LSD but lied to him about what drug he was taking. Apparently, it started off at a low dosage, but he increased it quickly because of his altered DNA's natural immunity to most drugs. Whenever Levi called him, confused or in the middle of a hallucination, Rowan played into and manipulated his delusions to study the outcome."

That asshole! To play with her stepbrother's life so badly after everything he'd already suffered...to abuse both her and Levi's trust...

"Is Levi awake?" she asked.

She was sure her brother probably had police *and* Tyler's team guarding his door...but she had to see him. As soon as possible.

CHAPTER 32

*E*merson stepped into Levi's room. She was finally being discharged, but she wanted to see her brother before she went anywhere. Several of Tyler's teammates were by his door, guarding him, and he'd already assured her that Levi would be assessed by a psychiatrist before they arrested him for shooting the officer.

Emerson sat beside the bed, and Tyler remained close behind, his heat pressing into her, his hand on her shoulder. He didn't like her being so close to her brother, but he understood her need to talk to him.

Slowly, Levi's eyes opened. He looked tired, but he also looked alert. She wasn't sure how that was possible.

"Hey," she said quietly, her voice thick with emotion.

"Hey, Em."

Her hand twitched to take his. "How are you feeling?"

"Not great. But I haven't been feeling great for a long time."

She couldn't *not* touch him. She lifted her hand and covered his. Tyler's fingers tightened on her shoulder, but he didn't say anything or try to pull her away.

"Is it true? You've been in contact with Rowan this entire time? And he's been giving you drugs?"

Levi's gaze shifted to the ceiling. He looked like he was in pain. Not physically. A deep, emotional pain. "After what happened in Iraq, I felt like I was drowning. I didn't want to be living anymore. When Hylar offered me the chance to be part of something bigger than myself...he said it would ease my PTSD symptoms and help tip the odds of war in our favor, make our soldiers indestructible."

The bastard.

"But he failed. I was stronger, faster...but still plagued by the same feeling of hopelessness. I didn't want to drag you or Mom into my mess, but I needed to talk to someone. Rowan listened. He acknowledged how I was feeling. And he offered me something to take away the pain."

Rowan had abused Levi's trust just as much as Hylar had.

His eyes scrunched, as if just thinking about it all brought him too much pain. "The drugs made the pit in my gut disappear. They made me feel human again. Almost superhuman. It wasn't until a couple months in that the delusions came, but by that time... I needed the drug more than I cared about the side effects. They helped me ignore all the negative thoughts inside me."

"Levi..."

Finally, he looked at her. "I'm sorry, Em. I'm sorry I couldn't drag myself out of that hole without Rowan and the drugs."

She squeezed his hand. "You had PTSD, and your trust was abused not once, but twice. I'm going to fight for you to get the therapy you need, Levi. That's what I've *been* fighting for. I know you haven't been well for a long time. You *need* help."

His gaze shifted between her eyes, his own desolate. "I don't deserve that kind of loyalty, Em."

"You do. I love you, and I'm not giving up on you."

Emerson remained with her brother for another hour. Just talking. Trying to understand. Every so often, he looked like his mind was wandering elsewhere, and she had to bring him back to the conversation.

It was heartbreaking.

When she finally stepped out of the room, an odd mix of emotions swirled in her stomach. Relief that Levi was here and not out in the community, hurting others or himself. Gratitude that she'd finally gotten to talk to the old Levi. But also anger. *So much* anger.

All directed at her ex-husband.

Tyler stood in front of her, his arms sliding around her waist. "Are you okay?"

"I want to see him." She hadn't been expecting those words to come out of her mouth, but now that they had, they felt right.

Tyler tilted his head. "Who?"

"Rowan."

Tyler's muscles tensed, and she knew before he spoke what the answer was going to be. "Em—"

"Please." She took a step forward, pressing her palms to his chest. "I need to ask him something, and I need to see his face when I do."

Tyler's jaw clicked through a heavy beat of silence. Her stomach did a little roll because she wasn't sure which way he was leaning. Finally...

"I'll see if I can make it happen."

She lay her head on his chest, instant relief like a lightning strike inside her. "Thank you."

The next twenty-four hours moved quickly. Tyler got hold of his contact in the FBI, and he pulled some strings to get them access to Rowan.

Tyler continued to ask her throughout the evening and following morning if she was sure she wanted to do this. He wanted her to wait. Wait until she was completely better. Not coughing every few breaths and when her throat stopped burning.

But it was only when they were finally standing outside the interrogation room that doubt started to flutter in her chest.

Tyler heard it in her heartbeat. He cupped her cheek. "It's okay to change your mind."

The idea flirted with her sense of self-preservation, teasing her. But the second it did, she straightened her spine. "No. I need to do this."

Tyler studied her for another second before turning to the officer and nodding. The guy opened the door. She took a quick breath of courage before stepping into the small room.

Her heart thumped at the sight of Rowan sitting at a small table. His hands were cuffed. An orange jumpsuit covered his body. His face was completely devoid of emotion. It reminded her of those minutes in the barn.

Anger rose in her chest, and she had to breathe through it before lowering to a seat opposite him. Tyler sat beside her, remaining close.

"Hi, Emerson."

His voice...it had changed from comfortably familiar to something that evoked danger.

She'd been going over what she was going to say all morning, but now that she was here, now that she was looking her would-be killer in the face, her head felt empty.

She swallowed, feeling the burn of her throat. "You've been in contact with Levi this entire time and supplying him with LSD."

It wasn't a question, and the statement burned her throat.

Still no emotion on his face. None. "I had to see how far your loyalty went. The drugs were a concoction of a few things. At first, it was just a small amount of LSD. But I increased the dose when he proved...resistant. I wanted him to do something terrible. It was the only way to determine what it might take for you to finally turn against him." A flicker of something...not remorse or regret. Almost *intrigue*. "But you never did. I led you to believe he'd *killed* someone. A police officer. A father and husband. And still you wanted to help him."

She ground her jaw, trying to stop herself from leaping across the table and strangling him.

As if Tyler could read her thoughts, he reached over and squeezed her thigh.

"You're sick. We were *married*, Rowan. Best friends for years!" And he'd manipulated her and her stepbrother with the intent to *kill* them.

Rowan leaned forward, his tone still utterly calm. "You divorced me because I loved my work more than I loved you. Because I loved my work more than anything. Abnormally focused. Obsessive. Calculating. They were all labels you gave me during our marriage. Nothing I did should've surprised you."

"A lot of people love their work. They're not psychopaths who go around killing people."

"Not everyone has my dedication."

Really? He was talking about what he'd done like it was something to be admired?

"You're a monster," she growled.

"No. I'm a man who's thirsty for knowledge. You should be proud. It was only after realizing the depth of your loyalty to Levi that I finally figured out my thesis." He tilted his head. "He was part of this reprehensible program. You knew he was allowing people to suffer. Yet you not only defended him afterward, you wanted to save him."

She shook her head, trying to comprehend this man's attempt at justifying his actions.

He sighed. "I can see you're disgusted in me, and even I can admit, my methods were somewhat extreme."

Her eyes bulged. "Extreme? You let innocent people burn to death!"

"I killed murderers, and people who defended murderers.

Their deaths will not be mourned. And I always gave the loved one a choice. Only one person chose to save herself."

"It's called *love*, Rowan. Something you don't have even the tiniest grasp of."

"How did your assistant come into it?" Tyler asked, speaking for the first time.

Rowan lifted a shoulder. "Mike was a student of mine. He idolized me and my work. He thought it was just as unfair as I did when I got dismissed from the PhD program. I knew I needed help, so I proposed to him that we continue my work together, and he agreed."

She shook her head, leaning back in her seat. "What was the end goal here? You were kicked out of your program. You couldn't publish your work thanks to the methods you used."

His eyes lit up for the first time. "My *goal*, as you put it, was for my work to outlive me. I want my literature to be used in neuropsychology for years to come. People around the world will speak of me. They'll talk about the neuropsychologist who went to such extremes to learn about the brain, and the connection between emotions and morality. And naturally they'll talk about my results, because they'll want to know what was so important that I gave up my freedom for it."

Rowan's eyes got wider as he spoke, as if he was excited about the prospect of being remembered for something so horrible. Like the idea of people dying in the name of *research* was not only okay but good.

"Were you always like this?" she asked quietly. "Or did you change somewhere along the way?"

"It was only these last few years that I felt the higher calling to leave something behind that would be more meaningful." There was a moment of quiet before he spoke again. "Thank you for inspiring me."

That's when she realized.

She'd been feeling so guilty since she'd woken up in that

hospital bed. Guilty because she'd inspired this little *thesis* of Rowan's and created the connection between him and her brother.

But this wasn't her fault. There was something deeply wrong with the man sitting across from her. And if it wasn't this study, it would have been something equally abhorrent.

"You're wrong," she said, a new calm threading through her words. He raised a brow in question. "I didn't divorce you because you loved your work more than me. I divorced you because I realized *I* didn't love *you*. You were so insignificant to me, and I knew I wouldn't miss you if I left."

She rose, and Tyler rose beside her.

"And you know what? You are just as insignificant to every other person in the world." She leaned forward. "Your work won't be published. It will be buried. *No one* will read it. No one will know why you were put away for the rest of your life. Because I will make it my personal mission to ensure your research never sees the light of day. Your work, and everything you did," she lowered her voice, "will be for *nothing*."

And there it was. The first glimpse of strong emotion in Rowan.

Anger.

Good.

She stepped away. "Enjoy rotting in a cell for the rest of your insignificant life."

Then she slid her hand into Tyler's and left, ignoring Rowan's angry shout behind her.

TYLER WATCHED Emerson closely as he drove to The Grind. He wanted to take her home. She'd only been discharged from the hospital yesterday, and she had a lot of recovering to do. But his team was at the coffee shop, and she wanted to be there so she could thank them.

God, he was proud of her. The way she'd stood up to her ex and wiped the smug grin off the asshole's face.

The guy was a psychopath. Recreating real-life ethical dilemmas? He needed to be locked up, never allowed a taste of freedom again.

Tyler pulled into the parking lot. But before they got out, he touched her thigh. "You're absolutely sure you want to be here?"

She turned, and what he saw on her face just about wrecked him.

Strength. Courage. Love.

"Yes. I want to thank your team. And a good double-shot iced latte wouldn't be terrible. The stuff in the hospital tastes like feet."

So. Damn. Strong. "Okay. One quick stop for a latte and thank you's, then I'm taking you home and forcing you to bed rest."

She grinned. "Will you be with me on that bed rest?"

"Yes." *Hell yes.*

The smile slipped from her lips. "Good."

God, this woman…

He got out of the car because otherwise he'd do something stupid, like drive her home and never let her leave again. He held her hand tightly as they crossed the lot. He needed her as close as possible for a long damn time after almost losing her. He'd almost been too late. But he'd made it. She was here. She was safe.

He forced away the thoughts of Rowan and his assistant and how close his woman had come to death.

She was about to enter the shop when he pulled her to a stop.

Her brows flickered. "What are you doing?"

"Before we go in, I need to kiss you." He needed to kiss her right this second, to give the angry parts of his world some peace.

Her eyes softened. "I'll never say no to a kiss from you."

Thank God. He threaded his fingers through her hair and snaked the other hand around her waist. Then he lowered his head and sealed his mouth to hers.

The second they touched, Emerson hummed. Her lips were soft and supple, and when he slipped his tongue inside her mouth, he tasted her sweetness.

And there it was. The peace that had evaded him for days. The reassurance that she was here, in his arms and okay.

Someone cleared their throat beside them. He wanted to growl at the person. Maybe he actually did, because they laughed.

Emerson pressed at his chest, and when he looked beside him it was to see Flynn and Carina.

Really? A second time?

Carina smiled, her hand in Flynn's. "Wow, this feels familiar," she chuckled.

It was exactly the same scenario when they'd almost shared their first kiss. But, unlike then, when everything he felt for Emerson was too new to name, this time he knew it was love.

He smiled, pressing a hand to the small of Emerson's back. "Come on, let's get inside."

He stepped into the coffee shop, and his entire team shouted their greetings. Yep, this was peace.

CHAPTER 33

*C*allum pulled into the library parking lot. He'd just left his friends at The Grind. Everyone had been happy and relaxed, which made *him* damn happy. A couple of days ago, that was far from the case. Emerson's brush with death had been too close. If something had happened to her, it would have destroyed Tyler.

Anger still pulsed through him at the memory of what her ex-husband had set up, not only for her and her stepbrother but others too. It still shocked him how damn sick some people were. You'd think after years in the Special Forces, then going through Project Arma, he'd have grown immune to the evils of the world. Apparently not.

He grabbed his book from the passenger seat. It was his latest borrow, a thriller about two neighbors who had witnessed a murder.

It was good. But then, he'd known it would be. It had Fiona's sticker of recommendation on it. They were the only books he paid attention to.

The thought of the hot-headed librarian who liked to ride his ass made a smile tug at his lips. He wasn't sure if it was the deep brown of her beautiful eyes, the dimples in her cheeks when she smiled, or just the fact that she was one of the only people who put him in his place, but he liked her. A lot.

He climbed from the car. The library was in a small, older building. It was never busy. Which worked for him. No one else to steal the woman's attention.

He pushed open the door and spotted her the second he was inside. She stood near the back, slotting a book onto a shelf. She wore a knee-length aqua dress, and her long brown waves were pulled up in a tight ponytail.

Cute. Damn cute, especially in those bright red shoes with just the hint of a heel.

The incident at the bar flashed through his mind. Levi holding a gun to her head, an arm around her throat while she stood there, skin pale and fear in her eyes.

His jaw clicked. He'd been a second away from tearing Levi's head off. Thank God she'd gotten out of there unharmed. He'd driven her home that night, and she'd been shaky as hell, her usual smart mouth silent. He'd wanted to stay with her, make sure she was okay, but she'd sent him away, claiming she was fine.

She hadn't been fine.

He moved forward. When she stretched up to place a book on the top shelf and couldn't quite reach, he stopped behind her, slid the book from her fingers, and set it on the bookshelf.

She gasped and spun. The second their gazes met, her eyes flared and her heart took off in her chest. The flare only lasted a second before a cool, familiar mask slipped over her face.

You can't hide the racing heart, though, sweetheart.

He grinned. She was attracted to him, but she didn't want to admit it. Why did that make him want to work even harder to capture her attention?

"Callum." That formal tone made his grin widen. Fuck, he

wanted to break through her icy walls so damn bad. "Here to return another damaged book?"

He held it up. "Nope. All in one piece today."

Her eyes moved over the cover. "Well, it sometimes *looks* like it's all in one piece, then I open it up to find folded pages or a coffee stain."

Oh, yeah. He'd done both of those things. But to be fair, it was never intentional. "Check it yourself."

There was a beat of pause. Hesitation even. Did the woman not want to take it from him? In case their hands touched?

He raised a brow in challenge. She gave a little huff and grabbed the book, and when their fingers grazed, he felt the hot pulse of awareness. Damn, her skin was soft. And he knew he wasn't the only one affected. Not if the flush of her cheeks and the spike of her pulse was anything to go by.

Her throat bobbed as she flicked through the pages before looking up. "Good work, Callum."

His name rolled off her lips, and he almost looked down at them. Almost. He just stopped himself, because if he looked at her lips, he might do something stupid…like step closer.

"See?" He smiled. "I can take care of your babies."

Her lips twitched. *Go on, you can smile for me, honey.*

She cleared her throat. "Did you like it?"

"Loved it. You never fail me with your recommendations."

Another throat bob. His gaze dropped to her delicate neck. When he looked back up, it was to see her chestnut eyes were a shade darker. She took a quick step back.

Running away from him?

"I'm glad you enjoyed it. I've put a few more recommendation tags around the library. Feel free to check them out."

She turned, but before she could walk away, he wrapped his fingers around her arm, stopping her in her tracks. A half second passed before she turned back to him. It was a half second that others wouldn't even have noticed. He did.

He took a small step closer and lowered his voice. "I also wanted to check on you. Are you doing okay after the other night at the bar?"

Something flashed through her eyes. Something that came and went quickly. Not quickly enough for him to miss it, though.

Demons. Just from that brush with death? Or were there other reasons?

"I'm fine."

Those words came too quickly for him to believe them. He gave her his most serious look. "Okay. But if you're not, I'm here. And I'm a great listener."

And man, he enjoyed listening to this woman's words. Her voice was like silk. It brushed over his skin, making him so damn hot he thought he'd burn to ash.

For a moment, her eyes lost their hard edge and her lips softened and separated, and he wondered if she might say something important.

Then she pasted on the well-practiced smile that he didn't believe for a second, and the moment was gone.

"Thank you, Callum. I'll keep that in mind."

She stepped away from him. His hand fell. And he watched the woman walk into another aisle of books and disappear.

It was okay. He'd be back. Checking on her. And trying to crack that tough exterior she worked hard to keep intact. The woman wasn't escaping him just yet.

Order CALLUM today!

ALSO BY NYSSA KATHRYN

Jackson

Declan

Cole

Ryker

JOIN my newsletter and be the first to find out about sales and new releases!

~https://www.nyssakathryn.com/vip-newsletter~

ABOUT THE AUTHOR

Nyssa Kathryn is a romantic suspense author. She lives in South Australia with her daughter and hubby and takes every chance she can to be plotting and writing. Always an avid reader of romance novels, she considers alpha males and happily-ever-afters to be her jam.

Don't forget to follow Nyssa and never miss another release.

Facebook | Instagram | Amazon | Goodreads

SEP 2023

CPSIA information can be obtained
at www.ICGtesting.com
Printed in the USA
LVHW031441090723
751942LV00040B/462

9 781922 869623